A DAUGHTER'S SECRET

THE SECRET SERIES - BOOK 2

TINA HOGAN GRANT

TINAHOGANGRANTBOOKS

Edited by Lou Ann Fox, *Fox Paws*, Editor

Cover Design by T.E. Black Designs

http://www.teblackdesigns.com

 Formatted with Vellum

For my incredible daughter-in-law,
Alejandra (Alex)
By marriage you joined our family,
by love you entered our hearts.

BIBLIOGRAPHY

ALSO BY TINA HOGAN GRANT
THE TAMMY MELLOWS SERIES
First Fall - The Prequel
Reckless Beginnings - Book I
Better Endings - Book 2
The Reunions Books 3
Waves And Memories - A Short Story Collection

THE SABELA SERIES
Davin - Prequel
Slater - Book I
Eve-Book2
Claire - Book 3
Jill - Book 4
All Of Us-Book 5
Vegas Bound - Book 6
Open Arms - Book 7
Dream Big - Book 8 (Final book in the series)

THE SECRETS SERIES
Secrets Told - Book I
A Daughter's Secret - Book 2
A Boyfriend's Secret (Coming soon)

REVIEWS

"We follow Molly and her secret all the way to Montana to start a new life, but there is more. I felt I was part of this beautiful story and the women who were in it. I also love a surprise.....did not see that coming at all." - *Agnes Shapiro*

"What an amazing book! It is such a heartfelt story filled with secrets, lies, unexpected events, and love. It brought happy tears to my eyes when a certain something came to the surface. I just wanted to keep reading to find out what would happen next and what the daughter's secret was. The quote below from Patricia is my favorite!" - *Karen Wright*

Quote - *'Live your life to the fullest and do it for you, surrounded by the people you love. Do what makes you happy, not what makes others happy."*

"I really enjoyed this book. I didn't have it all figured out. Looking back, there were clues. I have always loved Ms. Grant's books and this was no different. It is an easy read and one that you won't want to put down." - *Kris Rubi*

CHAPTER 1

Molly stared at the screen of her laptop, her hand shaking as she hovered the cursor over the "Submit" button. She shook her head vigorously, tossing her long, straight black hair away from her shoulders, allowing her neck, moist from sweat, to breathe. She rubbed her brow; it, too was moist.

"Just do it," she told herself, still hovering over the submit button on the screen, wiping the wet palm of her other hand on her grey sweatpants. This was the third time she'd filled out the same application in the last month. Each time exiting the site before submitting the form. But not this time. "Third time's a charm, right?" she said aloud, her voice firm, eyes fixed on the screen.

Molly shifted in her seat, pulling the neck of her white t-shirt away from her neck to ease the strangling feeling, uncrossing her legs and removing her reading glasses. She looked out the kitchen window next to the small table where she sat in her one-bedroom apartment. The sky had darkened since she'd first sat down to once again try and complete the daunting task before her. She saw only shadows of the roof tops of the adjoining two-story apartments. The familiar sounds of dogs barking and children playing began to emerge now that the temperatures had begun to cool from a scorching 105 degrees for most of the day to a more tolerant 70 degrees. Cooped up all day in their air-conditioned apartments in Round Rock, Texas, children and pets were now able to expend their energy and enjoy the cooler evenings.

Staring out the window, she watched as two Jack Russells chased a young boy through one of the courtyards of the apartment buildings. Molly giggled; it was a regular scene every night, brightening up her lonely days while working from home as an event coordinator for trade shows. It was a temporary job that paid the bills, as well as a steppingstone for her bigger plans of leaving Texas, where she'd spent all 29 years of her life. There were too many memories here, many not good ones. She was still young enough to start fresh, with a clean slate, in a new state where no one knew her. No ties, no family, no friends.

The one person she considered a friend was her neighbor, Stacey, in the adjoining apartment. They moved into the building on the same day three years ago, striking up a conversation as they unpacked their cars in the parking lot. Both were thankful their apartments came furnished and were able to fit all their worldly possessions in their cars. They were the same age (29), and a friendship immediately blossomed.

Molly had been planning to leave Texas for the past three years, ever since she was forced to leave home and face the world alone after losing both her parents in a house fire. She wasn't home when the fire broke out. Her father had fallen asleep smoking a cigarette in bed, her mother, asleep next to him. They both perished in the fire, and Molly, who had recently moved back home after a breakup, returned home later that night after dinner with friends, to find the family home burnt to the ground.

Surprisingly, Ted, their landlord of 24 years, showed nothing but compassion for Molly as she ran from her car, screaming for her parents. Blinded by the flashing lights of the many fire trucks and choking on the intense smoke filling the air, Molly's tears and agonizing screams brought her to her knees. She watched in horror as the firefighters dispersed gallons of water on the remaining burnt ruins of her childhood home. There was nothing left - it was now just a pile of smoldering ashes.

Ted rushed to her side and knelt beside her. Taking her in his arms, he held her tight, allowing her painful tears to fall. Molly clung to his shirt, grasping the material in her clenched fist and saturating it with her tears.

"What happened?" she cried, her voice shaking.

Ted continued to hold her tight, her head pressed hard against his chest. "We don't know yet."

Molly pushed back her tears and sniffed hard so she could speak. "And Mom and Dad?"

Ted slowly shook his head, tears welling up in his eyes. He wasn't one to show his emotions, but his heart was breaking for Molly, who was just 26 on the night of the tragedy, and Stan and Fiona's only child. "I'm afraid they didn't make it. I'm so sorry, Molly."

Molly screamed, "No! Oh my god, please god, no!" She pushed away from Ted, stood up and screamed for them again. "Mom, Dad!"

Ted quickly stood and pulled her into his arms again. "Molly, they're gone. I'm taking you to my house. My wife will set you up in the spare room, and you can stay as long as you need to."

Molly managed to compose herself and looked up at Ted. "And what about this house? It's your house, and it's gone. I'm so sorry."

"It's okay, I have good insurance. Don't you worry about me. It's you I'm worried about." Ted was taken aback by her apology for the loss of his home. At a time where she had just lost everything, she still thought of others, and it touched him deeply. "I'm not going to leave you here knowing you have nowhere to go. Doris and I are here for you," he told her.

After losing everything, Molly stayed with Ted and Doris for three months, allowing her to save enough money to move into her own place, which is where she was now. It hadn't been easy, but she had grown stronger since the fire, even more determined to live the life she was meant to have.

She remained in the same neighborhood where she grew up, just

15 minutes from where her childhood home had been scorched. It was the only place she'd known, but avoided going anywhere near her old street, always taking the longer route to avoid it when she was in that part of town. Knowing Ted and Doris were close by also kept her in the familiar neighborhood. They were there for her during her darkest days and told her when she left that they'd always be there for her, just a phone call away. His words brought Molly comfort and a sense of security, as well as a reason why she never left Round Rock. Since moving out she'd called them at least once a month, letting them know she was doing okay. Every holiday since the horrific fire was spent with Ted, Doris, and their family.

But now she was planning another move; it would be life-changing for her, but the hardest part would be saying goodbye to Stacey, Ted, and Doris.

Stacey had been the only person Molly had confided in and shared her plans with. She didn't know how to tell Ted and Doris, and wasn't sure if she ever would. Stacey understood why Molly's life now revolved around planning the life-changing move but feared it might destroy her if the outcome did not live up to her hopes and dreams.

Molly's apartment had served its purpose of solitude, allowing her to pave the way to her future. Even though the neighborhood wasn't the greatest, and the only views were other apartment buildings and a strip mall, the rent was cheap, allowing Molly to save money for her move and start her new life.

After three years of intense research, numerous phone calls, emails and countless pages of notes, the application had fallen into her lap, and Molly believed it would provide many answers for her research and finally bring her happiness. So why was she so damn afraid to act and submit the form? Molly wondered. Putting her glasses back on and returning her focus to the laptop screen, Molly knew the answer. She was expecting only one outcome; anything else would be heartbreaking. Would she be able to handle it if the results weren't what she hoped for? Molly didn't think so.

Overcome with fear and anxiety of the unknown, Molly once again quickly left the website and closed her laptop. Her emotions had won again.

CHAPTER 2

Feeling disgusted with herself, Molly immediately stood up and began pacing the small kitchen, fixing her eyes on the closed laptop. After circling the room six times, she marched over to the computer, opened the lid and stared at the black screen before taking a seat at the table again.

Taking a deep breath, she typed the website's domain and waited for it to load. Staying focused, determined to do the task, she quickly filled out the online form, and with no hesitation, hit the submit button before she could think too hard about it. "My god! I did it," she whispered, her voice shaking. "There's no turning back now." She took another deep breath. "Now I just have to wait for a reply." Will I even get one? She wondered, still staring at the screen. "I wonder how many applications they've received?" continuing to talk to herself aloud, shocked she'd finally done it.

She'd tried her best to list her qualifications, expressing how much she loved reading books, planning someday to write her own. Perhaps that would give her a boost to be hired as a manager for the indie bookstore in Montana.

Through her research, Molly already knew a lot about the owner, Caroline Moors. It wasn't Molly's dream job, but it would place her in the town where Caroline lived, the focus of her research. Thanks to the internet, which led to many successful leads, Molly could write a book about Caroline. She knew she was 44 years old, where she was born, the schools she attended, her parents, and the time she served America when she enlisted in the army. Last year Molly discovered she'd been married for ten years, and was the owner of the "Read More Books" indie bookstore.

For the last six months, Molly had been trying to figure out a plan to meet her in person. Traveling all the way to Montana to pose as a customer in her bookstore with the possible chance of a one-time encounter with Caroline would be expensive and not guaranteed. What if she wasn't in the store that day, or out of town for her entire trip? It was an expense she couldn't afford which would include airfare and accommodations. But as she continued her research, she discovered Caroline was looking for a store manager. Molly couldn't believe her luck - it was the answer to all of her questions and simplified everything. She'd be a fool not to apply. Molly believed it was meant to be, and assumed her chances of being hired were pretty good.

After staring at the screen for a few minutes, numb from finally completing the application, Molly reached for her cell phone and called Stacey.

After three rings, she heard Stacey's perky voice. "Hey, Molly. How's it going?"

"I did it!"

There was a pause. "Did what?"

"I filled out the job application and actually sent it! It's done, Stacey."

"You did, oh my god – congratulations! I didn't think you ever would. Now what happens?"

Molly shrugged her shoulders. "I'm not sure. I guess, wait for an email. I just had to tell someone, and you're the only person that knows about this."

"I'm glad you told me. You know you can talk to me about anything; I've told you that." Stacey took in a deep breath and exhaled. "Now, you must tell me when you've heard back from them. You can't leave me hanging, okay?"

Molly chuckled, feeling more relaxed after telling Stacey. "I won't. That would be pretty mean of me, don't you think?"

"I'll say," Stacey laughed. "Hey, I'm all by myself tonight. Doug's not coming over, he's working the night shift again. Do you want me to come over to your place with a bottle of wine and we can celebrate? We can hang out, watch Netflix and get drunk," Stacey laughed.

"Sounds good to me. Just come on in, the door will be open."

"I'll be there in ten minutes. I need to feed Henry," Stacey replied. "I'm already ten minutes late, and his inner clock has him wired, he won't leave me alone," she giggled.

"How's that little Pug doing? When I think of getting a dog, I just come visit you and Henry," Molly joked. "He satisfies my needs when I think I want a dog."

"You should get one," Stacey urged.

Molly shook her head in protest. "Oh no, I can't; I need to focus on the most important mission of my life. I can't have any distractions, you know that."

"I know, but a dog would be a good companion for you."

"Stacey, you always worry because I'm alone. I've lost count how many times we've had this conversation. It's my choice. There'll be plenty of time for boyfriends and dogs," Molly told her, chuckling. "Now, go feed Henry. I'll see you in a bit."

Stacey laughed. "I think you're the smart one between us. I'm loving these night shifts Doug is getting. This is his third this week. Don't get me wrong, I love him and all, but it's nice to have some me time."

"Why all the night shifts all of a sudden?" Molly asked.

"They've had several break-ins at the car dealer, so they've increased their security at night. Anyway, let me go feed Henry and I'll be right there."

"Okay, I'll see you soon."

CHAPTER 3

Molly was checking her emails when she heard the front door open. She wasn't expecting a reply from the application so soon, but wanted to check for a confirmation of her submission, pleased to see she'd received one.

She looked over her shoulder and smiled at Stacey, dressed in a pink bathrobe and matching slippers. She was carrying two glasses and a bottle of white wine. Her long, straight, dyed blonde hair was tied back in a ponytail.

"Hey, come on in," Molly said, laughing at her attire. "You didn't tell me it was a pajama party."

Stacey looked down and gave her wardrobe the once over. "This is when I'm most comfortable, and around you I can be myself," she chuckled.

"So, when I see you in your bathrobe, I know Doug isn't coming over," Molly laughed.

Stacey nodded. "Pretty much," she agreed, heading over to the kitchen where she placed the glasses and bottle of wine on the counter. "Do you want me to pour two glasses?"

"Sure, I was just checking my emails. They sent me a confirmation for my application. I hope it's not too long before I get a reply."

"Well, I'm here to help unsettle your nerves if it does," Stacey said, handing Molly a glass of wine and a caring smile.

Molly stood up and took the glass. "Come on, let's go find something to watch on the TV," she said, walking over to the grey couch in the small living room which consisted of a couch, a matching armchair, a walnut coffee table, two standing lamps in the corners, and a flat screen TV on a matching entertainment stand.

Stacey followed Molly, carrying her glass and taking a seat next to her on the couch.

"What are you in the mood for?" Molly asked, picking up the remote.

Stacey turned and faced Molly. "Let's talk about how you're doing first before we watch a movie. This is a big ordeal. You actually did it!" she squealed, nudging Molly's arm. "How do you feel?"

Molly shrugged her shoulders and took a sip of wine before speaking. "I'm not sure. I feel pretty numb. I'm still trying to let it sink in. The waiting game is going to be torture. I'm not sure which is worse - submitting the application or chewing my fingernails down to nothing while waiting for a reply."

Stacey paused. "Have you thought about what you'd do if you don't get the job? I know it's early, but it's something you need to think about. Do you have a Plan B?"

Molly shook her head. "I don't. I'm putting all my energy into getting this job. I can't think about that right now. If that's the case, then I'll think of another plan then."

"And what if you move all the way to Montana and you don't like her? Or even worse, she doesn't like you?"

Molly rolled her eyes. Stacey's questions were beginning to irritate her. These were questions that had haunted Molly ever since she began her research, and one of the reasons why it was so difficult to submit the application. She had so many *what ifs,* and she didn't need Stacey reminding her. "Why all the negativity?" Molly asked, an edge to her voice.

"I'm just looking out for you. I've known you for three years, and in that time your entire life has revolved around this. I just want you to be prepared if things don't go the way you had hoped or planned on."

Molly instantly felt guilty for her sharp tone. "I'm sorry, you've been a great friend, spending hours talking with me when I was a mess. I think about those things all the time - day in, day out. Even in my sleep," Molly chuckled, changing her tone to a more serious one. "If that happens, I won't lie; I'll be devastated, but I'll find a way to handle it."

"Well, if it doesn't work out, you can always come back here and stay with me for a while."

Molly smiled. "Thanks, but I hope that won't be the case, and not because I don't want to see you. You're the only friend I have. And, if I do end up moving to Montana, leaving you is going to suck."

Stacey leaned in and gave Molly a hug. "Aww, I'm going to miss you too." She quickly pulled back, waving her hands in the air. "I don't want to think about it. Let's find a movie," she said, standing up and grabbing the now two empty glasses on the coffee table. "Why don't you look for one while I go refill our glasses."

Molly picked up the remote, leaning back and began scrolling in search of a comedy. She needed to turn her mind off and shake off the worrisome thoughts Stacey had ignited again.

CHAPTER 4

Molly enjoyed Stacey's company and had been hanging out with her more often since her boyfriend of two years, Doug, had been working more nightshifts. When Molly was alone, she struggled to turn her mind away from the same negative thoughts Stacey mentioned. It was the first time Stacey had shown any bitterness towards her plans, and Molly immediately shut her down. But she did look forward to Stacey's visits. It was her only escape from her thoughts, and she wanted it to remain that way.

After scrolling through the Netflix menu, they both decided on the movie *Hangover*.

"I don't know how many times I've seen that movie," Stacey grinned, "but it's the best for when I need a good laugh."

"Me too," Molly replied, selecting the play button. "And I really do need a good laugh tonight," she added, turning to Stacey and squeezing her arm. "Hey, I'm sorry I got upset with you. I have those thoughts all the time when I'm alone, and honestly, I enjoy being able to shut off my mind temporarily when you come over."

Stacey smiled and patted her arm. "Hey, it's okay. I totally understand, but, like I said, I'm here if you ever need to talk, and don't you forget it, okay?"

Molly smiled. "Thanks. I know." She picked up her phone from the coffee table and checked the time. "It's 7:00. Do you have to work tomorrow?"

Stacey nodded before taking a sip of wine. "Yes, I'm doing the breakfast and lunch shift. I hate the morning shift, but I have classes tomorrow afternoon and evening." She suddenly bolted up and looked at Molly. "Which reminds me, can you feed Henry tomorrow and maybe take him for a walk? I hate the thought of him being cooped up all day in the apartment."

"Sure, not a problem," Molly said, nudging Stacey's arm. "Don't I always, unless Doug is there?"

"Yeah, you do, and thanks. I know I can always count on you." Stacey suddenly had a thought. "You still have your key, right?"

"Yep," Molly replied, taking a sip of wine.

"Great! I only have two more months of classes, then hopefully I can start my own web design business and be done waiting tables." Stacey threw her head back against the couch and moaned. "God, I hate it. People can be so damn picky when it comes to their food." She took a sip and continued to complain. "You know, yesterday, I had a guy ask me to take his soup back because it wasn't hot enough. You could see the damn steam rising from the bowl! He was just being an ass." She leaned into Molly and chuckled. "So, you know what I did?"

"No, what?"

"I put his stupid soup in the microwave for three minutes." Stacey leaned back again, throwing her head back, laughing loudly. "That shit was bubbling like a damn volcano!"

Molly's jaw dropped. "You didn't!"

"I sure did, and he didn't say a damn word when I went back to his table and asked if the soup was hot enough. He wouldn't even look at me!" Stacey laughed again. "He just nodded. That'll teach him."

"I could never do that," Molly confessed. "I wish I had your guts."

"When you deal with arrogant people all day who think they're better than you, you need to grow a tough skin and acquire a sassy attitude, I suppose."

An evening of laughter and alcohol was just what Molly needed. By the end of the movie, she was feeling relaxed and a little tipsy after drinking four glasses of wine. When she stood up, her body swayed, her head was light, and she giggled as she tried to make her way to the kitchen, holding an empty glass. "I hope I don't wake up in Vegas, like the movie," Molly laughed. "But one thing I do know for sure is that I'm definitely going to be waking up with a hangover!"

Stacey, also feeling the effects of the alcohol, roared out in laughter. "Where are you going?"

Molly turned and stared at her; her eyes glazed. "I don't *know*," she giggled, pressing her hand down on the arm of the chair for support. "I just felt a need to stand, but now I'm thinking it might have been a bad idea." She giggled again, struggling to hold on to her glass. "I think I'll stand here for a few minutes until the room stops spinning."

"It's not spinning for me."

Molly slurred her words. "That's because you didn't get up." She laughed again. "I have some advice."

"What's that?" Stacey said, her words garbled.

"Don't get up. It sucks up here." Molly straightened her body and slowly released her grip on the arm of the chair, taking baby steps and walking slowly towards the kitchen where she placed her glass on the nearest counter. "Why did you go and get a second bottle of wine from your apartment?" she said, holding on to the edge of the counter.

"Because you told me to," Stacy giggled.

"And you listened!" Molly said sarcastically, turning her head. "What time is it anyway?"

Stacey leaned forward and grabbed her phone from the coffee table, glancing at the screen. "It's almost 11:00. Shoot - I gotta go! I have to be out the door by 6:00 am tomorrow," she said, struggling to stand.

"And I need to go to bed," Molly said. "Maybe everything will stop spinning once my head hits the pillow."

Dragging her feet across the carpet, Stacey approached Molly and gave her a friendly hug. "Thanks for taking care of Henry tomorrow, I owe you one. I'll be home by eight and call you then."

Molly nodded, walking towards the front door, pulling it open. "Don't you worry about Henry, he's my buddy," Molly replied, her words still slurred.

After Stacy had left, Molly turned and looked at the mess in the kitchen. Empty wine bottles and glasses sat on the counter, along with open bags of chips, dirty bowls and salsa dishes. She waved her hands in the air. "I'll deal with that crap in the morning. I need sleep," she said, staggering to her bedroom and flopping onto the bed like a rag doll. Within minutes she was sound asleep.

CHAPTER 5

As Molly had predicted, she woke up with a splitting headache and a hangover. The bright sunlight beaming through her bedroom window blinded her, causing her to shadow her eyes as she slowly pulled back the sheets and crawled out of bed. "God, my head hurts," she moaned, dragging herself over to the window to close the drapes.

Once the room was darker, Molly let out a sigh of relief, dropping her hand away from her eyes and opening them completely. She shook her head, hoping it would erase the pounding, swirling headache. To her dismay, it did not. "I need coffee," she groaned, heading towards the kitchen where the reminders of last night greeted her: empty glasses and dirty dishes. She turned and walked away, avoiding the mess. "Coffee first," she mumbled, reaching for the can of Folgers on the counter.

While waiting for the coffee to brew and without a wall clock in her apartment, Molly checked her phone for the time and saw it was almost eight. She noticed there was a text from Stacey.

Molly read the text.

Don't forget to feed Henry, he likes to go out before he eats around 7:00. Thank you, I'll see you tonight.

"Oh, crap!" Molly hissed. Wearing only her underwear and a t-shirt, she marched to the bathroom, grabbed her sky-blue bathrobe from the back of the door, the keys to Stacey's apartment, then slid on her navy-blue slippers by the front door.

As soon as she inserted the key into the lock of Stacey's place, an angry bark was heard on the other side. "I'm sorry, Henry. I know I'm late!" she hollered, struggling to turn the key. Henry continued to bark as she pushed open the door and entered the apartment. "Hey buddy, it's okay, I'm here now. Do you want to go outside?" Molly petted Henry's head when she approached him and then suddenly stopped, raising her nose in the air when a rank smell engulfed her sinuses. "What is that smell?" she cried, trying not to gag. She inhaled deeply and followed the smell that seemed to be coming from the kitchen, and, within minutes, found the cause. "Oh, Henry, you didn't!" Molly screeched. "God, it stinks," she cried, holding her nose tightly. Henry walked over to his business on the kitchen floor, looking proud. "Oh god, Henry! Don't sniff it." Molly shook her head. "It's not your fault. I'm late, and I'm sorry I yelled at you," she said in a softer voice, petting his head again. She reached for a roll of paper towels on the counter. "Well, this is one way to snap oneself out of a hangover. Clean up dog poop before coffee."

After gagging the entire time, and with Henry looking on, Molly completed the awful mission. With one hand carrying a plastic trash bag at arm's length and Henry on a leash with the other, she headed down to the courtyard to take care of the stinky trash and let Henry roam around on the grassy area. Once Henry was free, Molly panicked and quickly checked her bathrobe pockets, thankful to find Stacey's keys in one of them, fearing she'd left them in Stacey's apartment. "Thank god," Molly whispered with relief.

Molly spent 30 minutes with Henry, allowing him to roam, go to the bathroom two more times, then fed him. By the time she returned to her apartment, she discovered her coffee was now lukewarm after taking a sip and spit it out in the sink. "Damn it," she hissed, placing the cup in the microwave. Once heated, she took a large sip and sat at the table. She opened her laptop to check her emails, anxious to see if she'd had a reply from her job application.

Holding her breath, she opened her email inbox and scanned through the abundance of scams and junk mail that seemed to be the majority of her daily emails. Her heart sank when she saw there was nothing. "This waiting game sucks," she moaned, closing the laptop in frustration.

Determined to fight her anxieties and not be controlled by them, Molly finished her coffee, took a long shower to clear her head, and spent the rest of the morning emailing clients for the upcoming Home and Gardening Show she was assigned to. She was talking to the show's officials about booths and pricing, but every time she heard the familiar ping of an email coming in, she immediately stopped and checked to see who it was from. To her disappointment, they were all junk.

Relieved when it was finally noon, Molly closed her laptop, grabbed her phone and headed over to Stacey's apartment to take Henry out again. "We're going to make this quick, okay, boy? It's over 100 degrees outside," she told him, putting on his leash.

Now dressed in Denim shorts and a white tank top, Molly sat on a wooden bench in the shade close to the grass while Henry roamed freely. She pulled out her phone from her back pocket to check her emails once again. Disgusted to see only more junk mail, she abruptly returned the phone to her back pocket. "God, what's taking them so long to reply? Is this a bad sign? Perhaps they have hundreds if not thousands of applicants?" Molly shook her head, disagreeing with her fears. "Nah, it's an indie bookstore, not a big corporation. I can't stand this waiting game," she snapped, wiping the sweat from her brow before standing. "Okay Henry, I'm burning up out here, I hate this heat. Let's go inside, buddy."

After filling his water and turning up the air in the apartment, Molly returned home to fix herself some lunch and begin the second shift of her workday, which consisted of writing more emails to clients and sending out floor plans and prices for the show. Her days consisted of the same routine five days a week, spent alone in her apartment, only venturing out to go to the store, check for mail at her mailbox, and have the occasional dinner out with Stacey. It was a lonely life, but Molly had convinced herself it was only temporary. She would start living again once she'd moved to Montana where her new life would begin. The job at the indie bookstore would get her there the quickest, but if that didn't go to plan, she was determined to get there somehow. She wasn't sure how yet, but she wasn't relying on a plan B or given it any thought, hoping she wouldn't need one.

At 5:00, just like any other day, Molly signed out of her job website and called it a day. A few minutes later she heard the familiar ping of an email notification and quickly switched her screen to the inbox. She instantly froze when she saw an email from a woman called Lucy Davis who was with the indie bookstore. Holding her breath, Molly opened the email and read the letter.

CHAPTER 6

Dear Molly,
    We have received your application for the position of Store Manager at the Read More Books indie bookstore. I'm Caroline Moors' personal assistant, and I oversee the applications. I'd like to schedule a phone interview with you and would like to know if next Thursday, July 12th at 10:00 am works for you. This will be a 30-minute interview, so please schedule your time accordingly.

Please confirm by email to let me know that I have the correct phone number.

I look forward to speaking with you.

Best,

Lucy Davis

Molly gasped. Leaning back in her chair as she clasped her hands in front of her mouth, her eyes were wide, filled with shock. "Shit! I have an interview! Does everyone get one?" she wondered.

In a panicked state, she pushed back her chair, stood up and paced the room. "Okay Molly, calm down," she told herself. "It's just an interview. You've had plenty of them. This isn't anything different," she added, lying to herself. "Hell, yes it is!" she hollered. "This is my damn future, and I can't screw this up." She quickly returned to her seat and read the letter again before hitting the reply button. Unsure of what to type, she was concise and to the point.

Dear Lucy,

Thank you for the quick reply. Yes, next Thursday works, and that is the correct phone number.

I look forward to meeting with you.

Sincerely,

Molly Rosswell

Without giving it a second thought, Molly hit the send button, then heavily exhaled. Her first thought was to call Stacey, but she quickly remembered that she was still working. "I need some fresh air," she said aloud, and with temperatures cooler outside, she decided to take Henry for a walk.

When she approached Stacey's front door, Henry's familiar bark could be heard on the other side. "Well, you don't need a doorbell, Stacey," Molly chuckled, turning the key and opening the door.

Henry greeted her with joyful jumps, pressing his front paws on her thighs. "Hey buddy," Molly said sniffing the air. "No more accidents?" she said, gently placing Henry's paws on the ground. After checking all the rooms, Molly was pleased to see there weren't and grabbed the leash from the hook by the front door, causing another outburst from Henry. "Okay, Henry, settle down. Yes, we're going for a walk," Molly laughed, hooking the leash to his green collar.

Both she and Stacey lived on the second floor of the building, but Molly always chose to take the stairs since the fire. The thought of being trapped in the elevator if the building ever did catch on fire terrified her. She'd much rather make three trips from her car with groceries than risk that happening. Molly never realized how much she'd been affected by the fire, other than the tragedy of losing her parents, until she began changing some of her everyday routines and habits. When she moved into the apartment, she made sure every room had a fire extinguisher, smoke detectors, and knew where all the fire escapes were in the building. When she left her apartment, she checked that all appliances were unplugged, and she no longer burned any candles, something she did most nights before the fire.

Outside in the courtyard, Henry made his way to the grass, pulling Molly behind him. She had a firm grip on his leash, and shouted, "Okay, Henry! Quit pulling." There were a few residents sitting on benches, enjoying the cooler temperatures. Molly nodded and waved with her free hand at an older gentleman who lived alone at the end of the hallway on her floor. "Hi, Jeff. I'm glad to see it's finally cooled off."

He nodded and returned the smile. "Yes, I'm ready for the fall. I've had enough of this heat."

"I hear you." After Henry had finished his business, Molly gave a gentle tug on his leash. "Come on, boy," she said, waving goodbye to Jeff and heading towards the front gate.

She planned on taking Henry to the main park two blocks away where she could let him run loose and have some space. The courtyard was too small, and there were too many resident cats roaming the property that Henry couldn't resist chasing.

Standing on the other side of the gate, Molly tugged on it to make sure it was securely closed, then walked over to the nearby crosswalk to cross the street. She lived in the heart of a community that was nothing but apartments. Both sides of the street were lined with apartment buildings, most being two-story like the one she lived in, except for the newly built, ginormous, six-story building at the end of the road. To her left and across the busy intersection was a supermarket and local businesses. Being late in the afternoon, the four-lane road was at its busiest with people returning from work. Standing at the curb, she told Henry to sit, pushed the button on the crossing sign, and waited for the light to turn green.

Within seconds, Henry began barking profusely, his body stiffening, with the fur on the back of his neck standing up. Shaking his head and using every muscle in his body, Henry pulled hard on the leash towards the road. "No! Henry, stop!" Molly screamed, struggling to control him. She gripped the leash hard, tugging on it to try and pull him back, but before she could wrap it around her wrist, Henry had broken free, his leash dragging behind him. He charged into the middle of the road, running towards a ginger cat strutting down the sidewalk on the other side in front of a three-story apartment building. "Henry, NO!" Molly screamed, and without looking, she panicked and rushed into the road to chase him.

Molly was oblivious to the deafening sounds of car horns and screeching brakes surrounding her as she ran out into traffic, her only focus being on Henry. That was the last thing she remembered before the world went black after a large, grey Ford 250 truck was unable to stop in time and hit her hard, knocking her instantly to the ground.

CHAPTER 7

Sitting in her car, after finishing her shift, Stacey tried texting and calling Molly for the third time in the last hour. It wasn't like her to not answer her phone, especially since Stacey knew she always had it with her. Stacey needed to stop by the store on her way home and had texted Molly, asking if she needed anything, Molly never missed an opportunity to avoid going to the store, and always thought of something for Stacey to pick up. Stacey was mildly concerned and decided to make it a quick stop, grabbing only milk and food for Henry. She decided that as soon as she got home, she'd check on Molly.

Thankfully the store was just a few blocks from her work, and she spent less than ten minutes shopping, grabbing just the necessities, and driving 20 minutes home. She quickly stepped out of the car, flung her purse over her shoulder, and grabbed the two bags of groceries from the back seat, kicking the car door closed with her right foot. Not wanting to wait for the elevator, she took the stairs and came to an abrupt stop when she saw an envelope taped to her front door with her name on it. She didn't recognize the handwriting and looked up and down the corridor before pulling it off the door,

"What's this?" she said aloud, noticing that Henry wasn't barking on the other side - something he never failed to do.

"Henry, I'm home," Stacey called out, setting the bags on the floor and stuffing the letter into one of her jacket pockets while pulling her keys out of the other. The silence was deafening. "Henry, mommy's home," she called again, turning the key in the lock. "Something's wrong," she said, her voice shaking as her heart raced with fear, unsure of what waited for her inside. *Was Henry hurt?* Was her first terrifying thought. "Please let him be okay," Stacey cried, pushing the door open. She was greeted with silence. Leaving the door wide open and the grocery bags sitting in the hallway, she raced through the apartment in a panicked state calling his name. "Henry, where *are* you?"

She searched in every possible hiding space; under the bed, behind the drapes, under the kitchen table, behind the couch, and in every closet. Desperate to find him, she even looked in every lower kitchen cabinet, as well as outside on the narrow balcony, thinking maybe Molly had let him on the patio and accidentally locked him out. Exhausted of possible hiding places to look, tears welling in her eyes, Stacey raked her fingers through her hair, pulling it way from her face. She was about to go over to Molly's apartment thinking maybe Henry was with her, but surely she would have left a note. "The letter!" Stacey shrieked, pulling it out of her pocket.

She quickly sat down on the nearby couch, and with shaking hands struggled to open the envelope. Once the letter was free, she tossed the envelope on the floor and unfolded the letter. She quickly began reading.

Stacey, this is your neighbor Jeff. I live at the end of the hallway in apartment 214. Molly was hit by a truck. I have your dog, and he's okay. They took Molly to the hospital. Come by when you get home.

Stacey gasped; her jaw dropped as she read the letter a second time, not believing what she was reading. "Oh my god! Is she okay?" she hollered, quickly standing up. She began pacing the apartment in search of her keys. "Where the hell did I put them?" She suddenly noticed the front door was still open and remembered she'd left the bags of groceries in the hallway. She marched to the doorway and noticed her keys dangling in the lock as she leaned over to pick up the bags. "I need to put the milk and eggs in the fridge, "she mumbled, walking over to the kitchen. "The rest can wait," she said, leaving the bags on the counter. "I need to get my Henry and find out what happened to Molly." She shook her head in disbelief. "She got run over!" she cried. "I can't believe it," she whimpered, closing the door to the fridge.

After grabbing her purse and the keys out of the lock, she double-checked that the door was locked after closing it, and with long strides walked down the hallway to Jeff's apartment. She didn't know him well. They'd shared the occasional nod and friendly greeting when passing in the hallway and the courtyard. She'd never seen him with anyone, but he was always courteous to her, giving her a friendly smile whenever they bumped into each other.

When Stacey reached his front door, she took a deep breath before knocking and waited nervously for him to answer. The sound of Henry's bark on the other side of the door melted her heart and brought a huge smile to her face. Jeff answered the door within seconds, dressed in blue jeans and a navy sweatshirt. Behind him was Henry, greeting her with excited barks and leaps of joy.

"Henry! Baby!" Stacey cried, kneeling to greet him. "Mama was so worried about you."

"He's doing just fine," Jeff said, smiling. "He's sure happy to see you," Jeff told her, leaning against the door jamb, enjoying Stacey and Henry's reunion.

Still kneeling next to her faithful friend as she was engulfed with puppy kisses, Stacey looked up and smiled. "Thank you so much for taking care of him. What happened?" she asked as she stood up.

"No problem. He's lucky he didn't get hit, too. I was sitting in the courtyard and heard the whole thing. I'd just seen Molly walking your dog, and a few minutes later I heard her yell and scream your dog's name."

"Oh no!" Stacey cried. "So what happened?" she asked again.

"Well, I didn't see the actual accident, but as soon as I heard the commotion and horns honking, I raced out to the street to see what was going on, and it was then I saw Molly out cold in the middle of the road surrounded by people. The traffic had come to a dead stop, and the man that hit her was on his phone, calling the police. I didn't see your dog anywhere, so I began looking up and down the road, then quickly spotted him on the other side, sniffing the grass in front of a building. It looked like Molly was in good hands, so I ran across the street and grabbed Henry."

"Thank you so much," Stacey said, looking down at Henry lying next to her feet. "And Molly, is she going to be okay? What the hell happened, do you know?"

"After grabbing your dog, I walked back to the crowd and talked to a few people. The man that hit her was distraught and kept saying to anyone that would listen that *she just ran out in front my truck. I didn't have time to stop.* I approached him and tried to calm him down, and he told me that your dog had broken loose from Molly and ran out into the road with Molly racing after him, which is when she got hit."

"Oh my goodness, this is all my fault," Stacey gasped. "If she wasn't watching Henry this would never have happened. I feel awful."

Seeing how upset Stacey had suddenly become, Jeff gently rested his hand on her shoulder. "Hey now, don't you go blaming yourself. This is no one's fault. I'm sure Molly will be fine."

Stacey wiped her moist cheeks with her hand. "Do you know which hospital they took her to? I want to go see her tonight. She has no family, and the thought of her being all alone is really upsetting."

"Yes I do. I asked the ambulance driver before he left, and he told me they were taking her to St. David's Hospital."

Stacey closed her eyes, embraced her chest and let out a great sigh of relief. "Thank you!"

"Don't you think you should call first and make sure she's allowed visitors?"

Stacey nodded. "Good idea. I know where the hospital is, it's about 15 minutes from here." She looked down at Henry who was still resting. "Again, thank you so much for rescuing Henry and taking care of him. I don't know what I would've done if he went missing too."

Jeff gave her a caring smile. "My pleasure. Hey, hold on a second," he told her before disappearing into his apartment. He returned a few minutes later and handed her a piece of paper. "Here's my phone number in case you need anything, and please let me know how Molly is doing. I don't know either one of you too well, but I'm happy to help in any way I can."

Stacey took the paper and tucked it in her jacket pocket. "Thank you so much. I appreciate it. I will definitely let you know how she's doing. Well, I should get going. I'm anxious to call the hospital."

"Of course, and you take care now. Call me if you need me."

CHAPTER 8

Refusing to let Henry out of her sight, Stacey held his leash tight until she was inside her apartment and the front door was closed. Before setting him free, she knelt beside him and petted the top of his head. "Don't you ever scare me like that again. I don't know what I'd do if something happened to you." Her heart melted when he looked at her with his big, bulgy brown eyes and licked the top of her hand before trotting off to his water bowl in the kitchen. When he returned, Stacey held him close to her on the couch while she called the hospital.

She listened to the voice-generated menu impatiently, frustrated that calls to any business nowadays were never answered by a real person. Finally, after an endless list of options, she pressed six for patient information. After a few rings a female voice came on the line.

"St. David's Hospital. How may I help you?"

Stacey stuttered nervously as she spoke. "Yes, hello, I'm inquiring about my friend that was hit by a truck this afternoon and taken to your hospital. I want to find out how she's doing and if I can come and see her?"

"Are you a family member?" The woman asked.

"No. She has no family, and I'm her only friend. Please, I want to see her," Stacey begged, raising her voice a notch, but remaining polite.

"What is her name?" The woman asked, her voice flat.

"Molly Rosswell."

"One moment please," the woman advised, putting her on hold and replacing her voice with classical music.

After a few minutes of listening to the repetitive loop of music, the woman came back on the line. "The patient is sleeping at this time, but you can visit her tomorrow between the hours of 8:00 am and 9:00 pm."

Stacey took a deep breath, "So she's okay? What are her injuries?"

"I don't have that information, but when you visit the nurse in the ward can tell you."

"Okay, thank you, I'll be there tomorrow," Stacey said, ending the call, elated that Molly was alive and was assumed to be okay.

Still holding her phone, Stacey looked down at Henry lying beside her and smiled when she saw he'd finally fallen asleep after his traumatic day. She checked the time on her phone and saw that it was almost 9:00, and then suddenly remembered. "Fuck! Doug is supposed to come over tonight. Shit, I don't feel like having company, and I'm *certainly* not in the mood for sex." She found his number in her phone and called him. "I'm sure he'll understand." she mumbled, waiting for him to answer.

"Hey babe, I'll be there soon. I just took a shower and I'm heading out the door in a few minutes. I've missed you," Doug said.

Stacey ignored everything he said. "Oh good, you haven't left yet. Listen, Molly was hit by a truck today and is in the hospital, and Henry was almost lost, too. I'm super tired and just want to go to bed. Can we get together another time?"

"Oh shit! Is Molly okay?"

"I haven't seen her yet or talked to any nurses. I'm going to the hospital tomorrow, which is another reason why I want an early night. Please say you don't mind," Stacey begged.

"It's fine, baby. I understand, but I won't see you until the weekend 'cause I'm doing graveyard all week."

"Really? That sucks. I'll miss you, but there's no way I can stay up late tonight. I'm going to take a hot bath and call it a night."

"Wish I was there to wash your back."

Stacey giggled. "Me too. I'll call you tomorrow after I've seen Molly."

"Okay, babe. Love you."

Stacey smiled at his words but hesitated when she replied. "I love you too. Goodnight."

He was 31, two years older than her. They'd first met at the restaurant where she worked almost two years ago. He was having dinner with his mother to celebrate her 60th birthday, which Stacey thought was really cute. Stacey was instantly attracted to Doug when he was seated at a table in her station. He was tall, around six feet; not muscular, but well toned. His hair was dark, mid-length and wavy. He wore a dark beard and mustache that complimented his silver framed sunglasses which he removed as he looked at Stacey and smiled. They struck up a friendly conversation, whereby Stacey learned that his father had passed away when he was only 12 from a car accident when he was hit by a drunk driver on his way home from work. He looked at his mother proudly when he told Stacey that she'd done an incredible job raising him and his four brothers alone.

It was when Molly served them each a piece of pie with a candle in his mother's that Stacey giggled from embarrassment when Doug's mother smiled at her, then looked over at her son. "You should ask her out on a date. She seems like a nice young lady, and she's already got your mother's approval."

Molly turned away and giggled at her words but was then surprised by Doug's reply.

"Well, I always do what my mother says," he said, looking at Stacey, wearing a sweet smile. "Would you like to go out on a date with me?"

Stacey accepted without hesitation and their relationship had blossomed since that first date. Talk of moving in together were quickly crushed when Stacey told him early in their relationship that she was focusing on school and getting her website design business off the ground after graduation, before thinking of settling down. Doug understood and showed his support by telling her he didn't see the need to rush into elevating their relationship to the next level when everything was going so well. "Why spoil a good thing?" he'd said on one of the nights he was at Stacey's, which is where they usually spent time together as he lived 20 miles away but worked only four miles from Stacey's place.

Relieved that Doug hadn't given her a hard time about not getting together tonight, Stacey was anxious to call it a night and put away the rest of the groceries she'd left on the counter. She ran a bath before taking Henry out on the balcony where he could do his business on the fake piece of grass before putting him on her bed, where he slept close to her every night. After her soothing bath she joined him, feeling more relaxed. She soon fell asleep, anxious for tomorrow to arrive so she could go see Molly.

CHAPTER 9

Like clockwork, Stacey woke up at 6:00 to the sound of Henry's persistent barking, letting her know he needed to go outside.

"Okay, Henry! Give me a minute," she hollered, rubbing her eyes before pulling away the warm, cozy blankets from her body. When she stood up and slid her feet into the slippers next to her bed, Henry immediately jumped on the floor, raced over to the door and began scratching. On her way out of the room, she grabbed her bathrobe draped over a chair and wrapped herself in it, embracing the warmth of the soft fleece.

After letting Henry out on the balcony, she closed the sliding glass door to keep the chill out and headed over to the kitchen to make a pot of coffee, leaving Henry outside to take care of business. She had a few hours to kill before visiting hours began at the hospital and made use of her time cleaning up her neglected apartment. Holding down a job and going to summer school left her little time to be a homemaker.

By 9:00 she was dressed in blue jeans and a red tank top, ready to hit the road. After grabbing her purse, she looked over at the sliding glass door to check it was open a bit so Henry could go in and out, made sure his water bowl was full, and pet him gently on the head as he followed her to the front door. "Don't give me that look, Henry. I'll be back this afternoon." She held the door open as she looked down at him again. "Now you be a good boy, okay?"

It took her less than hour to reach the hospital, and even with the morning rush hour, she was third in line to talk to the nurse at the front desk. Temperatures were already beginning to rise outside, and she was grateful to be in the air-conditioned building since the a/c in her car wasn't working at full capacity, and she didn't have the funds to get it fixed. It had been a grueling hot summer when commuting.

She was greeted with a friendly smile by a middle-aged female nurse with short, chestnut brown hair. "Hello, how can I help you?"

Stacey returned the smile. "Hi, I'm here to see my friend Molly Rosswell. She was hit by a truck and was admitted yesterday."

The nurse looked at her computer monitor and began typing. "One moment, please."

After a few minutes the nurse smiled again. "She's on the 5th floor in Room 508."

"Can you tell me how to get there and how she's doing?"

"The nurses on that ward will update you on her condition. You'll see them as soon as you step out of the elevator." She stood up, leaned forward over the desk, and pointed down the long hallway on Stacey's right. "Take any one of the elevators at the end of the hallway to the 5th floor, one of the nurses will tell you how to get to her room."

"Okay, thank you so much," Stacey said, scurrying off.

She shared the elevator with five other people; two women, one with a young boy, and two men. The silence was deafening as they rode to their respective floors. Stacey was the only one left after the fourth floor and immediately spotted the nurse's station when she stepped out of the elevator onto the fifth.

Again, she was greeted with a friendly smile by another nurse, this one of color, as she approached the counter of the station.

"Hi, how can I help you?" the nurse asked.

"Yes, hi, I'm here to see my friend Molly Rosswell. They told me downstairs at the front desk that she's in Room 508."

"Aah yes, Molly. We've been trying to locate her family but have had no luck."

Stacey's smile disappeared. "She doesn't have any and I'm her only friend. Can I see her?"

"Oh, I'm sorry to hear that. Well, I'm glad she has you," the nurse said, releasing another smile. "Yes, you can see her. I was just in her room administering her medication, so she should still be awake."

"How's she doing?" Stacey asked.

"She's doing okay. She has some facial bruising and swelling, so don't be too alarmed when you see her. She has three broken ribs which is causing most of her pain, and some swelling and grazes on her arms and legs. She's a lucky young lady, it could have been much worse," the nurse told her.

"Oh wow!" Stacey gasped. "When can she go home?"

"Maybe later today, but she'll need a ride."

"I can do that."

"Great - I'll have the doctor come to her room and he will tell you more."

Stacey smiled. "Thank you, I appreciate it. So, how do I get to her room?"

After following the nurse's directions, Stacey reached Room 508 and saw that the door was open. She walked in quietly and found Molly sitting up in bed, her eyes closed. She tiptoed to the edge of the bed, horrified by the purple and blue bruises across her cheeks and the swelling around her eyes.

She leaned in and whispered, "Molly, are you awake?"

Molly didn't respond, and Stacey contemplated leaving, not wanting to disturb her. She whispered her name one final time. "Molly, it's me, Stacey. I can come back later if you're sleeping."

Molly slowly opened her swollen eyes. "Hey Stacey, you can stay. I'm awake, I just feel like shit." She tried to smile, and quickly stopped as the pain kicked in.

Stacey chuckled at her last remark. "You look like shit, too. My god Molly, I'm so sorry. I feel awful."

Even through the swelling, Molly's confusion could be seen. She spoke slowly, struggling to speak, her words somewhat slurred. "Why do *you* feel terrible? You didn't run me over."

Stacey slid a chair next to the bed and took a seat. "No, but if you weren't walking Henry, this would never have happened. I talked to our neighbor Jeff, and he said he'd talked to the man that hit you, and that Henry ran away and you tried to chase him."

"Yeah, he did, but I don't remember anything after that." Panic consumed her face. "Oh shit. What happened to Henry? Is he okay?"

Stacey rested her hand on Molly's arm. "Relax, he's at home safe and sound. Jeff heard the accident from where he sat in the courtyard and went out to the street. He was able to catch Henry and kept him at his place until I got home."

Molly released a huge sigh of relief. "Oh, thank god. I wouldn't be able to live with myself if anything had happened to him." She turned and looked at the dresser next to her, wincing from the constant pain she felt through her entire body. "What time is it? There're no damn clocks in this place, and I have no idea where my phone is," she complained.

"It's almost 10:30," Stacey replied, opening the cupboard to the end table. "There's a green plastic bag in here. Looks like a hospital bag," she said, pulling it out.

"What's in it?" Molly asked, straining to see.

Stacey set the bag on the bed next to Molly and looked inside. "It has all your things in it," she said, pulling out the items. "Here are your clothes, and yep, here at the bottom is your wallet and phone," she said, displaying them on the bed.

"Oh good. I need to email my job and let them know what's going on. I'm supposed to log in at 9:00, but every time I move it hurts like shit."

"I can do it for you," Stacey told her. "Can we do it on your phone?"

"Yes, we can, and I will need you to check my emails. I have an interview next week with the bookstore. Oh dear, it's via Zoom - how can I do it looking like this?"

Stacey gasped. "You got it? Oh my god! I want to read it, when is the interview?"

"I don't remember, which is why I want you to check for me," Molly told her, hoping she'd have time to heal before the crucial day.

CHAPTER 10

Stacey was able to email Molly's work and tell them about her accident. She was surprised when they replied so quickly, telling Molly to take the rest of the week off and check in next week.

"Wow, what a great company! The restaurant where I work would have wanted me to bring a doctor's note. I wouldn't put it past them to insist I come into the restaurant and show my injuries in person. They're such assholes; I can't wait until I'm finished with school to get my web design business off the ground."

"Yeah, they're a good company," Molly told her. "I love that I can work from home. That's what clinched the deal when I took the job." She tried to move her right leg but then screamed in pain. "God damn it!"

"Shit! Are you okay? Should I get a nurse?" Stacey said as she quickly stood, unsure of what to do.

"No, every time I move any part of my body, my friggin' ribs kill me. This is the worst. I can handle cuts and bruises, but broken ribs suck." She winced again from the excruciating pain as she sucked in air trying to ease it, but nothing worked. "Have you ever had broken ribs?" Molly asked, trying to grab her side.

Stacey shook her head. "No, but I've heard how painful it can be and that there's nothing you can do, right? How many did you break?"

"Three too many. I don't know how the hell I'm going to sleep at night or even walk for that matter. I've never experienced pain like this before, and yeah, there's nothing they can do, I just need to wait for them to heal."

Stacey gave her a caring smile. "Well, I'm going to help you as much as I can."

Through the constant pain she was experiencing, Molly managed a weak smile. "Stacey, I appreciate the offer, but you work and go to school, I can't ask for your help."

"Who said you needed to ask? I'm offering. You're a good friend, and I want to take care of you as much as I can. I'll go shopping for you, do your laundry, cook you some meals, clean your apartment, and anything else you need."

"You don't have time to do all that," Molly stated, surprised by her gesture.

"I'll make time," Stacey persisted. "Don't be so stubborn, Molly, you need help." She looked at her from head to toe. "Look at you - you're a mess. You can barely move, and when you do, you scream out in pain. How do you expect to take care of yourself? Now, I'm not taking no for an answer, okay?" Stacey insisted.

"Well, you told me, didn't you?" Molly said, trying her best not to chuckle, because any form of laughing or sudden body movement resulted in intense pain. She put on a weak smile. "Thank you, but don't kill yourself over me. Take care of yourself first, and any time left over I'll gladly take."

Stacey folded her arms and gave her a friendly nod. "That's better. That's the attitude I want to see." She returned her focus back to Molly's phone in her hand. "Now, let's see when your interview is."

Stacey checked the email, and after reading it told Molly her interview was next Thursday at 10:00 am.

"What's today?" Molly asked, her memory still fazed from the accident.

"It's Friday."

"So, I have six days. Do you think these bruises and swellings will be gone by then? And how the hell am I supposed to sit still for 30 minutes with broken ribs?"

"The rib thing I'm not sure about, but I'm pretty good with makeup. I'm sure I can make you look decent," Stacey told her. Her eyes lit up. "Hey, maybe we can practice having you sit at the computer for 30 minutes at a time and see how you do?"

"That's a good idea." Molly replied, liking her suggestion.

A few minutes later they heard a knock on the open door. They both looked over at the same time and saw a middle-aged male doctor wearing a white overcoat and blue scrub pants. "Hello, I'm Doctor Lewis. May I come in?"

"Yes, of course, Doctor," Molly said, trying to sit up more, quickly deciding against it due to the sudden, intense pain.

Doctor Lewis quickly put out his hand to stop her. "Please don't move, you're fine. You need to limit movement to the bare minimum for the next few weeks."

"Few weeks!" Molly gasped. "I have a Zoom job interview next week which I can't miss."

Doctor Lewis approached the side of her bed. "You're going to be in a lot of pain for quite some time. Ribs take time to heal, just take it easy. If you're able to sit for the interview, go ahead, but don't overdo it. Listen to your body. If you experience any pain stop whatever you're doing," he told her.

"When can I go home?" Molly asked.

"If you have a ride, I can release you this afternoon." He turned and looked at Stacey. "Are you a relative?"

Stacey shook her head. "No, but I'm her neighbor and best friend. I informed the nurse that I could give her a ride home, and I'll be taking care of her as well."

"Excellent. She's a very lucky young lady. Her injuries could have been much worse. The broken ribs are going to give her the most trouble. The pain can be excruciating if she pushes herself too much." He turned and looked at Molly. "It's important that you don't lift anything heavy or do any strenuous exercise. The bruising and swelling will go away over the next couple of weeks, but the ribs will take the longest to heal."

"I'll make sure she doesn't, Doctor," Stacey confirmed.

"Okay then, I'll have the discharge papers written up and you should be able to go home in a few hours."

Molly smiled. "Thank you, Doctor." She then gave Stacey a grateful smile, relieved to have her in her life.

CHAPTER 11

On the day of the interview, Molly was a nervous wreck on top of dealing with the injuries and constant pain she was experiencing. She'd thought of nothing else all week except the interview, counting down until the day arrived.

Like every morning since arriving home, she'd inspected her facial bruises and swelling in the bathroom mirror. Today, she was relieved to see that most of the swelling had subsided, but she still detected traces of yellow bruising around her eyes and her left cheek. "Shit!" she said aloud. "Well, Stacey is going to have to do her magic," Molly said, talking to her reflection in the mirror and remembering Stacey was off today. She had told Molly last night that she would stop by after her boyfriend Doug left around 8:00 for work. It was only 6:30, which gave Molly enough time to get some much-needed coffee.

Molly was truly thankful for Stacey; for the past week she'd not let her down and kept her promise, being there for her every day. Molly didn't know how she did it. Before leaving for work she came by every morning with sandwiches for her lunch, grabbed any laundry she had, and spruced up her apartment. On her way home, she called and asked if Molly needed anything from the store.

Together they practiced having Molly sit in a chair at the computer for at least 30 minutes. At first, Molly screeched in pain after five minutes, and had screamed, "I'm not going to be able to do this!" Stacey had pushed her and insisted they practice morning and night, every day. Yesterday was the first time she'd managed to sit at the table for almost an hour.

"See, I told you that you could do it!" Stacey had squealed, pleased with herself for pushing her.

It had been almost a week since the accident, and even though she was still in pain, Molly was finding it a little easier each day to move around, but not quite ready to run a marathon or even push a vacuum around her apartment. The swelling on her thighs had also diminished, but they were still severely bruised, and her legs continued to ache constantly, which made standing or walking for any length of time a struggle.

After making her coffee, she took a large sip of the delicious liquid before running a bath. Feeling insecure and still in pain, she hadn't tried taking a shower since arriving home from the hospital. She took her time in the bath, not making any sudden moves, and turned on the showerhead while sitting in the tub to wash her hair.

Stacey arrived shortly after 8:00. She let herself in and found Molly in the bedroom, staring at her clothes in the closet.

After tossing her purse on the bed, she approached Molly and asked her if she needed help picking something out to wear.

"Sure, but I only need a top, I'm going to wear my pajama bottoms."

Stacey cracked a laugh. "You're joking, right?"

"No, I'm not. They're loose fitting and the most comfortable thing I have to wear. You won't be able to see them when I'm sitting at the counter."

Stacey nodded. "Well, you've got a point there. Okay, let's see what you've got here," she said, sliding the coat hangers along the rail while looking at Molly's clothes. "You should wear something cheery and colorful."

"Oh yeah, I'm feeling super cheerful with broken ribs and bruises." Molly suddenly remembered her face. "Speaking of which, you need to fix my face - you can still see the yellow bruises."

Stacey stopped going through her clothes and took a closer look at Molly's face. "Oh, we can fix that, don't you worry," she said, turning back to the clothes and pulling out a sage green blouse with white pearl buttons. "This is pretty. How about this?"

"Wow! I've not worn that in a long time, I forgot I even had it. When I worked in an actual office, we had to dress in business attire, like real people," she laughed. "I didn't last long at that advertising and event company," she added.

"Okay, come on. Let's do your hair and makeup. Your interview is in a few hours," Stacey told Molly, laying the chosen blouse on the bed. "I'll grab the stuff from the bathroom and meet you in the kitchen. I think it'd be easier if you sit on one of the bar stools at the counter."

"I agree. It's where I've been sitting most of the time, and where I'll sit for the interview."

While waiting for Stacey, Molly poured herself another cup of coffee and hollered, "do you want some coffee?"

"No thanks. I've had my quota," she shouted back. "I'll be there in a minute. Where's your hairbrushes and combs?" she yelled from the bathroom.

"Second drawer down on the left," Molly said, taking a sip of coffee.

A few minutes later Stacey entered the kitchen carrying an array of cosmetics, hairbrushes and scissors.

"What are the scissors for?" Molly asked, creasing her brow.

"I'm going to trim your ends; they're all split. When was the last time you got a haircut?"

"I don't remember, it's been a while."

"Well, it's no wonder you have split ends," Stacey remarked, shaking her head. "Come on, sit down."

Still feeling the pain in her ribs, Molly persevered, managing to stay seated as Stacey trimmed her hair and worked on her face, hiding the bruises and applying light makeup to her eyes, cheeks and lips.

Stacey smiled when she was finished, standing back to admire her work. "Not bad, I must say. You should wear makeup more often; you look really pretty."

Molly looked up, her eyes bright. "Really? I want to see," she said excitedly, getting up slowly.

Stacey followed her to the bathroom, anxious to see her reaction.

"Oh my god, how did you do that?" Molly squealed, slowly leaning forward to get her face closer to the mirror. "I don't see any bruising! And where did you find this ruby red lipstick? I don't remember ever using this color, but I like it."

"It's mine. I grabbed it from my purse, and you can keep it. It's definitely your color with your long, dark hair."

Molly ran her fingers through her hair. "I love what you did with my hair, it looks so full and bouncy, and the ends look great."

"That's because I used a blow dryer, which I know you never do."

"I don't recognize myself," Molly said, still wearing a large grin. "Thank you so much."

Stacey matched her smile, pleased with her work. "You're welcome. Now, I'm going to let you get dressed - well, half dressed," she joked. "Call me when your interview is over. I'll be waiting anxiously for all the details."

Molly turned and gave her a large smile. "I will, and thanks again. Wish me luck," she added, as Stacey grabbed her purse from the bed, wished her luck and left the room.

Left alone in her apartment to gather her thoughts and calm her nerves, Molly changed her top from the white t-shirt she was wearing to the pretty sage blouse and took one final look in the mirror. Pleased with what she saw, she returned to the kitchen and took a seat at the counter, booted up her laptop, and took a deep breath before logging in for the interview. "You've got this," she whispered, waiting for the website to load.

CHAPTER 12

M olly soon found herself face-to-face on the screen with a slender, middle-aged woman. Her light, auburn hair was short, the ends curling below her cheeks. Like Molly, she wore little makeup; only a brush of pink lipstick, some black mascara to accentuate her lashes, and a little blush. Her jawline was prominent and her cheekbones high. Molly relaxed when she gave her a friendly smile.

"Hello Molly, I'm Lucy Davis. Thank you for taking time out of your day for this interview."

Molly sat with her clammy palms clasped together in her lap, and in her best professional voice, replied, "Hi Lucy, and no problem. Thank you so much for considering me for the position."

"It's my pleasure," Lucy said, picking up some notes and taking a moment to scan them. "Let me tell you a little bit about the position and what it involves. I want to ensure it's something that interests you, okay?"

"Okay," Molly replied.

"Caroline Moors, the owner of the bookstore, is dealing with some family issues and is seeking a person to overlook the entire store during her absence. This will include staff management and scheduling, restocking and ordering new releases of books. She needs someone who has experience in promoting the bookstore and bringing in more business. Quite frankly, the bookstore is on the brink of closing its doors, and Caroline is unable to do any events currently due to her personal affairs. Her hopes are to hire someone who can prevent this from happening, and to basically turn the bookstore around and save it. Do you think you have the qualifications and experience to achieve her expectations?"

A rush of adrenaline raced through Molly's veins, she knew she could do this. She had the experience and loved a challenge. She smiled. "Yes, I do. I've worked in advertising and planned many events for family-owned businesses and big corporations. I've also organized many charity events for a variety of businesses, and I currently work for a trade show company and help businesses plan their booths. I've also designed and worked many booths at events for my clients. Promoting businesses in diverse ways is all I've ever done. I'm not afraid of hard work, and I already have many ideas that may help the bookstore."

"Can you give me a couple of examples?" Lucy asked.

"Yes, certainly. I'm sure the town has many local authors - we could host a meet-and-greet night with book signings and wine. Maybe a weekly book club held at the store with live readings from authors. And I'm sure I can come up with many more ideas," Molly said excitedly.

"Well, I like the few you've mentioned," Lucy said, giving her a friendly smile.

"One concern I have is your age." Lucy looked down at her notes and continued to speak. "You're only 29. What we're asking of you is a huge responsibility."

Molly nodded. "Yes, it is, but I've never been afraid of hard work and have led many successful campaigns and events for many businesses; from small bakeries, clothing stores, coffee shops, yacht brokers, Old Navy and many more. I've been working since I was 16, and I entered the advertising business when I was 19. I have over ten years of experience."

"Very impressive, I must say." Lucy looked at her notes again. "Another thing that concerns me is that you live in Texas, and we're in Montana. Are you willing to leave everything behind, including your current job, to come work for us? It's quite a sacrifice to make. What if it doesn't work out? Why would you want to make such a change in your life and move so far away? I'm not sure I could do that. I'd like to know why you're willing to do that?"

Molly took a deep breath; she sensed she hadn't convinced Lucy to hire her. Her age was a concern, as well as her living so far away. She had to pull out all the stops and lay it on thick. She wasn't planning on using this leverage, but felt she must now.

"I'm ready to make a change because I have no family here, just bad memories and solitude. Three years ago, I lost my parents in a devastating fire. I have no siblings, and I live alone. Texas holds nothing but bitter and sad memories for me. I'm young enough that I can begin a brand-new life away from here and start over. Leaving what I have will not be a sacrifice - I look at it as closing a chapter and beginning a new one." Molly paused and took a deep breath. She felt the beads of sweat forming on her brow, and when she began to speak again, she was unable to hide the tremor in her voice. She didn't want to resort to begging, but she was desperate and felt she had no choice. She looked straight into the camera, locking eyes with the woman who held her future in her hands. "Look, Lucy, I know I can do this job. I can promise you that and I won't disappoint you. I have no distractions. No husband or family. No children and no pets. I will put one hundred percent of my time and focus on rebuilding the bookstore, and, in fact, make it better than it ever was. From what you've told me about Caroline; I want to take away her worry and stress and let her focus on her personal issues. When she's ready to return, I plan on having the bookstore thriving. Please, let me prove myself to you and give the bookstore what it deserves, a second chance." Molly quickly wiped her brow, her hands shaking as she waited for Lucy to respond.

With misty eyes, Lucy spoke. "I'm so sorry for your loss. That is such a tragic story, and my heart goes out to you. Thank you for sharing with me an extremely difficult time in your life. It makes all the sense in the world to me why you're willing to move and start fresh. Moving to Montana sounds like it would not only be a way for you to heal, but, like you said, it would provide you with a new beginning. I'm going to make a note of this on your application and discuss it with Caroline. I appreciate your honesty and expressing to me what we can expect from you." She gave Molly a caring smile. "You said all the right things, and believe me when I tell you I'm taking notes, and that you have definitely got my attention. I'm intrigued by your enthusiasm, your work ethics and your promises. I can assure you; they will not go unnoticed when I meet with Caroline."

"Thank you, it's been extremely hard, but I've always been a strong person. Losing my parents at such a young age has only strengthened me and made me realize that we need to be the best we can be, because none of us know how long we have on this earth, and I apply that to my work as well."

"You are absolutely right. A great rule to live by." Lucy gave Molly another caring smile before leaning back in her chair." Well, Molly, I have everything I need. It's been a pleasure talking to you and getting to know you better. I have a few more interviews to do, and I'll be meeting with Caroline next week to go over the applicants. I will be in touch shortly afterwards with our decision."

"Will you let me know either way, whether I have the job or not?"

"Yes, of course," Lucy confirmed.

"Okay, thank you, and it was pleasure to meet you, too. Thank you for your time and your consideration. I truly appreciate it. I can't tell you how much this will mean to me if you decide to hire me. I would be forever grateful." Molly tittered nervously. "I'm sorry, I shouldn't beg."

"It's okay, I get the impression this may be a long-term position for you, which is something that is important to us when making our decision."

Molly's eyes lit up and doubled in size. "Yes! Most definitely. I want to make Montana my new home; meet new friends and become a part of the community where the bookstore is located. I have no intentions of coming back to Texas."

"That's good to know. I will be in touch, and thank you."

"You're welcome, and again, thank *you*."

Molly waited for Lucy to sign off first and sat there numbly, looking at the blank screen and reading the banner across the bottom, "*Session has ended.*" She nervously sucked in air and vigorously rubbed her clammy palms together. "God, I hope I didn't come across too heavy with my sob story," she said aloud before slowly standing and pacing the small kitchen in circles. "I need a drink," she said, her hands still shaking. She headed to the fridge and found a lonely can of Coors Light. After hastily pulling back the tab, she leaned back against the counter and took a huge swig, her eyes closed. Beer had never tasted so good, she thought to herself as she took a second large gulp. Soon after, savoring the flavor of the beer, her nerves began to calm, and her hands became steady. She set the can on the counter and scanned the area for her phone, spotting it next to her laptop. "I need to call Stacey. She's probably dying to know how it went." Walking over to the kitchen bar to her laptop, she quickly slowed her pace as she was reminded of her broken ribs by the piercing pain shooting through her abdomen. "Ouch! Fuck!" she screamed, as she reached for the phone and held her side with her other hand.

Trying her best to ignore the pain, she located Stacey's number and called. After four rings it went to her voicemail. "Damn it!" Molly hissed, waiting for the prompt to leave a message. "Stacey, where are you? I'm all done with the interview. Call me as soon as you get this message." Disappointed that Stacey didn't answer, Molly returned the phone to the counter and looked at the screen on her laptop again. The banner was still there, telling her the session had ended. Looking at the screen again, she replayed the interview again in her head, questioning herself about having left a good impression on Lucy. She had never been so raw and honest in an interview before, and she worried that she may have overdone it. "God, I hope I didn't scare her off, but, as they say, honesty is the best policy. Well, let's see if it's true," Molly said to herself. She clasped her hands together and raised them to her chest. "Please hire me, I'm begging you," she whispered, still staring at the screen before closing her eyes and saying a short prayer. The sound of her phone ringing snapped her out of her thoughts.

CHAPTER 13

When Molly saw Stacey's name flash across the screen, she quickly picked up her phone and answered. "Stacey! Where are you?"

"I'm at home. I was out on the balcony with Henry when you called. So how'd it go?" Stacey asked, excited to hear all the details.

"I think it went okay," Molly replied anxiously. "She was really nice, and super friendly, which I wasn't expecting. I thought she'd be a stuck-up corporate snob for some reason, but she was totally the opposite."

"What kind of questions did she ask you?"

"The usual - my work experience, my skills, then I got really nervous when she asked me why I wanted to leave Texas and start a new life in Montana."

"Oh, shit! What did you tell her?" Stacey gasped.

"Well, I couldn't tell her the real reason, I'd never get the job."

"So, what *did* you tell her?" Stacey repeated, raising her voice a notch.

Molly hesitated before answering. "I told her about the fire and losing my parents."

Shocked by Molly's confession, Stacey gasped again. "Wow! You never talk about that."

"I know, but I felt like the interview wasn't going in my favor. I had to do something, I felt desperate."

"So you played the sympathy card, you wanted her to feel sorry for you?"

"Yes, I guess I did. You know how important it is that I get this job. Everything will finally fall into place if I do, we both know that. So, I told her about the fire, and that I needed to get away from here and start over."

"Was she sympathetic?"

"She was shocked and yes, sympathetic, too, and she actually got a little teary eyed - I wasn't expecting *that*. Whether it helps my chances or not, I don't know. She told me she has a few more interviews, and she'll let me know in a week or so. God, another waiting game. I hate this."

Hearing the frustration in her voice, Stacey tried to calm her down. "Hey now, look how far you've come since you started this obsession of yours three years ago. What's a few more weeks?"

"It's not an obsession; it's my life, god damn it, and stop calling it that. It's the life I'm supposed to have," Molly countered.

Shocked by her outburst, Stacey was quickly consumed with guilt. "I'm sorry. I know how important this is to you, and I honestly hope it all goes in your favor."

"It has to," Molly snapped. "I have no other plans if it doesn't." Panic swept through her. "God Stacey, what if I don't get the job?"

"Let's not go there, we've had this conversation numerous times. You just need to hold it together for the next few weeks and try not to stress out about it."

Molly gave a sarcastic laugh. "Ha! Easy for you to say. We're talking about my life, not yours."

"I know that, and I support you one hundred percent." She paused, feeling sorry for Molly knowing she'd gone through a lot in the past week with the accident, and now the stress of not knowing the outcome of the interview. "Listen, why don't I treat you to lunch so you can take your mind off all of this?"

"No, you don't need to do that, besides, I'm not sure if I can sit at a table for too long, my ribs are still killing me."

"Oh, come on, you need some cheering up. We can go to Denny's. Not the fanciest of places, but they have a counter where the seats are high, *and* it's within my budget," she joked. "You just sat at your kitchen counter for the interview, so you should be fine to eat a meal," Stacey reminded her.

"You're right. I need to get out of this place. I've been cooped up all week. Give me about 15 minutes to get changed."

"Great. I'll be over in a bit, and we can take my car."

MOLLY WAS glad she listened to Stacey. It felt good to get out of the apartment and be a part of society, even if it was just for a few hours to share a meal. They arrived at the restaurant close to 1:00. It was still busy with the lunch rush, but they avoided waiting for a table by taking two open seats at the counter.

"Are you comfortable?" Stacey asked, watching Molly sit down slowly.

Molly nodded. "Yeah, it just takes me a minute to find a position that doesn't hurt."

Stacey handed her a menu from the chrome holder on the counter. "Order whatever you want. It's on me," she added, smiling.

Molly returned the smile. "Thanks. This was a good idea you had; I'm already feeling better."

"I knew you would. You've been spending too much time alone inside that crazy head of yours." She gave Molly's arm a gentle nudge. "Things will work out, no matter what the outcome is. You must keep telling yourself, even if it doesn't go the way you hope, at least you gave it your all and you'll be able to move on."

"The moving on part will be hard," Molly confessed.

"Yeah, it will be, but I'll be there right beside you, supporting you and helping you along the way. Either way, you've got this."

"God, I hope you're right," Molly replied, feeling appreciative of Stacey's friendship. Then she smiled. "Okay, enough talk of my woes. Per your instructions, we came here to take my mind off the interview and everything else keeping my head in the mud, so let's order and change the subject." She cracked a laugh and smirked, "I know, we can talk about your love life."

Stacey rolled her eyes and laughed. "How about you get a boyfriend so we can discuss yours." She grinned and nudged Molly's shoulder. "Doug is coming over tonight, so we can have that discussion tomorrow," she joked.

"Hopefully without too many details," Molly chuckled, looking at the menu.

CHAPTER 14

For Molly, the following days and weeks peaked her anxiety having not heard from Lucy. She was beginning to wonder if the position had already been filled and they'd decided not to inform the applicants of the outcome. Maybe they just had too many people apply and it would've been too much work for them to reach out, Molly told herself. She'd considered emailing Lucy and asking her if they'd reached a decision but decided against it, not wanting to come across as too pushy. Instead, she tried to keep herself busy with work, having returned 12 days after the accident as the pain had subsided. She was finally able to sit comfortably at the table with her laptop, and she was driving again, depending less on Stacey's help with running errands and shopping. But Stacey still insisted on coming by every day to check on her, always staying for a cup of coffee or a glass of wine. A few evenings they treated themselves and dined out.

Molly had already decided that if she didn't get the job she wouldn't give up but would continue on with her quest. It could take a bit longer with more hours of research, but she wasn't a quitter. She was in it for the long haul, no matter how long it took; this was too important to give up on and just quit. No, she needed to follow this through and see what would happen and accept it, no matter what. Molly hadn't told Stacey of her plans, hoping she wouldn't need to. Everything relied on getting hired.

Molly was thankful she'd be working at the Home and Garden Show this weekend, a show she'd been coordinating and booking vendors for. She had many clients that she'd reached out to and knew their businesses well. She was often hired to design their booths and assist them at events. These were side jobs and were not related to the company she worked for. They paid her well, and it was additional funds towards her savings, and someday, her new life.

This weekend she would be setting up the booth for Fred and his wife Rita, who owned a recycled furniture business. They were also going to pay her to tend the booth with Rita while Fred went out of town in search of unique items for new products. Molly loved their creativity and the joint business adventure they shared, finding nostalgic items and refurbishing them for modern times. Vera handled the business side - finances and booking shows - while Fred worked his magic creating beautiful pieces as he and his wife shared ideas. They were a great team, and Molly had a knack for dressing the booth that showcased every piece beautifully. She'd done numerous shows for them in the area and each one had been a success. This one was at the convention center in the city of Austin, which was about a 30-minute drive for Molly if traffic was good, and a roughly two-hour drive for Rita, who'd be driving alone since Fred would be out of town. Molly planned on meeting her at the convention center at 6:00 am. Because of Fred's absence and Molly's broken ribs which were still healing, they were grateful the convention center had a crew that would help vendors unload and take their items to the booth.

Tomorrow being Friday and the 15th day with still no word from Lucy regarding the job, Molly planned on working in the morning and calling it a day by noon so she could spend the rest of the day planning for the show. She'd have to figure out what to wear, make sure she had the necessary tools to hang things knowing that Rita lacked a sufficient supply, and pack an ice chest with food and drinks, remembering from previous shows that lines were long and food was expensive at these shows. Molly also planned on taking an early bath and being in bed by 8:00 since she'd have to leave at 5:00 am. She always gave herself an extra 30 minutes in case of accidents or unforeseen traffic, which was always a given driving to Austin, no matter what time of day it was.

As she sat at the table in the kitchen writing her list for the show, her body jerked when her phone rang. "Ouch! she screamed from the sudden movement of her body as sharp shooting pains racked her ribs. "Shit! I can't be moving like that!" she hollered, holding her abdomen to ease the pain. Using her other hand, Molly reached for her phone on the table and glanced at the screen. She gasped when she saw Lucy's name and took a deep breath.

"Oh my god, she's calling me." Negative thoughts immediately consumed her. "Do I want to talk to her? What if it's bad news and she's calling to tell me I didn't get the job?" Sweat beaded up on her brow and her hands shook. Holding her phone with both hands fearing she may drop it, Molly continued to stare at the screen, unsure of what to do. She took another deep breath to calm her nerves, and before the last ring, swiped her finger across the screen to take the call.

CHAPTER 15

M
olly spoke in a soft, nervous tone, clutching the phone with both hands. "Hello."

Lucy's voice was quite the opposite - upbeat and happy, calming Molly's nerves. If she had bad news, she wouldn't sound so joyful, Molly thought to herself.

"Hi Molly, it's Lucy. How are you doing?'

Still in pain from her recent sudden moves, she lied. "I'm good, thank you. I'm not going to lie though, I'm anxious to hear the verdict. Did I get the job?"

Lucy chuckled. "That's one of the things I like about you, Molly, you don't beat around the bush, always straight to the point."

Molly felt at ease talking to her and felt comfortable enough to crack a little joke. "Are you like me? You're not going to beat around the bush about the job, are you?"

Lucy laughed again. "No, I'm not. The position is yours if you're still interested."

Molly gasped and sucked in air before releasing a loud scream, but refrained from any sudden body movements. "Oh my god! Are you serious? I have the job?"

"Yes Molly, I went over all of the applicants with Caroline, and we both agreed, you're perfect for the position. You're young and ambitious, and from the tragedy you've endured as well as the loss of your family, I can see you're a strong woman and a fighter. I appreciated your honesty when you told me the story about your family, and we understand completely why you'd like to leave Texas and start over. The fact that you'd like to make our little town your next permanent home gave us confidence in hiring you. None of our other applicants could commit to even a couple of years. We don't want to have to do this again in a few years, and it sounds like you'd be around for a while and make a wonderful asset to our business. I loved the ideas you came up with so quickly for the bookstore, and can't wait to hear more after you settle in."

Molly couldn't hide her excitement. "Oh, I have all kinds of ideas, from making the store inviting and attractive to potential buyers to holding events that will bring people in to the store. I've been going to sleep every night since my interview thinking about it, and I'm so excited. Thank you so much!" she squealed. She'd never remembered being this excited about *anything*.

"We're not only excited to meet you, but very excited to get you on board. I have a good feeling about you, and I'm sure that we've made the right choice."

"Thank you, and I promise I will not disappoint you. I have a lot of questions, but the most important one is when do I start? I have so many things to take care of before I leave."

"We realized when we made our decision that this would be a big move for you, so we want to give you plenty of time to pack, find a place to live and get settled. Caroline said she would be okay for a while with the staff she currently has in the store. She's very excited and is willing to work with you to make this a smooth transition for all concerned. She doesn't want you to be under any stress during your move."

"Oh, thank you; that was very nice of her, and I can't wait to meet her," Molly said, her hands shaking from a combination of excitement and nerves.

"She's great," Lucy replied. "It's why I've been working for her for over ten years. She's not only an amazing person, but a wonderful friend and boss, too." She paused. "Now, how much time do you need?"

Molly quickly calculated everything she needed to do. Find a place to live in Montana, which she'd have to do online, give notice to her landlord in Texas and to her employer, and pack. "Oh gosh, is 45 days too long? I could maybe do 30," she added.

"I think 45 days works, but if you can be settled within 30 days, of course we'll have you start then. How does that sound?"

"Fantastic!" Molly cried, tears of joy trickling down her cheeks.

Lucy had an idea. "How about I call you in two weeks for an update and you can tell me how things are going? In the meantime, I have a dear friend, Vera, a real estate agent and property manager. She's the 3rd generation in her family, and they've resided in this town for decades. She knows this place inside and out, and is well known in the community. I'm sure she can help you find a place. Would you like me to send you her email and phone number?"

"Oh, yes please, that'd be wonderful!" Molly gasped. "There are so many scams online, you never know who you're doing business with. A referral would be great! Thank you, I appreciate it."

"You're welcome. I'll send it straight away. In fact, I should let you go, I'm sure you're anxious to begin making your list," Lucy joked.

"I am, and I can't thank you enough." She released a nervous laugh. "I can't believe this is happening. Thank you so much for believing in me."

"You made it easy, Molly. I'm excited for you, too. I'll check in with you in two weeks, okay?"

"Sounds great. Have a great night, I know I will," Molly laughed.

After ending the call, Molly sat frozen in her seat, numb from the life-changing conversation. All the grueling, lonely hours she'd spent on her laptop; her research had led her to this moment. This is what she'd been dreaming about and wanted, so why was she so scared? Molly knew why - fear of the unknown. She had the job, but what if they didn't like her? Or even worse, what if she didn't like them? She just couldn't let that happen.

What if she hated the town of Riverbanks? She'd never lived anywhere but Texas, it was all she knew. Where she lived was a busy suburban town: how would she adapt to living in a small rural town? She had spent many hours researching Riverbanks on the internet and looking at Google Earth. It sounded charming, nestled in the Beartooth Mountains where everyone knew everyone. With a population of 3,000, the nearest city was Billings, 60 miles away. Molly wasn't sure if she'd get accustomed to that. There was no Walmart, Target or any of her other favorite stores. Family-owned stores and restaurants including the Read More Books bookstore where she would soon be the manager, was what kept Riverbanks thriving. "Was this really happening?" Molly whispered under her breath, her mind drowning in negative thoughts.

Other than the fear of the unknown, just making the life-changing move alone terrified her. She'd be leaving everything she'd ever known behind, including her only friend, Stacey. She'd be driving by herself across four states with all her worldly possessions in her eight-year-old Honda Civic. She wasn't worried about the car not making the journey, it only had 60,000 miles on it, and Molly had always been adamant about getting regular oil changes and tune-ups. She also had AAA Roadside Assistance, but driving that many miles alone unsettled her. Maybe she should have listened to Stacey and got herself a dog, it would have made the ideal companion.

Molly couldn't shut her mind off. Her list was growing by the minute, and fearing she might forget something, she reached for the notepad next to her laptop and quickly began jotting down notes. She suddenly felt overwhelmed. There was so much to do and she had no idea where to begin. While adding to her ever-growing list, she suddenly stopped and gasped. "Shit! I need to tell Stacey," she said aloud. Molly checked the time on her phone and saw that she'd still be at work. "I'll leave her a message," she decided, grabbing her phone. After letting the voicemail play, Molly spoke. "Stacey, you're not going to believe this! I sure as hell don't believe it. I got the job! Call me and come over as soon as you get home." Tears welled up in her eyes. "It's happening, Stacey. I'm so nervous, but at the same time, I'm excited, too. Somebody pinch me," she chuckled, ending the call.

CHAPTER 16

Molly wasn't expecting to hear from Stacey for at least a few hours, knowing she was working at the restaurant till 5:00. She continued to add to her list which had now grown to over two pages. She checked the calendar - if she really pushed herself to get everything done within 30 days, she'd be starting her new life in Montana by the middle of September, right before the winter season began. Living in Texas, she never had to deal with snow, but from her research over the past few weeks, she learned that the small town of Riverbanks endured quite a bit of snow every year. She just hoped it wouldn't be as bad as an ice-storm, something she experienced a few years ago in Texas that left her with no power for days. Molly was actually looking forward to getting snowed in, curling up beneath a cozy blanket and losing herself in a good book as the snow silently fell outside turning everything white.

Molly spent the next few hours prioritizing her list and decided that the first rule of order was to give notice to her job and to the landlord. She would do both first thing in the morning, then call Vera the real estate agent in Riverbanks who Lucy had recommended. The rest of the day she planned on checking out rentals in Montana and getting ready for the show this weekend. It would be the last commitment she made. She had a new life to plan, and nothing was going to stand in her way.

Now that her prayers had been answered and she had the job, Molly spent another hour on the computer browsing websites about Riverbanks, knowing it would soon be her new home. She downloaded photos of what seemed to be a charming little mountain town on the riverbanks of Yellowstone River, hence the name. Main Street was lined with turn-of-the-century buildings that had been converted to gift shops and restaurants, reminding Molly of a small town in a Hallmark movie. They even had a movie theatre that played all the classics which Molly was a huge fan of. Being only an hour from Yellowstone National Park, the town benefited from tourists in the spring and summer who were visiting the park, fishing on the river, or hiking the many trails surrounding Riverbanks. Being a popular ski resort, the town also attracted winter tourists, and boasted numerous hotels and fine places to dine.

Reading up on the town and studying the photos more closely, Molly was excited about the new life ahead of her. She could see herself fitting in and hopefully making new friends that would evolve into close friendships like she had with Stacey. Sadness suddenly crept in; Molly would truly miss her. It was the only downside to her move.

While checking her emails she discovered Vera had emailed her, letting her know she'd call in the morning. Molly's phone rang; she smiled when she saw it was Stacey and quickly answered the call.

Stacey screamed into the phone causing Molly to hold it away from her ear. "Oh my god! I can't believe it; you got the job! When do you start?"

Molly laughed at her excitement. "They've given me 45 days to get settled in Montana, and I'm going to try and do it in 30 days, but there's so much to do, I may be pushing myself."

"I'm coming over. I'm about ten minutes away from home. I'll feed Henry really quick and take him out to go potty, then I'll come over. Shall I pick up a pizza?"

"Sure, I've not even thought about eating since I got off the phone with Lucy. I can't believe this is happening, Stacey! I don't know where to start and I need your help. My brain is going a thousand miles a minute," she laughed.

"We'll make a list of everything you need to do."

I've already started one, and it keeps growing. I don't know how I'm going to get everything done."

"I'll help you," Stacey told her, and continued to show her support. "We've got this, I'll be there in a jiffy. Now go make yourself a cup of coffee or have a beer and shut that mind of yours off for a bit."

"I can't," Molly laughed, "but I'll try. I'll see you in a bit."

While waiting for Stacey, Molly took her advice and poured herself a glass of wine, it was the only alcohol in the fridge, and she needed some spirits. In an attempt to shut off her mind, she turned on the TV and selected The Andy Griffith Show; one of her all-time favorites. Holding her wine, Molly settled on the couch with a pillow behind her back to ease her ongoing pain, and soon lost track of time enjoying the show. She was startled when she heard Stacey come barging through the front door.

"Hey Molly, I'm here with pizza!" Stacey yelled, marching over to the kitchen counter.

"Damn girl! You scared the shit out of me."

"Sorry, I figured I'd just use my key knowing you're still in pain; I didn't want you to get up to answer the door."

"Yeah, scaring me is much better," Molly joked, slowly rising from the couch to meet Stacey in the kitchen where the aroma of pizza filled the air. "Damn, that smells good. I'm starving," Molly said, opening the lid of the pizza box.

"I'll grab two plates. What are you drinking?" Stacey asked.

"I just had a glass of wine, so I'll take some milk. I don't want to get buzzed and possibly injure myself again," Molly laughed.

Stacey stopped in the middle of the kitchen on her way to getting the plates. She turned and smiled at Molly. "I'd give you a big hug right now, but I don't want to hurt you with your broken ribs, and I'm really happy for you. You've worked so hard for this moment, and I feel like crying. Then, as I was driving home, it suddenly hit me -

you're moving, and I'll probably never see you again. I know it's selfish of me, but I'm really going to miss you."

Molly returned the smile and wiped away a tear that'd trickled down her cheek. She was touched that Stacey felt the same way she did. "I'm going to miss you, too. It's the only part that sucks about this whole move." She paused, giving Stacey another smile. "Promise me you'll keep in touch. I'm going to call you every week, and maybe you can come out for a visit someday?"

Stacey wiped her misty eyes. "Yeah, of course I'll keep in touch, but we all know how that goes. We'll call every week for a while, then it'll be every two weeks, then every month until we no longer call each other. That's what always happens."

Molly approached Stacey and gave her a hard stare. "Then we need to make a promise to ourselves that we won't ever let that happen. Do you promise?"

Stacey nodded. "I do, but it still sucks that you're leaving."

"I agree, it does, but I honestly believe our friendship is strong enough to survive this and that we'll remain best friends for years to come."

"I'm going to do whatever it takes to ensure it does," Stacey agreed. "Now, come on, let's eat some pizza, then I want you to show me your list." She grinned. "I bet I can add to it!"

CHAPTER 17

Stacey was right, she'd added lots of items to Molly's list that Molly had overlooked, including mapping out her drive to Montana which would be a long, 1,400-mile drive.

"You're also going to have to book a room in some hotels along the way where you can rest and have a good meal. You can't drive that many miles without resting," Stacey told her after they'd finished their pizza and sat at the counter going over Molly's list.

"You're right," Molly replied, updating her list.

Stacey leaned back and folded her arms. "And you'll need to call the Gas and Electric company and request they turn off your utilities on the day you leave," Stacey reminded her.

Molly rolled her eyes. "God, there's so much to do. Maybe I'm pushing myself too hard to try and be in Montana within 30 days."

Stacey gave Molly's arm a gentle squeeze. "Don't stress over it, each day you'll be crossing a few items off your list, and in a few weeks, you'll know where you stand and will have a better idea of when you'll arrive in Montana." Stacey shrugged her shoulders. "If it takes 45 days, so be it. Your new boss is okay with that, so you should be, too."

Molly appreciated her words of wisdom and knew she needed

someone to keep her grounded. "You're right, I tend to push myself too hard sometimes." Molly smiled. "Thank you, I needed to hear that. Tomorrow I'm just going to focus on getting ready for the Home and Garden Show this weekend with Rita, then I'll call Vera, the real estate agent in Montana, and give notice to my job and landlord."

Satisfied with Molly's goals, Stacey smiled. "There you go. That's enough for one day, and you know I'm here to help, too. Doug's coming over tomorrow night, he's working nights all weekend, so maybe this weekend while you're doing the show I can help with something?"

Molly thought for a moment. "Do you want to map out my drive and some possible places to stay on the way, seeing as how you mentioned it?" she said with a cheeky laugh.

Stacey's eyes lit up. "I would love to. I love maps, and Google Maps makes it so easy. I will have everything organized by the time you get back from the show. You'll just have to book your rooms. Is it a one- or two-day show?"

"It's a one-day show, thank god, but it will take me a few hours to help Rita tear down the booth, which means I won't be home until well after midnight. The show ends at 7:00 pm."

"Okay, then on Sunday I'll come over and we can go over what I plotted out for you."

"Sounds good, but not too early, I'll want to sleep in after a late night at the show."

Tossing her head back, Stacey laughed. "Don't worry, I'll let you sleep in. Why don't you call me when you're up and have had your coffee quota?"

"That works," Molly said with a bright smile.

Stacey scanned the kitchen and glanced over at the adjoining living room. "It's a good thing you don't have to take any of the furniture, and you don't have many pictures on the walls, another plus. What about your other stuff, dishes and such; are you going to be taking them all?"

Molly leaned back, pleased she was feeling less pain which told her that her ribs were healing. "I don't know. I'll have to go through everything," she said with a heavy sigh. "I've accumulated so much crap since I moved here, and I still have the same car. It's not all going to fit, so I'm going to have to let some of it go."

"Like what?" Stacey asked, looking around the kitchen.

"Things like dishes - I can buy new once I'm settled in my new place. I'm afraid they may get broken on the drive, so I don't mind using paper plates for a while."

"That's a good idea, and just take a few cooking pans, you don't need a whole set. I'll help you go through everything if you want."

Molly smiled. "Thanks, I don't know how I'd do any of this without you."

"You don't have to thank me silly, that's what friends are for. I'm happy to help. Now, let's go over your list one more time before I go home. I'm working the morning shift again tomorrow and have classes. Doug is coming over at 8:00."

AFTER A SURPRISINGLY GOOD night's sleep, Molly woke up anxious to begin her day and start checking things off her list. It was early, 6:00 am, and she didn't need to log into work until 9:00. Her list had grown immensely thanks to Stacey's help last night, and to freshen her memory, Molly looked it over as she sat at the counter drinking her coffee.

Once fueled with caffeine, she remained in her bathrobe and called her landlord, leaving a message that she was moving and giving him a 45-day notice. After some thought, she added that she may be leaving in 30 days if she could get everything done. Leaving the message made everything suddenly feel so surreal. This was it, there was no turning back now. She just gave notice, and in a month, maybe a month and a half, this place would no longer be her home. The hairs on the back of her neck tingled and her palms began to sweat with anxiety. She rubbed her hands together to calm her nerves, shook her head to stop the tingling, and opened her email. It was time to notify her job.

It took Molly almost half an hour to write her letter of resignation. She wanted to word it just right, making sure to include how much she'd enjoyed working for them, and appreciated the experience they'd given her, as well as how much she'd learned while she was employed by them. She went into detail as to why she was quitting, and about her new job in Montana, stating that it was an opportunity she couldn't pass up and hoped they would understand and give her a good reference to add to her resume. Satisfied with the letter, Molly read it three times before hitting the send button. Hearing the "woosh" noise as it made its way through cyberspace gave Molly the chills. She'd just crossed another stepping-stone. Everything she knew about her life was about to change. A new chapter was beginning, she thought, reaching across the counter, grabbing the list and crossing off two items.

The next thing she wanted to do was call the real estate agent before logging into work. She checked the time and saw that it was almost 8:00, then remembered Texas was one hour ahead of Montana. "Damn it, it's only 7:00 there. It's too early to call," she hissed, and decided she'd call during her lunch break. Disappointed, she pushed the list aside and spent the next hour on the line with Rita to make last minute arrangements for the show tomorrow before starting work.

Much to Molly's delight the morning went by quickly, even though she found it hard to concentrate on her work. Her mind was consumed with her list and everything that needed to be done. Making her morning even better was receiving a pleasant email from her employer, wishing her luck on her new adventure and confirming that her last day would be August 31st and that they would indeed give her an excellent reference.

Molly counted the minutes down to noon and quickly clocked out for lunch, anxious to call Vera in Montana. After making herself a turkey and cheese sandwich, she grabbed a Sprite from the fridge and made herself comfortable at the counter. She located Vera's number in the email she'd sent and keyed it in her phone.

After three rings a pleasant female voice said, "Hi, this is Vera speaking. Thank you for calling Riverbanks Properties, how may I help you?"

"Hi Vera, this is Molly Rosswell in Texas. You emailed me and said I should call you about finding a place to rent. Lucy at the bookstore referred you to me."

"Yes! Hi Molly, I'm glad you called, and congratulations on your new job! You're going to love it here, and Caroline and Lucy are fabulous! I'd be happy to help."

Molly instantly felt at ease with Vera's friendly voice and her endorsement of the town and Caroline. "Thank you so much. I'm a little nervous about moving so far away to a place where I don't know anyone and of which I know nothing about. I've never been out of Texas," Molly confessed.

"Oh, don't you worry, young lady. You're going to make many new friends here. It's a small town, and we all know each other's business," Vera laughed. "I'm sure you'll fit right in, and everyone knows the bookstore."

"Everyone's business, eh?" Molly said, nervously, thinking about the real reason why she was moving to Montana.

"Oh, I'm just kidding, it's just a tight-knit community. We all look out for one another. Now why don't you tell me your budget and what you're looking for and I'll see what I can find."

"Okay," Molly replied. "It's just me, I'm single and have no pets, so a one-bedroom apartment would be fine. I don't need a yard, either. As far as my budget goes, I'm not really sure yet. Where I live now, I have a one-bedroom apartment, and I pay thirteen hundred a month."

"Rent here is going to be a bit more expensive, I'm afraid. Being close to Yellowstone Park and a ski resort, we're a tourist town. We have very few apartments, but we do have some town houses that have one- and two-bedrooms, and some cute, small one-bedroom homes just out of town that may be available. Let me see what I can find, and I'll email you some listings to look at."

Molly was thrilled with how easy Vera was making this for her. "Thank you! That would be great; I really appreciate your help."

"It's my pleasure. You sound like a wonderful young lady, and I'm looking forward to meeting you and welcoming you to Riverbanks. My family has lived here for decades, going back to my great-grandmother, and let me tell you, I wouldn't want to live anywhere else. Most people that move here never leave," she laughed.

"It sounds wonderful, and I'm very excited. Now, if I see something I like, what do I do? Do I call you?"

"Yes; if there's a rental that interests you, give me a call and I'll tell you more about it, I know every building in this town," she joked. "If there's nothing you like, then I'll keep looking."

"Thanks again. I need to get back to work in a bit, but I'll start looking at them tonight."

"Great! I'll talk to you soon."

After ending the call, Molly leaned back in her chair and took a sip of her Sprite, feeling more relaxed about the move. One of her worries was finding a place to live as she was now so far away in Texas. But Vera had instantly eased her mind, and her anxiety since accepting her new job quickly disappeared. She smiled, leaned forward, grabbed her list and checked off another item before eating her sandwich and returning to work.

CHAPTER 18

Molly's prediction of feeling exhausted after the Home & Garden Show was an understatement. By the time she returned home she could barely stand. Every muscle in her body ached, her feet were numb and swollen from standing all day, and her ribs hurt more than they had all week. Driving home had been a challenge - her eyes were heavy, and she feared she might fall asleep at the wheel. She rolled down the two front windows, wanting to feel the cross-breeze, and played music from her phone through the speakers of her car at full blast.

Even though she was exhausted, she refused to take the elevator and instead pushed herself to climb the two flights of stairs to her apartment, where her ears buzzed from the calming silence that instantly soothed her when she closed the door behind her. She leaned back and closed her eyes, embracing the quietness of the room. "Oh, it feels good to be home," she whispered under her breath. She had done many shows and knew what to expect. It was always non-stop from the minute she left in the morning until finally arriving home late at night. Unloading the merchandise, setting up the booth, dealing with potential customers all day then taking down the booth at the end of the day and driving home took a toll.

It was good to see Rita again and spend the day with her running the booth. She hadn't seen her in six months since the last show they'd done together along with her husband Fred. She was still her flamboyant self, dressed in a bright, multi-colored long dress and wearing large hoop earrings and an assortment of colorful beaded necklaces and bracelets, reminding Molly of the hippy days. Much to Rita and Molly's delight, it was a successful event. Rita sold many items, received orders for some custom pieces, as well as some leads on buying items for new pieces to refurbish. The only damper for Rita that day was when Molly told her she had a new job and was moving to Montana next month.

"I'm afraid this will be the last show I'll be able to help you with," Molly said regretfully.

"Oh no! I'm going to miss you. You have such a knack for these shows, and you always make the booth look so beautiful and inviting. I have to say, I've learned a lot from you."

Molly smiled. "Thanks! I'm going to miss you too, but I'm looking forward to a change in my life. I'm sure you'll find someone just as qualified."

"Oh, I'm not so sure about that. You've set the bar pretty high when it comes to running these things. I never have to worry or question anything you do. If your new job doesn't work out, promise me you'll call, okay?"

Molly shuddered at the thought. It MUST work out she reminded herself, and faked a polite smile. "I promise."

Now at home in the solitude of her apartment, Molly was too exhausted to eat, even though she hadn't had anything since lunchtime. It was after 11:00, and all she wanted to do was peel off her clothes and feel the softness of her pillow and blankets. Molly didn't hesitate with her wishes, and within ten minutes she was sound asleep.

~

MOLLY SLEPT in until after 10:00 am, feeling fully rested by the time her eyes opened to greet the world. There was something about Sunday mornings that comforted her. Was it the sleeping in with no alarm, or lounging around all day in her pj's if she'd chose to? It was a day with no rules or schedules, and definitely her favorite day of the week. After giving her body a good stretch, she grabbed her phone off the end table and saw that Stacey had texted her at 7:00. "Why did she text me so early?" Molly mumbled, pulling the covers off and leaving the warmth of her bed before reading the message.

Molly read the text, "*Let me know when I can come over. We need to talk.*"

"Well, that doesn't sound good," Molly said aloud, walking to the kitchen to make a pot of coffee, then remembered that Stacey was going to map out her drive. Molly assumed it was something about that and continued on with her morning routine before texting back.

Enjoying her morning of solitude, Molly was in no hurry to call Stacey and decided to browse through the listings that Vera had emailed as she drank her coffee. She gasped when she saw the price of the first rental. A one-bedroom, one-bath duplex in the *Madison Creek Courtyard*. "Twenty-four hundred dollars!" she screeched, almost gagging on her coffee. "That's insane, and it's smaller than this place." Molly quickly calculated what she'd have left over after taxes from the salary she'd discussed and agreed to with Lucy. "That's over half my wages. I'll have just over one thousand dollars to live off of for the whole month. Shit! That sucks," she hissed under her breath, quickly moving on to the next listing in hopes of finding something less expensive.

Molly quickly became discouraged after going through all of the listings Vera had sent her. To her dismay, the only one cheaper was an old, rundown shack eight miles out of town on a half-acre. The rent was twenty-one hundred dollars. Molly studied the listing; the house had seen better days and there were no neighbors nearby. The thought of being that far out of town, alone in the middle of nowhere and not knowing anyone was a definite no. "Scratch that one," she said, closing the browser. "Well, none of these are going to work.

Surely there's something cheaper," she whispered under her breath, closing her laptop in discouragement.

Molly stared at the blank wall of the kitchen across the room, contemplating calling Vera and asking if she knew of anything less expensive but decided against it, realizing it was Sunday, and she'd most likely not be in her office. Disheartened by the rental prices, Molly stewed over the numbers – she calculated her living expenses, including gas, food, and utilities and insurance, and concluded that she'd be eating beans and rice every night. Upset by the numbers and knowing she couldn't talk to Vera until tomorrow, Molly refused to have her Sunday ruined by the expensive listings and looked at her list to see what else she could tackle. The first thing she saw on the list was *Map Out Drive*. Her spirits suddenly flipped for the better. "There we go!" she said, reaching for her phone, hoping Stacey had some better news about her drive.

Molly was about to hang up the phone after five rings with no answer, when Molly heard Stacey's voice.

"Hello," Stacey said in a sleepy voice.

"Hey Stacey, it's Molly. Did I wake you?'

"Yeah, that's okay."

Molly chuckled. "I guess you had a good time with Doug. You're certainly sleeping in."

"Don't talk to me about that fucking asshole!" Stacey snapped, her voice fueled with anger. "It's because of him I've *not* slept." Then she began to sob. "I'm a friggin' mess. How could he do this?"

Molly had never heard Stacey so angry and upset before. "Hey, what's going on? What happened?"

"He fucking dumped me!" Stacey cried between sobs.

"What? You're kidding! Why? I thought everything was going good for you guys."

"So did I. I feel like such a fool. He played me, Molly. How could I have been so stupid!"

Molly was about to reply with some soothing words to comfort her when she was startled as her front door opened and saw that Stacey was standing in the doorway with her phone to her ear, dressed in red pajamas dotted with blue stars. Her blonde hair was a tangled mess, and smudges of mascara and eyeliner shadowed her eyes.

Molly's jaw dropped. "My god, you look terrible," she said, hanging up her phone.

Still holding her phone to her ear, Stacey ran over to Molly, her face drenched with tears, her sobs tearing at Molly's heart. "How could he?" Stacey cried.

"Oh Stacey, I'm so sorry," Molly said, as she took Stacey into her arms and held her tight.

Stacey set her phone on the counter and cried heavily on Molly's shoulders, her tears uncontrollable. Within a minute Molly's shoulder was soaked. Molly remained silent, holding Stacey's trembling body and allowing her to release the hurt she was feeling. After a few minutes Molly spoke in a soft soothing voice, stroking Stacey's hair. "It's okay. That guy is a fool for breaking up with you. He'll never find anyone better than you."

Stacey lifted her head away from Molly's shoulder and let out a loud, sarcastic laugh. "Ha! Apparently, he already did."

Molly was shocked. She pulled away from Stacey and gave her a hard stare. "What? What do you mean?"

"I mean, he dumped me for another woman." She raised her hand to her brow, closed her eyes and sobbed as she spoke. "Can you believe it? He wasn't working nights, he never did. All this time he was seeing *her*." She raised her voice. "He lied to me! I am such a god damn fool!"

Molly couldn't believe what she was hearing. "You're kidding! But I thought he'd been working nights for months; so all this time he was seeing another woman?"

Stacey nodded between tears, holding her hand up to her mouth.

Molly could feel the anger rise within her. "What a fucking jerk! And he told you all of this on Friday when he came over?"

Stacey nodded again. "Yep. He was all nice and sweet when he got to my place. He had a bottle of wine and made me a steak dinner. Then over dinner he casually says, '*I can't do this anymore, I've been seeing someone else and we're really happy, and I want to break up with you."'*

Molly gasped, "Oh wow! That's pretty heartless."

Stacey wiped her eyes and began pacing the room. "Oh, that's not the kicker. When I got upset and began crying, because stupid me, I actually liked the guy and thought we loved each other, he got angry and said I was making this harder for *him*." Stacey's eyes narrowed, her nostrils flared. "Can you friggin' believe it? Then he goes on to tell me about how working nights was a big lie, but he didn't know what else to do." She burst out with another sarcastic laugh. "He even had the audacity to tell me to grow up, that couples break up all the time, and that I was just making things worse by crying like a little girl." Stacey's tears came on strong. "He was so mean to me, and I did nothing wrong."

"Oh Stacey, I'm so sorry. I didn't know him that well but, by god, you deserve so much better. I'm sure you'll meet someone deserving of you."

"Oh, screw that! I'm not dating for a while; I'm done. From now on it's going to be just me and Henry."

Standing in the middle of the room facing each other, Stacey became more composed after releasing her hurt and anger. Molly folded her arms and gave her a caring smile. "I know you'll be okay, I just wish I wasn't leaving in a month during this difficult time you're going through. Now I'm going to be worried about you."

Stacey's eyes lit up, concerning Molly. "I want to go with you! she shrieked; her eyes wide.

CHAPTER 19

Molly was stunned by Stacey's request and didn't react immediately; unsure she'd heard her correctly - *Did she just say she wanted to go with me?* Molly asked herself.

"You want to *what*?" Molly finally replied.

"Go with you!" Stacey squealed in a high-pitched voice. "I'm done with this place. There's nothing here for me, and you're my best friend. If you go, where does that leave me? No boyfriend, no friends. I'll be miserable. I want to start fresh, like you."

Shocked, Molly didn't know what to say. She couldn't be serious. "Stacey, you can't just pack up and leave, what are you talking about?"

"Why can't I? You are," Stacey pouted.

Molly disagreed with her reasoning. "Stacey, I have a job when I get there, and a new home with Vera's help. Not only that, but I'm also doing this, as you well know, for other reasons which you've known about for years since I've confided in you. I'm not doing this on a whim because I've had a bad day, I've been planning this for years. You can't just pack in your job, and what about school? You only have a month left and then you can start your own business. You've worked really hard - don't throw it all away now because some guy dumped you. He's not worth it. No guy is."

Stacey shook her head, refusing to listen. "I can get another job. There're many restaurants in town, being the tourist spot it is. I'm sure I'd have no trouble finding a waitressing position."

"And what about school? You're not thinking straight," Molly advised, raising her voice and throwing up her hands in frustration.

Stacey remained calm; she had it all figured out, she just needed to persuade Molly. "I can finish the course online. That's always been an option, but I wanted the in-person experience. I'm more disciplined if I'm physically in class, but I can knuckle down at home and finish the last month without being distracted."

Molly gave her a piercing stare. "And where's home going to be?"

Stacey ignored the evil eye Molly was giving her and grinned. "Well, with you of course. We can get a place together." Stacey grinned again. "It'll be so much fun."

Molly couldn't believe what she was hearing. "Stacey, do you have any money saved for such a big move? If we get a place together, it's going to have to be a two-bedroom, and I can barely afford a one-bedroom. I can't support you until you find a job *and* pay for the gas *and* the food for the drive to Montana. It's a ridiculous idea, just stop," Molly insisted.

Stacey's smile disappeared. "It's only a bad idea if you let it be. You're right, I don't have any money saved and I don't expect you to support me. I've been with you the entire time on this journey, helping you with your research, supporting you, and giving you words of encouragement when you've had doubts and concerns. I'd like to continue to be there for you. What if your plans don't go the way you'd hoped? You'll be stuck in Montana all by yourself, miserable and alone, but not if I go with you."

"Not gonna happen," Molly snapped. "I'm determined to make this work. It has to!"

"I KNOW THAT, but there's no guarantees in this world. We can make this work Molly; we can support each other. I want to start fresh just as much as you do, I know we can do it together," Stacey pleaded.

Molly rubbed her brow and closed her eyes, pivoting her body in a circle, unsure of Stacey's idea. "I don't know Stacey, you still haven't said how you're going to pay for anything. It's not a bad idea; I don't disagree with that. I'll admit, driving through four states with someone versus going alone when I've never even been outside of Texas does sound appealing, and much safer. But the reality is you're not in a position financially to move, and like I just said, I can't afford to pay your way." Molly shrugged her shoulders. "It's that simple."

Stacey wasn't giving up. "I can come up with the money."

Molly gave Stacey a hard stare. "How? It took me years to save what I have."

Tired of standing, Stacey sat down at the counter. "I'll sell my car. It's a good car with low mileage, and it's paid for. I know I can get at least six thousand dollars for it."

Molly shook her head in disbelief. "You can't sell your car!" she hollered. "How are you going to get around in Montana?"

Stacey leaned back in her chair, clasping her hands together. "It would be too expensive to drive two cars there, and from what I've seen it's a small town. I have no problem walking until I can buy another car. The money I get from the car will help pay for gas, food, and rent until I get a job, which I promise will be the first thing I do."

"I'll tell you right now, half of that money will go towards the rent of a two-bedroom apartment. Rent is a lot higher there."

"Then we'll get a one-bedroom, and I'll sleep on the couch. I'm telling you, I know we can make this work."

Molly had to admit she was warming up to Stacey's idea. Selling her car made sense. She was right, it'd cover her costs, but being crammed in a one-bedroom place unsettled her. "I don't know, it might be over a year before we can afford a bigger place. I can't see you sleeping on a couch for that long."

"Aren't you forgetting I lived in my car for a month a few years ago before I met you when I lost my job? If I can live in my car, I sure as hell can sleep on a couch."

"I *had* forgotten about that, sorry. That was a difficult time for you." She gave Stacey a caring smile. "The other thing I'm afraid of is our friendship."

Stacey wrinkled her brow. "What do you mean?"

Molly took a seat next to her at the counter. "I'm worried that living together, especially in cramped spaces, may affect our friendship. I've never lived with you, and we get along great now, but what if we get on each other's nerves or want some space? We get along well because we have our own apartments to escape to. That won't be the case if we rent a place together."

"Well, we'll just have to make sure we never let that happen. We can honestly do this Molly, and you must admit, doing this with someone you know would be much better than doing it alone."

"I don't know. You make it all sound so easy," Molly said with uncertainty.

Stacey laughed. "That's because it is. You're overthinking everything. Any obstacles or challenges we come upon on our way we can figure out and conquer, together. Come on, Molly. You know this is a better plan."

Molly hesitated. She still had many concerns, but what appealed to her most was not being alone on the fourteen hundred-mile journey she was about to embark on, and as much as she hated to admit it, Stacey was right: what if the job didn't work out, or worse, she and Caroline didn't get along? It would be nice to have a shoulder to cry on and have someone to help her through what could very well be her darkest days. She smiled at Stacey and raised her hands. "Okay, you win. You've convinced me. Let's do this. Sell your car and start packing, 'cause you're coming to Montana with me!"

Stacey's jaw dropped, her eyes big as saucers. "Really?" she screamed, throwing her arms in the air with joy as she jumped off her seat and did a small dance around the room. She ran over to Molly to hug her. "This'll be so much fun! A road trip, a new state, a new home, and a new job. I can't wait!" She spun around the room, excitement engulfing her. "I'm going to list my car today and give notice to the landlord and the restaurant. I'll put in the work with school and get most of my classes completed before we leave. I know I can," she beamed, her eyes bright.

Molly laughed at her enthusiasm. "Don't push yourself too hard; like you said, you can finish them online."

"I know, but I'm so excited about everything. An hour ago, I felt like my world had ended, and now everything is coming up roses - life is good again!"

"I'm excited too. I'll admit, I've been nervous and somewhat scared about making this trip on my own. Now, because of your brilliant idea, I can't wait to say goodbye to this place and Texas and start anew," Molly smiled. "Thank you," she said, embracing her.

Stacey returned the hug. "This will be good for both of us. We're going to be there for each other no matter what, right?"

Molly squeezed Stacey's hand. "No matter what."

CHAPTER 20

Molly was excited with the plans she and Stacey had made, and within minutes the room was filled with smiles and excitement. What had started out as a terrible weekend for Stacey had turned into a future of adventure, and a new beginning for both of them. Molly had concerns about being able to afford a place in Montana, but her worries quickly slipped away as fast as they'd appeared.

"Did you have a chance to figure out the route?" Molly asked, pouring herself a second cup of coffee.

Stacey shook her head. "No, sorry, not with the shitshow Doug pulled. Do you want to do it together?"

"Sure! It'll be fun, then we can look at rentals. We'll make a morning of it," Molly smiled.

"Great! Do you mind if I bring Henry over? He's all alone at my place. He knows his mama was upset over the weekend and he wouldn't leave my side." She glowed with a loving smile, thinking of Henry. "He snuggled with me in my bed all night."

"Of course. Do you want me to pour you a cup of coffee while you go get him?"

"That'd be great, thanks. I'll be back in a minute," she said.

Alone with her thoughts, Molly took a sip of her coffee and smiled. She was pleased Stacey had had the idea of joining her, and the more she thought about it the more it made sense, not only for safety reasons, but driving through four states and sharing expenses would also help. They'd shared a lot, and Stacey was the only one who knew the real reason why she was about to make such a bold move. It was only right she'd be there to the end, no matter the outcome.

As she waited for Stacey to return, Molly poured her a cup of coffee and placed her laptop between the two barstools, then grabbed a pad and pen to take notes. A few minutes later the front door opened; Henry rushed in ahead of Stacey and raced over to Molly sitting at the counter entering their destination on the MAPS app.

Molly looked down and smiled at Henry who was jumping excitedly at her feet. "Hey Henry, I'm happy to see you too," she laughed, looking over at Stacey. "Your coffee's on the counter."

Stacey approached the counter with Henry close on her heels and picked up her cup. "Go lie down, buddy," she told him, taking a seat next to Molly and glancing at the computer screen. "Oh great, you have the MAPS app up."

After a few hours of researching their options and endless cups of coffee, they were both satisfied with the route they'd planned out.

"The most I've ever driven is 200 miles to a show," Molly laughed. "One thousand four hundred and twenty-six miles is quite a jump," she laughed, putting down her pen.

"I think breaking it up into three parts and stopping overnight is a good idea," Stacey said. "That'll give us a chance to rest and freshen up."

"I agree - there's no way I want to drive fatigued. I want to enjoy it and spreading it out over more days will allow us to see more and have some fun while we're at it."

Stacey picked up the notepad and read their trip out loud to confirm everything. "So, on the first day we're going to drive 437 miles to Amarillo, Texas, and spend the night there. Then the next day we'll do another 434 miles to Denver, Colorado, and spend the night, then the last leg will be the longest - 555 miles to Riverbanks."

"Sounds good to me. We can take turns driving and stop to eat on the way." She leaned back in her chair. "Now we need to book the hotels, and I know you don't have the money right now."

Stacey shifted in her seat. "I'll pay you as soon as I've sold my car, I promise."

"I know you will; if you don't, I'll be driving alone."

Stacey wasn't sure if she was being serious, but she wasn't taking any chances. "This is the only thing you need to cover for us. By the time we leave, my car'll be sold, and I'll have cash for everything else."

Thirty minutes later their rooms were booked and the final details of their route mapped out and printed.

"We did it!" Stacey squealed, raising her palm for a high-five, which Molly gladly gave.

"Damn, that feels good," Molly said, beaming as she reached for her list, and grinning as she checked off another item. "I need a break - my head is spinning from figuring all that out."

"Me too. I'm going to take Henry for a walk on the grass. Do you want to join me?" Stacey asked, standing up and stretching.

The minute Stacey said the word 'walk,' Henry, who'd been sleeping soundly at her feet in front of the counter, jumped up and barked, spinning in circles excitedly.

"Well, he knows *that* word," Molly laughed. "Yes, a walk and some fresh air sounds good. Are you hungry? We can grab some sandwiches from the deli and bring them back. Then we can start looking at the rentals Vera sent me."

Stacey agreed. "Sounds good." She looked down at Henry as he continued to bark and jump up on his hind legs. "You wanna go for a walk, buddy?" She stood up and grabbed his leash from the counter.

CHAPTER 21

They returned an hour later to Molly's apartment with sandwiches in hand after walking Henry, excited to begin their search for a rental. Henry, satisfied from his walk, wasted no time claiming his spot in front of the counter at Stacey's feet and was soon fast asleep. Molly grabbed two beers from the fridge and plates for their sandwiches, taking a seat at the counter next to Stacey.

"Now we have to find something in town because you won't have a car," Molly said, shifting in her seat before opening her laptop.

"Close to town should be okay," Stacey replied. "It might be a little cheaper if it's not in the center of town," she grinned. "I'm not afraid to walk, it'll be good exercise for me."

Molly chuckled. "You might say that now but trust me, it'll get old real fast if you have to walk everywhere."

Vera had sent Molly eight rental listings. They immediately crossed off the first four as they were either too far from town or too expensive, leaving a one-bedroom in the *Madison Creek Courtyard*, and three priced a few hundred dollars more which were in town or less than a quarter mile away.

"The *Courtyard* one is the cheapest, but it's still two thousand four hundred dollars," Molly complained. "It's the only furnished one which is a huge plus," she noted.

"But if we split it, that's only twelve hundred each. That's cheaper than what we're paying here," Stacey reminded her.

"That's only if you find a job within the first month. If not, then I'm going to have to fork over your share of the rent." Molly let out a heavy sigh, leaned back in her seat and folded her arms. "I'm taking quite the risk here, Stacey. I said I can't afford to cover for you, and now I'm worried I may have to."

Stacey gave her arm a reassuring squeeze. "I will walk that town from morning till night every day until I find a job." Her tone was serious as she tried to convince Molly not to worry. "I will do whatever it takes." She squeezed Molly's arm again. "I'm not going to let you pay my share of the bills." She smiled. "Don't worry, okay?"

Molly managed a weak smile. "I'll try, but it's hard not to. I'm also worried about you sleeping on the couch with no bedroom or a space of your own. How long do you think that's going to last before you get sick of it and turn into a total bitch?" she laughed.

Stacey laughed. "I'm not going to turn into a bitch. I don't care where I sleep and neither does Henry."

As Molly leaned forward to look at the computer screen, she cried, "oh, shit!"

"What?" Stacey asked, her brow furrowed.

"Do any of these places take pets?"

Molly quickly scanned the listings, the *Courtyard* being the first. "Oh, thank goodness, that one does and so does this one, but the other two don't, so scratch those off. Now we're down to two, and out of those I'm going to say that I like the *Courtyard* which is right on the edge of town." She turned and looked at Stacey. "What do you think?"

Stacey nodded. "Sounds good to me. We can always look for a bigger place later."

"Which will cost more money," Molly added.

"Yes, but we'll be working and hopefully making more money than we do here. I don't care where we live as long as we have a place when we get there."

"True, good point," Molly agreed. "I'll call Vera and tell her I'm interested in the one-bedroom in the *Madison Creek Courtyard*."

Stacey clapped her hands. "Sounds good to me, I'm so excited!"

"Don't get too excited, we haven't got the place yet. It's the weekend, so she probably won't be in the office. I'll leave her a message and send her an email, too. I'm not expecting to hear from her until Monday."

"Okay, while you're doing that, I'll be at my place checking things off my list," Stacey said.

"Like what?" Molly asked.

"I'm going to call the landlord and give notice, call my job, then list my car for sale, but I'll state in the ad that it won't be available for a few weeks – I'll need it for work and stuff."

"That makes sense. I think I'll start going through my things and make a Goodwill pile." She paused and locked eyes with Stacey. "You do realize we'll have to leave more behind now that we're only taking one car?"

Stacey shrugged her shoulders. "That's fine. Most of my stuff is junk anyway."

Molly chuckled. "Mine too."

After Stacey left, Molly wasted no time in calling Vera. She was happily surprised when she answered the phone. "Hey Vera, I didn't think you'd be in the office today."

"Hi, Molly. I make exceptions sometimes as some of my clients work all week and can only see properties on weekends. You caught me just in time, I was getting ready to wrap it up after showing properties this morning. Did you get my email with the listings?"

"Yes, that's why I'm calling. I'd like to apply for the one-bedroom in the *Madison Creek Courtyard* if it's still available."

"I believe it is. Hold on one second, let me bring it up on my computer." There was a moment of silence before she spoke. "Yes, here it is and yes, it's still available. I can email you the application before I leave the office if you'd like."

"That'd be great, but there's been a change in my plans. My friend Stacey is moving with me - she's had enough of Texas and wants to start fresh too, so we've decided to make this a joint venture. It would be the two of us renting; that won't be a problem, will it?"

"I don't see why it should be, I think it's a wonderful idea. I look forward to meeting her. She'll also need to be on the rental agreement, so be sure to include her information on the application."

"I will and thank you so much. We'll fill it out together later today and I'll email it to you. I'm afraid if we wait too long it could get rented, and really, it's the only one that'll work for us. Stacey has a dog, and there were only two places that took pets; the other one is too far out of town and much more expensive."

"I understand. I'll look for your email and do enjoy the rest of your weekend."

"You too," Molly said, ending the call. "Well, that was easy," she whispered under her breath, feeling skeptical about how smoothly everything was going. She was waiting for something to shatter their plans and disrupt everything. Isn't that how it always goes when things are going so well, she thought to herself. She sent Stacey a text asking her to come over later to fill out the application. After hitting send, Molly had a terrifying thought - *maybe this is our downfall, and we don't get the apartment. Then what'll we do?*

CHAPTER 22

Molly was surprised when she heard a knock at her door. She heard Stacey's voice a few minutes after sending the text.

"Hey Molly, it's me," Stacey said, opening the door.

"Hey, did you get my text? You could have just texted back."

"I did, but I didn't want to write a long text. It's quicker to just come tell you in person."

A look of worry blanketed Molly's face. "What's going on?"

"I had no idea I had to be on the lease. My credit really sucks, and I'm afraid it may affect our application. Can't we just use your information and tell them I'm a guest for a short while?"

Molly rolled her eyes, "Oh crap, Stacey! I already told Vera you'd be staying with me. She's the one that said you'd have to be on the lease. Why didn't you tell me this before we decided to get a place together?"

"Because I didn't think about it, and I never thought it'd be an issue. I assumed *you'd* be the only one on the lease."

"Maybe this wasn't such a good idea," Molly snarled. "You have no money, your credit sucks; is there anything else I need to know?"

"Will you calm down? And no, there's nothing else. This is just a small snag that can easily be fixed. It's not that big of a deal, I think you're overreacting."

Trying her best to control her anger, Molly took a deep breath. "Look at us, we're already arguing, and we've only made this decision a few hours ago. We've never argued before and I've never been pissed off at you like I am now. What's it going to be like traveling together for three days and living in a tiny apartment? I don't know about this, Stacey."

"Oh, come on. You're going to give up that easily?"

"Who said I'm giving up? I'm still moving, I'm just having seconds thought about bringing you along. I don't want this to ruin our friendship, and it seems to be heading that way."

"We won't have a friendship after you move. Eventually we'll lose touch, and besides, need I remind you this is about supporting each other through the good and the bad?"

Molly raised her hands in defeat. "Okay, maybe I'm acting a little irrational, but I want everything to go smoothly." She gave a sarcastic smirk, still not pleased with Stacey. "Funny thing is, I was just saying to myself how easily everything was falling into place so far, and I was wondering what may happen to foul it up, and here we are."

"It's not fouled up, just give Vera a call and tell her I'd rather not be on the lease."

"And what if she insists?"

"If that's the case, then we'll figure it out, but let's see what she says first," Stacey suggested.

"Okay, we'll give it a try," Molly grumbled, grabbing her phone off the counter. "I'll call her right now."

Silenced by Molly's mood, Stacey quietly took a seat at the counter and allowed her to make the call.

"I'm going to be honest with her and tell her why we don't want you on the lease; I don't know these people and they don't know me. First impression is everything, and I'm not going to start telling little lies that may turn into bigger ones."

"We're not telling any lies," Stacey interjected.

"Saying you're a guest and only staying with me for a short while is a lie."

"No, it's not. After I get a job, I may decide to get my own place. We don't know yet what's going to happen a few months from now. All we're trying to do is get to Montana and start fresh, and we agreed that getting a place together is the cheapest and easiest way. Let's try and stick to the plan, okay?"

Molly scrolled through her phone contacts. "Let me call Vera and see what she suggests."

Expecting to leave a message, Molly was surprised when Vera answered the phone. "Hey Vera, are you still at the office? Last time we spoke you were just leaving."

"I had my calls forwarded to my cell. What's up?'

Molly hesitated. "It's about the lease. I just found out from Stacey that she doesn't have good credit and she's afraid it might ruin our chances of getting the apartment, so I wanted to ask you if we could just put everything in my name. Stacey will be living with me, but we don't know for how long, so I suppose she's kind of my guest."

"Of course. That's not a problem at all. Tenants have guests all the time, it's not required they be on the lease. Just send over your information."

"Really? Thank you!"

"No problem. They may have a different way of handling it in the city, but here in our little town we don't like to pry too much into people's lives."

"Oh, I'm loving Riverbanks already," Molly smiled. "Okay, I'll get the information emailed to you by the end of the day. I promise I won't bug you again."

"Hey, that's what I'm here for," Vera reassured her. "If you have any more concerns don't hesitate to give me a call, okay?"

"Thanks, I will," Molly replied, feeling relieved.

"See, I told you everything'd be okay," Stacey said, giving Molly a big grin. "Don't always think the worst about every situation. You made one simple phone call, and look, it's all been sorted. That silly argument we had could have been avoided."

Molly gave a slight nod, ashamed of her outburst. "Yeah, you're right, I owe you an apology. I just want everything to go as planned with no hiccups or problems."

"And it will. We've done okay so far. We have our route mapped, booked our rooms, and will hopefully get the apartment," Stacey said, crossing her fingers. "I'll have my car listed by the end of the day, I'll notify my landlord, and I'll let my work know tomorrow when I go in."

"That's great." Now working with a more positive attitude, Molly rubbed her hands together. "Okay, I promise not to be so negative or worry so much. You're right, we're getting things done, I'm just so nervous about it all."

"I know you are, I am too, but we've got this. Now, I'm going to leave you alone so you can send the application to Vera, and I'm going to write up an ad for my car."

"Okay, sounds good, and I'll let you know as soon as I hear back from her. I wonder how long it'll take?"

"It's a small town, I'm sure they work quicker than any businesses we've had to deal with here in the city."

Molly laughed. "You're probably right." She stood and opened her arms. "Give me a hug, I feel bad about losing my temper, I don't want any bad vibes between us."

Stacey smiled. "No bad vibes," she reassured her before meeting in a hug. "I'll talk to you later tonight, okay?"

"Okay."

After Stacey left, Molly grabbed another beer from the fridge and sat down at the counter. Before opening the rental application on her laptop, she savored a few sips of beer and soon was daydreaming about the journey ahead her and Stacey would be embarking on. Had she made the right decision letting Stacey tag along? Molly still had her doubts but couldn't share them with Stacey. As much as she cared for her, she feared she may become a burden, or maybe already had. Molly did some calculations in her head - she'd paid for the hotel rooms, used her credit card on the application for the apartment, which would be charged if they got it; Molly wondered what was next?

CHAPTER 23

Molly was surprised how fast the next few weeks flew by, but still skeptical at how smoothly everything was falling into place with no major issues as she and Stacey continued crossing things off their lists.

Two days after applying for the apartment in Montana, Molly received the good news that it was hers and immediately wired the funds to Vera along with the signed lease. Upon receiving them, Vera said she could pick up the keys in her office when they arrived in town.

In just one week, early Monday morning she and Stacey would begin their drive to Montana. Her last day at work was Friday which left her a week to finalize everything with no interruptions. She looked around her almost empty apartment. She had spent the last week making numerous trips to Goodwill, leaving only the essentials and the furniture that came with the apartment. Most of her dishes, glasses and pans were gone. Most of her knick-knacks and books, except for a few favorites, were also donated. This week she planned on downsizing her wardrobe, as well as cleaning the bathroom and food cabinets.

Stacey had also been busy donating things, and at the end of the week a couple she'd received a deposit from were coming to pick up her car. The last thing on their list was cleaning their apartments which they'd do the day before they left. They wanted to ensure they'd both get their deposits back which was a few grand and decided to make it a joint effort and clean each apartment together.

"Yours will take longer," Molly joked.

"Are you calling me a slob?" Stacey smirked, hands on her hips.

"Your place smells like Henry. We need to get that dog smell out and freshen up the carpet."

"Henry doesn't stink," Stacey laughed. "Poor Henry. Don't let him hear you say that," she said, looking at Henry with a pitiful look.

"You're used to his smell. Anyway, we'll do your place first because I'm not sure how long it's going to take," Molly said.

Today Molly had an appointment to take her car in for a tune-up, have four new tires put on, then take it to the carwash. Stacey was going to spend the day finalizing her online classes and making more trips to Goodwill.

"*I'll come over to your place tonight after I get back from the carwash and we can go over our lists to see what else needs doing,*" Molly texted.

"*I'm so excited!*" Stacey texted back. "*I can't believe we only have a week to go!*"

Molly laughed at her text before replying with a smiley emoji.

AFTER TAKING care of her car, Molly was relieved and impressed to see that Stacey's apartment was almost as empty as hers.

"Wow! You've been busy," she remarked, looking around at the bare walls, shelves and a couch that no longer had a pile of colorful pillows.

"I have, and I'm exhausted. I didn't realize how much crap I had until I started going through it. I must have made ten trips to the Goodwill, I swear."

Molly scanned the walls again. "You got rid of all your Marilyn Monroe pictures and memorabilia?"

Stacey sighed, looking at the empty walls. "Sadly, yes. I got rid of it all – it was really hard, but it's okay, I know we don't have enough room in your car."

Molly gave her a caring smile. "I'm sorry. I'm sure you can start another collection once we get settled."

Stacey shook her head. "Nah, it's okay. They're nothing but dust collectors anyway, and besides, our tiny place in Montana won't have any room for a collection of any sort," she laughed. "I also sold my TV to the couple who are buying my car. I'll give you half the money for the apartment and the rooms we booked for the drive this Friday after they pick them up."

"Great! I sold mine too, there's no room for a TV in the car. I sold it to our neighbor Jeff. I saw him in the parking lot last week when I was loading the car for Goodwill, and when I told him we were moving, I mentioned the TV and asked if he knew of anyone that'd like to buy it. He said he's been wanting one for his bedroom and jumped at the chance. I'm sure we can find a used one in Riverbanks."

"Well, that was easy."

"I know, he's picking it up Sunday evening, the night before we leave," Molly told her.

"Great! The only things I'm taking, besides my laptop of course, are clothes, and, I might add, I got rid of a lot of my favorite jeans, dresses, boots and shirts. You should be proud of me. I'm taking all my makeup; sorry I can't give up any of that, my nail polishes and some miscellaneous things I just can't part with, including a couple of my favorite blankets." She smiled. "I think I can fit everything in two or three boxes. I really *am* starting over!"

"I'm proud of you. You had way more stuff than me, but it looks like we'll end up taking about the same amount."

"I'll have Henry's things along with his bed, too," Stacey added.

"We'll make a special place for him and his bed in the car so he can look out the window."

"Aww, he'll love that, he's never been on a road trip. I know he's going to love it as much as we are, and he'll be good company for us." Stacey clasped her hands together. "I can't believe this happening!"

"I'm still waiting for the other shoe to drop," Molly confessed.

Stacey slapped Molly's arm. "Will you stop saying that? Everything will be fine."

"I'm sorry, I'm just a very pessimistic person. I'm constantly worrying about everything - the drive, my new job, what if I hate it, what if I can't stand Riverbanks, and what if Caroline hates me?" Molly rolled her eyes and raised her hands. "I sometimes wish I could just turn my mind off."

"I wish I could turn it off for you," Stacey joked. "You're driving me nuts with all your negativity. Just go with it and stop worrying about things that haven't even happened yet."

"I wish I could. I want it to be a year from now, then I'd have all the answers."

"You'll probably have them sooner," Stacey corrected her, deciding to change the subject. "So, the car is ready for its long drive and has no major issues?"

"The car's in good running condition and sparkling clean. I made an unexpected stop on the way home."

"You did? And where was that?"

"I drove past my parent's old landlords, Ted and Doris' place. I saw their car in the driveway and decided to stop by."

"Oh, how did it go?"

"Well, they've been on my mind a lot lately. They really helped me after the fire by taking me in and giving me a place to stay. They've been there for me ever since that horrible day, and I couldn't just leave without saying goodbye after everything they've done for me."

"Do they know about Caroline?"

Molly shook her head. "No, only you know. There's no reason to tell anyone else."

"I agree. It would only complicate things. So, how did they take it when you told them you were moving?"

"There were a few tears shed, and I told them I'd be forever grateful to them. They helped me through one of my darkest times and I'll never forget it," Molly smiled. "I'm glad I went by."

Stacey matched her smile. "Me too. Now, come on, let's go over our list. If you're staying for a while, I have a couple of frozen dinners I can pop in the microwave, and maybe you can help me go through the rest of my kitchen cabinets and box up more things for Goodwill."

"That sounds great," Molly said, removing her jacket.

CHAPTER 24

Much to Molly's surprise, Monday morning arrived quickly with no problems. Wanting to leave at 6:00 am, they'd loaded the car the night before with all their boxes. The apartments were both spotless after spending most of Sunday cleaning. When they called their landlord, they were told there'd be an inspection Monday afternoon, and if everything looked good he'd wire them their deposits.

"He's an asshole if he doesn't," Stacey said, getting in the car. "We spent hours cleaning, and they look better than when we moved in."

"I agree," Molly said, backing out of her parking space. Before putting the car in drive, she leaned forward and looked up through the windshield at the apartment building that'd been home for the past three years. "Goodbye old home of mine, I'm not going to miss you, and goodbye Round Rock."

Stacey rolled down her window and leaned out waving both arms with joy. "Goodbye! It's been fun, but we're off to better places, and I won't miss you either." She turned and looked at Henry standing up in his dog bed, looking out the window. "Henry? Are you ready to go to your new home?"

Henry tilted his head and looked at her, sending out a playful bark, as if he understood what she was saying. After sniffing around and doing a few circles in his bed, he finally lay down, curling his body inward to take a nap.

Already entered in her phone, Molly checked the distance and time of the first leg of their journey to Amarillo, Texas. "Okay. According to the map, it's 445 miles to our hotel, and if there's no traffic or accidents we should be there in seven and a half hours," Molly said, looking at the screen.

Stacey checked the time on her phone. "Okay, we should get there around 1:00 in the afternoon if we don't make any stops."

"I'm sure we'll make some stops," Molly stated. "We'll need to refuel, and the ice chest we filled only has drinks and snacks. It'll be nice to find a decent place to eat and stretch our legs."

"Don't forget we'll have to make bathroom stops for Henry, too," Stacey added.

"I'll be happy if we make it to the hotel by three or four," Molly said, heading towards the I-35 via the Frontage Road.

"Sounds good to me," Stacey agreed, leaning back in her seat. "Let me know when you want me to drive. I've told you numerous times that I don't expect you to drive the whole way."

"I will," she said, not taking her eyes off the road.

AFTER DRIVING for almost five hours on 280 miles of highways and interstates and making a few bathroom stops for Henry, they decided to find a place to eat in Snyder.

"Let me drive after we eat. You've driven the entire time since we left," Stacey insisted as they exited onto Coliseum Drive, driving towards the small town.

"Sure, I could use a nap - my eyes are heavy." She turned and looked at Stacey, "What do you feel like eating?"

"A sandwich sounds good at a place with an eating area outside. I don't want to leave Henry in the car, plus he needs to walk around a bit and stretch his legs."

"Keep your eyes peeled for such a place," Molly said, slowing her speed while scanning the buildings as they drove by.

A few minutes later they both spotted a Subway with tables and benches outside.

"There you go!" Stacey said, pointing out her window. "I love Subway."

"Sounds good to me," Molly agreed, slowing down as she pulled into the parking lot.

Molly went inside to order sandwiches while Stacey waited outside with Henry.

"Keep an eye on the car," Molly said. "Our laptops are in there, and mine has my entire life in it."

"No one's going to steal the car," Stacey laughed.

"You know me, I always think the worst, and we don't know this town. I'm just being cautious."

After lunch and a walk with Henry, they were back in the car and on the road again within the hour.

"Thanks for letting me drive," Stacey smiled as she pulled out of the parking space.

Molly leaned back in her seat and folded her arms. "I'm glad you offered. I didn't realize how tired I was. I'm going to take a nap, wake me up if you need me to drive."

"I'm fine, I took a two-hour nap earlier. I should be okay to drive the rest of the way to the hotel. According to the map it's 200 miles away, and we should get there in about three hours."

"We're making good time. I hope the rest of the trip goes just as smoothly," Molly said, closing her eyes.

"There you go again, always thinking something bad's going to happen," Stacey remarked as she drove to the highway.

Molly kept her eyes closed. "I can't help myself. I've always been this way."

Within a few minutes, Stacey heard subtle snoring sounds and knew Molly was asleep. She began to relax and turned on some light music, focusing on the drive.

As she drove along the desolate highway with no one to talk to,

Stacey began thinking about when she first met Molly, and how she did everything she could to make sure they became best friends. So far, her plan had worked, but when Molly told her she was moving to Montana, Stacey knew she had to find a way to go with her, not realizing at the time that Doug, her ex-boyfriend, had been the solution. She felt bad about lying to Molly, saying he was the one that broke up with her and broken her heart, when the truth was she'd been the one to end the relationship. She was desperate and needed Molly to feel sorry for her. The only disappointment was that Doug accepted it so easily and didn't show any signs of being upset about it. He answered with a simple "Okay, I guess I'll see you around." Stacey hated to smear Doug's name and make him out to be a total jerk, but she had no choice; thankfully Molly took the bait. Stacey leaned back in her seat and smiled. Not only were Molly's plans playing out perfectly, so were hers.

CHAPTER 25

After spending a much-needed night at the Holiday Inn in Amarillo where they feasted on a large pot roast and mashed potato dinner, then watched a movie in their room which had two queen beds, they called it an early night at 9:00.

They woke up at 6:00 ready to start the second leg of their journey. Molly hit the shower first while Stacey wrapped herself in a white bathrobe and took Henry outside to do his business.

When she returned to the room, Molly was already out of the shower and sitting on the edge of the bed putting on her jeans.

"Wow, that was quick," Stacey said, unleashing Henry.

"I want to get on the road as soon as possible. Why don't you jump in the shower and I'll start packing. We can get breakfast to go from the restaurant."

"I have to feed Henry first," Stacey said, grabbing his bowl and a bag of dry food from her duffle bag. "Give me 15 minutes and I'll be ready."

~

THEY WERE on the road again by 7:30 with Molly driving. Stacey checked the map on Molly's phone which had all the routes pre-entered. "Okay, so it's 433 miles to Denver, where we'll be spending the night at another Holiday Inn. According to this with no stops we should be there in six and a half hours."

"Well, we already know we're going to make some stops, so I'm guessing it's going to be about eight hours, which means we should get to the hotel around three or four this afternoon. How about we find a place around noon to eat lunch like we did yesterday?"

"Sounds good," Stacey agreed, turning her head to check on Henry, already fast asleep in his bed. "He sure has been good; he's never been on long trips before." She reached over and pet the top of his head. "He's such a good boy."

"He's been great. I thought he'd be barking and jumping around a bit more, but he's proved me wrong," Molly smiled, pulling out of the hotel parking lot.

Pleased the highways and interstates were clear with no heavy traffic or accidents, they made good time. Molly drove for the next four hours covering almost 260 miles, stopping only for bathroom breaks for their little group.

"Are you getting hungry?" Stacey asked, just outside Walsenburg off the I-25 in Colorado.

"I am, let's stop in this town. It'll be our first stop in Colorado," Molly said, feeling excited about getting out of the car in a new state.

After exiting the interstate, Molly turned onto Main Street. "We should find a place to eat down here."

Stacey sat up and looked out the window. "What a cool town. Look at all the historical buildings, I feel like I'm in the wild west," she laughed.

"It is pretty, and there's no traffic like there was in our old neigh-borhood. Look at those gorgeous mountains off in the distance," she said, pointing ahead.

"Hold on a second," Stacey said, picking up her phone. "I'm going to look them up." After entering the name of the town, she read from her phone. "They're the Spanish Twin Peaks."

"What a great view to wake up to every day," Molly said, taking in the magnificent sight.

"I bet Riverbanks has some spectacular views, and that town is a lot smaller than this one," Stacey said, also enjoying the amazing landscape surrounding the town.

"This is a city; Riverbanks is much smaller," Molly informed her.

After a few minutes of driving down Main Street, Molly spotted a family café and pulled into the parking lot. "This looks perfect, and they have tables outside so Henry can sit with us."

After turning off the engine, the silence woke Henry up instantly. He immediately sat up and stretched before looking out the window. Stacey turned her head and smiled. "Hey buddy, ready to go on walkabout?"

Henry seemed to understand what the phrase meant and jumped from the back seat into her lap, allowing Stacey to hook the leash to his collar before they got out of the car. She gave a big smile as her foot touched the ground. "Hello, Colorado," she said, filling her lungs with fresh air. "God, the air is so clean here, and look, no clouds up above," she said staring up at the clear blue skies.

Molly took the keys out of the ignition and reached in the back for her laptop and purse before stepping out of the car, and like Stacey smiled when she stepped onto Colorado soil. "This is amazing," she said.

Stacey turned and looked at the laptop in her hand. "Why are you bringing that?"

"My whole life is in here; I never let it out of my sight."

Stacey pointed to the wooden tables painted white with red benches to their left. "The car won't be out of our sight, it'll be fine. One of us can sit with Henry while the other goes inside and orders the food. Just lock the car up."

Molly checked the distance between the car and the tables and decided it was safe to leave the laptop behind. "Okay, I guess you're right, but don't let the car out of your sight while you're walking Henry.

"I won't, I promise. My laptop is in there too you know, and I'm buying lunch, seeing how our ex-landlord gave us our deposits back. I guess he wasn't a jerk after all," Stacey laughed.

Molly smiled. "Thanks! Let me go get a couple of menus, I'm starving."

After studying the menu, they both decided on the turkey melt. They took their time eating the oversized sandwiches while they were enjoying their new surroundings. The streets were a lot quieter than what they were used to back in Texas. Antiques stores, boutiques, thrift shops, and a variety of bars and restaurants lined the streets. Stacey nudged Molly's arm as a red pick-up truck with a happy Golden Labrador leaning out the passenger side window pulled into the parking lot.

"He's cute," Stacey whispered, eyeing the handsome man wearing shades and a brown cowboy hat, waiting for him to step out of the truck so she could get a full view.

Molly chuckled. "I thought you were talking about the dog, but now I see the guy behind the wheel," she whispered.

Stacey nodded and grinned. "Yep, the view just keeps getting better in this town."

Molly had to admit, he did look kind of cute, but she wasn't as bold as Stacey. They waited in anticipation for him to get out of his truck. After he pet his dog, he turned and opened the door. With the door blocking their view, the first thing they noticed was his tan cowboy boots beneath his jeans as he stood behind the open door and adjusted his hat.

"Come on, close the door," Stacey whispered, following with a giggle.

Molly smirked and shook her head. "You're too much," she said, not taking her eyes off the guy.

Before closing the door to the truck, the man turned and looked at his dog. "You be a good boy, okay Troy?"

"Aww look, see I'm not the only one that talks to my dog like it's human," Stacey said.

After what seemed an eternity, he finally closed the door to the truck and slid his keys into his back pocket. He was tall and slender, wearing a red-and-black checkered shirt with the sleeves rolled up over his muscular arms. His jeans fit nicely, hugging his well-toned legs. Dusty blonde hair shadowed his face.

"Wow!" Stacey whispered.

"Close your mouth," Molly laughed. "You look like a puppy in heat."

"Right now, I feel like a puppy in heat. He's friggin' gorgeous. Are all the men like this in Colorado? He's beyond sexy."

Molly silently agreed with Stacey. It'd been a long time since a man got her heart racing; then again, she'd removed herself from the dating world a few years ago to commit her time to her research and life-changing move.

Her last relationship ended when she was 27, shortly after the fire. Emotionally distraught from the devastating fire, she didn't have the energy to continue the relationship and ended it with Craig after five months of dating. Eventually she'd get back into the dating world, but right now she had no interest and wanted no distractions from her ultimate goal, but looking and drooling did bring some pleasure, and the man before her was certainly creating that feeling.

"He's good looking, there's no denying that," Molly agreed, watching the handsome guy walk away from his truck.

Using her elbow, Stacey gave Molly's arm a sharp jab. "Shit, he's coming this way - try not to stare."

"Well, it's hard not to," Molly giggled, taking a sip of her iced tea.

Molly's heart raced nervously as he neared their table, and to her surprise he stopped and smiled at them as he removed his hat, revealing a thick head of wavy, dusty blonde hair. "Morning ladies. Beautiful day, isn't it?" he said, his voice deep and muscular.

Molly looked up and smiled. "Sure is."

Not wanting to be left out of the conversation, Stacey gave him a huge smile. "Howdy, this is a really beautiful town."

The man looked over at Stacey and smiled, followed by a sexy wink. "You ladies aren't from around here I take it?"

Stacey shook her head. "No, we're just passing through."

"Where ya headin'?"

"Montana," Molly told him. "We're moving from Texas."

"That's quite a move. Montana's beautiful country, you're gonna love it. I'm Dylan, it's a pleasure to meet you both," he said, holding out his hand.

Molly quickly rubbed her wet palms on her pants and shook Dylan's hand. His grip was strong, and his hands were warm. "I'm Molly, and this is my friend Stacey."

Stacey held out her hand and smiled. "Hi, it's a pleasure to meet you, too. So, you live around here?"

"Yep, me and my wife, lived here our whole lives."

Even though she wasn't interested in dating, Molly's heart sank when he mentioned his wife, and she was certain Stacey's did too.

"You two traveling alone?" Dylan asked, rubbing the brim of his hat.

"Yes, we are," Molly said.

"Well, you ladies be safe out there and enjoy the rest of your day," he said, putting his hat back on.

"Thanks, we will," Stacey said, giving him another smile. She waited until he was out of earshot before she said, "Just our luck, he's married."

Molly cracked a loud laugh. "And if he wasn't? What were you going to do, stay here in Walsenburg and pursue him? Maybe settle down and marry him while I continued on to Montana by myself?"

"No, of course not, but I enjoyed the fantasy while it lasted."

"Yeah, me too. Alright, lets finish up and get back on the road. I'll let you drive to Denver, I'm ready for a nap," Molly said, taking a bite of her sandwich.

CHAPTER 26

As Stacey backed out of the parking space, they both took one last look at Dylan as he stepped into his truck. "I hope I find a guy like that someday," Stacey said, letting out a heavy sigh.

"Don't we all?" Molly giggled. "Hey, you haven't mentioned Doug since he broke up with you. I'm sorry it didn't work out, if you need to talk about it, I'm here." She paused, giving Stacey a caring smile. "It won't ruin our trip, I promise."

Stacey was surprised by her comment. She hadn't thought about Doug since, unbeknownst to Molly, she'd broke up with him. Everything was going according to plan easier than expected, she was much happier, but could *not* let Molly know this, not yet anyway, so she continued playing the sympathy card. "Thanks, I'm okay, I'm trying not to think about him. Leaving everything behind and starting fresh has really helped. If I was stuck in that apartment by myself, it would've been *really* depressing." She smiled. "Thank you for letting me come with you."

"I wasn't sure it was a good idea at first, but I'm glad you're here."

Stacey quickly changed the subject, "What about you? You

haven't dated anyone since Craig. When do you think you'll be ready?"

Molly strained to keep her eyes open and leaned back in her seat. "Oh, I don't know, I'm in no rush. I don't need the complications of a relationship right now," she said, feeling fatigue take over. "I'm tired, wake me up if you need me."

Molly slept for the next two hours as Stacey drove with no incident, listening to soft music while Henry snored quietly from his bed. The drive to Denver was 166 miles via the I-25, and according to the GPS it'd take two and a half hours. Stacey was relieved when Molly woke up just outside Denver. After driving for two days on wide open highways and stopping in small towns, she experienced somewhat of a culture shock. The skyline of the city with its magnificent tall buildings and the Peak mountains in the background made her feel somewhat anxious. The thought of driving in a strange city in traffic made her nervous. Stacey glanced over at Molly, who was in the middle of a yawn, as she stretched and sat upright.

"Hey, you slept for almost the entire drive," Stacey said, returning her eyes to the road.

Molly yawned again and looked out her window. "Is that Denver?"

"Yes, it's huge, isn't it?" She quickly looked at Molly again. "Hey, would you mind driving from here? You know how much I hate driving in the city, and to drive in one that I don't even know terrifies the crap out of me," Stacey confessed, her hands gripping the wheel tightly.

"Sure. Pull over wherever you want, I'll take over."

Forty minutes later they were pulling into the parking lot of their hotel, thankful it wasn't in the heart of the city, and just like the rest of the trip so far, the temperatures were mild with no wind and clear blue skies.

"I am so ready for a shower," Stacey said, stepping out of the car. Before she let Henry out of the back seat, she stretched her arms above her head and walked a few paces to loosen up her legs.

"Just grab what you need for tonight, I want to get a super early start tomorrow. It's our final drive on this trip, and I want to do it in one day if we can. Make sure you bring your laptop."

"Isn't that like over 500 miles?" Stacey asked, hooking the leash on Henry.

"Yep, 555 to be exact, and according to the Maps app it should take around nine hours, but that's without stopping."

"Okay, then we'd better get an early night in. We're going to need to make a few stops for Henry and at least one to eat," Stacey said, letting Henry lead her to a patch of grass underneath a tree. "I'm going to guess it'll take at least ten and a half hours."

While Stacey walked Henry and waited for him to do his business, Molly grabbed her laptop, phone and shower bag, as well as some clean clothes from her duffle bag.

"Here, can you hold Henry while I grab my things?" Stacey said, handing her his leash. "I'm going to leave his dog bed here and just grab his food. It's too much to carry. He can sleep in my bed with me," she added, rummaging through the back seat.

After checking in after their exhausting trek, thirty-five minutes later they finally opened the door to their room, welcoming the sight of the two queen beds.

"I should call Vera and let her know that we should arrive in Riverbanks sometime around 6:00 tomorrow night, but that's only if we leave here no later than 7:00 in the morning," Molly said, tossing her things on one of the beds.

"Okay. While you're calling Vera I'm going to take a quick shower. I feel so grungy from sitting in the car all day, and my hair feels likes straw," she said, running her fingers through her matted hair.

"Sounds good. Do you want to order dinner in tonight? I don't feel like going anywhere," Molly asked.

"Yes! I love that idea; I was going to suggest the same thing and maybe watch a movie, but I don't know that I'll be able to stay awake," Stacey replied, grabbing her shower bag and pj's. She turned and looked at Henry who was sniffing every inch of the room. "I'll feed you after my shower, buddy."

Before calling Vera, Molly kicked off her tennis shoes, plugged in her laptop and fluffed the pillows for support before stretching out on the bed. After a few rings Vera's familiar voice came on the line. "Hey Molly, how's your drive going? Where are you?"

"Hi Vera, it's going great. The weather's been perfect, and we're seeing so much. We just got to Denver and are spending the night here. We should be in Riverbanks sometime around 6:00 tomorrow night. Can I pick up the keys to the apartment when we get there?"

"Yes, of course. I live just a few minutes from the office. Call me when you're in town, and I'll meet you over there, then you can follow me to the apartment."

"That'd be great! Thank you."

"It's my pleasure. Caroline and I are looking forward to meeting you. Drive safe, I'll see you tomorrow."

"Will do, and I'll call you as soon as we arrive."

Excited and nervous at the same time, Molly ended the call and closed her eyes, thinking about her new life that was about to begin in Montana, hoping it would be everything she'd planned for. It couldn't be anything else. She'd worked so hard for this, and the outcome could only be a happy one.

CHAPTER 27

After a much-needed restful night, Molly was the first to wake up at 5:30 when she heard Henry jump off Stacey's bed and begin sniffing near the door.

"Hey Stacey, I think Henry needs to go out," she said, rubbing her eyes as she sat up.

Stacey stirred and let out a loud moan. "What time is it?"

"Five-thirty. Come on, get up; we'll eat breakfast on the way," she said, pulling the warm covers away from her body. "I'd like to be on the road in an hour."

Stacey moaned again. "Okay, okay, give me a minute."

Molly laughed. "Hey, if your dog pees on the carpet, *you're* cleaning it up."

Stacey quickly sat up. "Okay, I'm up," she said, rubbing her eyes. "There's a coffee machine in the bathroom; can you make us some coffee while I take Henry out?"

"Sure, coffee sounds good, I'm on it."

After drinking two small pots of coffee between them, Molly and Stacey were ready to begin the final drive of their three-day road trip. They decided to look for a McDonald's and grab breakfast to go before getting on the I-25.

After checking their room thoroughly for any forgotten items, they grabbed their bags, hooked Henry up to his leash and headed down to the parking lot where they planned on letting Henry go again before getting on the road. Being so early it was still dark out, and an eerie feeling lingered in the air as they walked through the parking lot illuminated by dimly lit overhead lamps.

"Shit! It's cold out here," Stacey grumbled, pulling her jacket tightly around her body.

"No kidding," Molly agreed, rubbing her arms and quickening her pace. "Come on, I'll turn the heater on in the car," she shouted to Stacey who was lagging behind. In a hurry to reach her car and get out of the cold, Molly was almost running until she came to a sudden stop.

"What's the matter?" Stacey asked when she finally caught up with her, confused as to why she came to such an abrupt stop.

Molly spun around, panic in her eyes, scanning the entire parking lot. "Where's my car?"

"What?" Stacey asked, her brow furrowed.

Molly spun around again, "My car! Where's my car? It's not here!"

Stacey scanned the parking lot. "Are you sure this is where you parked? We were so tired last night."

"Yes, I'm sure! This is my parking space." She pointed to a tree close by. "That's the tree where Henry took a dump." She walked over and pointed to Henry's business. "See? It's still here."

Stacey refused to acknowledge that the poop was Henry's. "That could be any dog's poop." She scanned the surrounding area again. "Let's walk around, I think you may have parked somewhere else."

Molly rolled her eyes and hissed. "Fine, but I'm telling you, I parked the car right here. Someone stole my fucking car!"

"Let's not jump to conclusions," Stacey said, trying to calm Molly. "Me and Henry will walk this end of the parking lot while you search the other side, then we'll meet back here," Stacey suggested.

"It's not going to do any good, my car's been stolen!" Molly shouted.

"We don't know that yet. Please, can we just walk the parking lot first? I don't believe anyone would steal your car."

"Why not? Car thefts happen every day, *especially* in a city like this!" Molly yelled, storming off to begin her search.

Panicked, Molly raced amongst the vast rows of cars, checking every silver car. "I can't believe this is happening!" she cried aloud. All these friggin' cars here and you have to take mine? Why?" Every time she came to a silver car and saw that it wasn't hers, her heart sank more, tears pooling in her eyes. By the time she reached the end of her search and there'd been no word from Stacey, she was convinced her car had been stolen. Trembling and full of despair, she pulled out her phone and called Stacey as she headed back to where they'd parted.

"Any luck?" Molly asked in desperation.

"No, I don't see it, but it has to be here."

"It's not Stacey, I've looked at every silver car here. I'm heading back to where we split up. Meet me there."

Stacey reached the spot first and Molly found her sitting on the curb that surrounded the tree where Henry had gone the night before.

"I can't friggin' believe this," Molly cried, raking her hands though her hair. "Everything we owned was in that car. Now do you see why I insisted we take our laptops with us?"

"This is so messed up," Stacey said, standing to her feet with tears in her eyes. "I have nothing but the clothes on my back, some dirty laundry and my shower bag, and thanks to you, my laptop. Even poor Henry lost his bed. What the hell are we going to do?"

"This is what I was talking about. I knew something bad was going to happen. Everything was going so well, but I didn't think it would be this bad. We have nothing! No car, no clothes..." Molly scanned the parking lot again; there was no one else around.

"I wonder when they took it. This place is like a ghost town, and I'm sure no one saw them," Molly said, her tone flat from disbelief. "We need to go back to the hotel and file a report and call my insurance. God, I hate dealing with insurance companies." She raked her hands through her hair again, wiped her moist cheeks and shook her head.

"Will they give you a rental so we can at least get back on the road?"

"They'd better. We're stuck here with nothing!" Molly hollered.

WHEN THEY ARRIVED at the front desk they were greeted by the same tall, skinny young man with short, light brown hair and glasses that'd checked them out.

"Hello again, did you forget something?" he asked with a courteous smile.

Molly placed her laptop on the counter. "No, my damn car's been stolen."

"Excuse me?" the young man replied, shocked by her comment.

"I said my *car* has been stolen. I need to file a police report. Do you have cameras in your parking lot?" Molly snapped.

"Are you sure? Maybe you parked it in another spot."

"I didn't park it in another spot," Molly snapped again, rolling her eyes. "My friend and I walked your entire god damn parking lot. It's not there. Someone stole it." She shook her head in disgust, her anger rising. "Does this happen often at this establishment of yours?"

The desk clerk understood her outburst and tried to calm her. "I'm so sorry to hear that. We *do* have cameras in the parking lot, and I'm sure the authorities will take a look at it and study the footage. I'll make the call right now. Would you mind taking a seat in the lobby until they arrive? I'd be happy to bring you both a cup of coffee."

"I don't want any damn coffee; I want my fucking car!" Molly said sharply, grabbing her laptop.

CHAPTER 28

Along with her laptop, Molly carried the few possessions she owned and marched over to the beige couches placed perfectly in front of the stone fireplace which sadly wasn't lit. Disgusted, she slumped her body onto the couch, keeping her computer on her lap. Stacey was a few feet behind and joined her. She told Henry to lie at her feet, which he obediently did, and was soon asleep.

Molly leaned forward and buried her head in her hands. "I can't believe this is happening. We are literally stuck here at the mercy of my insurance company. They get to decide our fate."

Stacey stretched her legs out in front of her, leaned back into the cushions and stared at the wooden beams and chandelier above her. "The thieves probably saw all of our crap in the back and figured they'd scored when they took our car."

Molly emitted a sarcastic laugh. "Ha! Imagine their faces when they discovered its mainly women's clothes and bedding and is of no value. What pisses me off is that they'll just throw everything we own in the god damn trash!" Molly grasped her hair with clenched fists. "I've never had my car stolen before, where the hell do I start with this shit?"

Stacey sat up and rubbed Molly's back as she leaned forward, her head buried in her hands. "Well, the guy at the front desk said he'd call the cops, so that's a start, and I'm sure they'll be here soon. I think you need to call your insurance company now," Stacey said, offering some guidance.

Molly raised her head and rubbed her brow before leaning back. "Yeah, I guess you're right." She closed her eyes. "I just need a minute."

"Take all the time you need, we aren't going anywhere," Stacey joked, trying to make light of their situation.

Molly closed her eyes and tried to gather her thoughts. Losing everything took her back to the house fire when she'd lost everything, including her parents. Now? Here she was again: she owned nothing and would be starting over for the second time in her life. Why does this keep happening to me? She thought to herself. After the devastating fire, she'd learned not to get emotionally attached to any of her material items, reminding herself that they could all be replaced, unlike her life. It was the attitude she'd lived with since the fire, and she reminded herself that everything in her car could be replaced. She tried to run a mental list in her head on what was in the car but could only remember her clothes and a few precious knick-knacks that sadly were irreplaceable.

She felt a tap on her knee, interrupting her thoughts. "Molly, the cops are here," Stacey whispered.

Molly stirred and opened her eyes. "That was quick, I've not had a chance to call my insurance."

"You've been asleep for 20 minutes," Stacey told her.

Molly quickly sat up, looked around the lobby of the hotel, and spotted two male cops talking to the guy at the front desk. "Shit, I have?"

After a few minutes of talking to the desk clerk, Molly watched him point in their direction and shifted nervously in her seat as she watched the two officers approach her.

"Good morning, ladies," the elder one said, his hand hooked over his belt.

Molly managed a weak smile. "Morning, officer."

The elder officer was slender, over six feet tall with short grey hair. "I understand your car was stolen from this hotel's parking lot."

"Yes, it was," Molly replied. "Can I file a police report?"

The officer smiled. "Yes, of course you can, and I'm sorry to hear that. My partner and I can help you. We'll need a statement from both of you; have you notified your insurance company?"

Molly shook her head. "No, not yet; I fell asleep. I'll do it right after I file the report with you guys."

For the next 30 minutes Molly and Stacey reiterated their stories and how they'd lost everything they owned and were now stranded at the hotel. The officers took down their information along with details of the car and its contents.

"What are the chances of getting my car back, officer?" Molly asked, her hands clasped together in her lap. "Do we have to sit around here and just wait?"

"Unfortunately, the percentage rate of stolen cars retrieved is very low. Most cars are stripped for parts within hours of being stolen. Depending what insurance coverage you have, you may be assigned a rental until the insurance company decides your car is a total loss and reimburses you the current value."

"How long could that take?" Molly asked.

"That all depends on your insurance company. We're almost done here; I suggest you call them right away. They'll be able to tell you more."

"Thank you, I will," Molly said, standing to shake the officer's hand, as he stood ready to leave.

After they left, Molly collapsed back onto the couch and rubbed her brow, "Shit! So, it looks like I'm never going to get my car back. This totally sucks. I hope my insurance gives me a rental, otherwise how the hell will we get to Montana? We can't afford to rent a car until they decide at their convenience to cut me a check. That could be months, and it'll cost a damn fortune."

"Call them right now and see what you can find out. I'm going to grab us some coffee and take Henry outside. Watch my laptop," Stacey said, pointing at it on the couch.

Thirty minutes later Stacey returned with two steaming hot cups of coffee with Henry following closely behind, his leash dragging on the floor. "So, how'd it go?" she asked, setting the cups on the table in front of the couch.

"Actually, not bad. I feel a little better after speaking with them." She picked up one of the cups and inhaled the soothing scent of the freshly brewed beverage. "Thanks for the coffee."

Stacey smiled. "Well, that makes me feel better. You seem much happier than when I left. So, what'd they say?"

Molly took a sip of her coffee before answering. "The good news is that I have comprehensive insurance which means I'll get a rental for 30 days. After I send them a copy of the police report they'll approve it, and it may take 30 to 45 days before they consider the car a total loss and cut me a check for its value. They won't cover the cost of the contents, which is understandable."

"That's great! I feel much better. We'll be okay."

"Oh, and right after the cops left and before I got on the phone with the insurance company, the guy at the front desk came over and told me that they're giving us a free room for the night, which means we can take care of this stuff in the comfort of our room. They also said they have guest buses that will take us anywhere we need to go within their limits, so we can get one to get to the car rental place tomorrow."

"That was awfully nice of them, but I can see why they'd do that; after all our car *was* stolen in their parking lot."

"Right!" Molly agreed. "Once we get a room, I'll call Vera and let her know what happened and that we'll be arriving in Riverbanks a day or two later." She took another sip of her coffee and then let out a heavy sigh. "You know, even though I'm feeling a little better knowing my insurance will cover everything we need, it still sucks. I loved that car; it was paid off, and with the cost of cars nowadays I probably won't be able to find anything decent with the pay-off I'll be getting.

It'll be a decent downpayment, but I'll have car payments again, an expense I wasn't expecting. We're going to be on a tight budget for a while, I hope you can find a job quickly," Molly told Stacey.

CHAPTER 29

Much to Molly's dismay it took two days to get everything sorted with the insurance company, and just as the cops told her, she'd have to wait 30 days before she was issued a check for her stolen vehicle. In the meantime, she filed the papers for a rental.

While they waited for a rental to be approved, they spent the next day taking the hotel bus to the nearby Walmart where they bought some clothes to get them by, a bed for Henry, as well as a few other necessities. They took turns shopping while the other waited outside with Henry.

The rental was finally approved the following day, but not until late in the afternoon, so they decided to spend another night at the hotel and get an early start in the morning. Much to their surprise, the hotel comped their room for the second night, too.

"Wouldn't it suck if our rental was stolen," Stacey joked as they walked through the chilly parking lot the next morning at 6:00, ready to start the final leg of their journey.

"Oh my god!" Molly shrieked. "Don't jinx it," she hollered play-fully, and gave a sigh of relief when she saw the black Honda Civic parked in its space. "There it is, I see it," she said, smiling. She quickened her pace, anxious to get inside the car and turn on the heater.

Being the only insured driver on the rental, Molly wasn't looking forward to driving the entire 550-plus miles in one day. After entering the state of Wyoming and taking some photos at the state line next to a huge welcome sign, Molly drove the next few hours on a wide-open highway surrounded by flat lands and fields.

"There's nothing out here, I've not seen a house in miles," Molly said, her eyelids heavy.

"It's pretty desolate," Stacey agreed. "Imagine breaking down out here - you'd die."

Molly pointed to a sign a few miles down the highway. "Look, next gas 20 miles." She smiled. "We're getting off - I need a break and I'm sure Henry needs to go the bathroom."

It was almost noon by the time they pulled off the highway. They'd been driving for six hours but had made an extra stop to give Molly a much-needed break.

"You look really tired," Stacey said, sitting at the bench across from her outside a Taco Bell with Henry lying at her feet. "Why don't you let me drive for a few hours so you can take a nap?"

"I can't. You're not on the rental agreement which means you're not covered."

"Who's going to know? We're in the middle of nowhere. I haven't seen a cop anywhere on this highway."

"Oh, I don't know. What if we get into an accident?"

"There're hardly any cars out here to hit. At least let me drive to the Montana state line, it's only a couple of hours away. You need your rest," Stacey insisted.

Molly contemplated her suggestion and agreed that she was having a hard time keeping her eyes open. A nap would feel good, and she reluctantly agreed. "Okay, but only to the state line," she said, using a sharp tone. "And no speeding," she said, pointing a finger at Stacey.

Stacey rolled her eyes. "Okay, okay. Now let's finish eating and get back on the road."

Molly was asleep before Stacey got back on the highway During a fitful nap in which she remembered nothing, the silence of the motor woke her. "Is everything okay?" she said, bolting upright from a deep sleep before looking out the window.

"Everything's fine. You slept like a baby, you were even snoring," Stacey laughed.

"No, I wasn't," Molly protested, still looking out the window. "Where are we?"

"Look ahead," Stacey said, smiling.

Molly looked ahead and gasped when she saw the huge sign 50 feet in front of them. Grinning, she read it aloud. "Welcome to Montana." She turned to Stacey - her jaw dropped. "Shit! We're here. I can't believe I slept the whole time, I guess I was tired."

"Like I said, you were snoring."

"I don't snore," Molly insisted, hitting Stacey in the arm. I'm going to call Vera and let her know where we are and tell her we should be in Riverbanks in a few hours. What time is it?"

"Two-thirty," Stacey told her.

"So, we should be there before 5:00, that's great!"

After calling Vera, they switched seats and Molly pulled away from the turnout and back onto the highway, excited to be driving the last leg of their journey.

Feeling rested from her much needed nap, Molly smiled as she drove down the open road. She lowered her window and breathed in the cool air. "Wow, the air smells so fresh here," she said, closing her eyes for a moment. Surrounded by open fields and the occasional farmhouse with cattle grazing and pine trees off in the distance, Molly took it all in, excited to be calling the surrounding area and state her new home. "It's absolutely gorgeous out here," she beamed.

Stacey agreed, mesmerized by the spectacular views. "This is incredible, and this will be our neighborhood," she said, looking over at a pond occupied by ducks.

"Yep, can you believe it? It's like a different world. So quiet and peaceful, and look, there's hardly any traffic."

"Henry's going to love this place with all the open spaces to run around instead of a cramped courtyard he shared with other dogs, cats, and people back in Texas," Stacey said as she made room for Henry on her lap, who also wanted to look out the window.

An hour later, they reached Main Street in the small town of Riverbanks.

"We're here!" Molly shouted, unable to control her excitement. "Will you look at this darling little town," she grinned, driving down the quiet, two-lane road.

"I feel like I'm in the Old West," Stacey said, in awe of what she was seeing.

Molly looked ahead at the spectacular view of the tall peaks of Bear Creek Mountain and the tall pine trees overlooking the quaint town. On either side of her were red brick buildings with flat roofs, all hosting a business of some sort. Driving down Main Street she spotted many restaurants; some were pizza houses, some steak restaurants, and coffee shops as well. All had hand-painted wooden signs, accentuating the country vibe. There was an abundance of antique stores, a small movie theatre that reminded her of the sixties, and a western clothing outlet.

"I can't wait to explore all these stores," Molly said, driving slowly through town, making sure not to miss anything.

"And the restaurants, too," Stacey added. "Look, there's an old-fashioned ice cream parlor," Stacey said, pointing out the window. "How cute is that?"

"Do you see a bookstore?" Molly asked, searching around. "It's the only one in town."

Stacey shook her head. "Nope, not yet."

Molly continued to drive down Main Street, taking note of the variety of stores and restaurants until the map app instructed her to make a left on Creek Drive. After passing a few more stores, the app told her she'd reached her destination, *Riverbanks Properties, 2038 Creek Drive.* Molly was relieved to see lights on in the building, telling her Vera was inside.

"What a charming building," Molly said, staring at what seemed to be a single family, white-painted, wooden cottage with green trim that had been turned into a business. Molly admired the colorful potted plants on the front porch and on both sides of the wooden steps leading up to the covered porch. White lace curtains hung in the windows, and on either side of the green front door there were pine benches. A luscious green lawn embraced the property decorated with a metal birdbath, feeders, and various wildlife lawn ornaments, all enclosed within a white picket fence.

"This is like something out of a Hallmark movie," Molly said. "It's so picturesque and perfect."

Before stepping out of the car, she took a deep breath to calm her nerves and racing heart. The life she'd been denied her entire life was about to begin.

CHAPTER 30

Lost in her thoughts, Molly felt the gentle squeeze of Stacey's hand on her shoulder. "Are you ready?" Stacey asked.

Molly turned and smiled. "As ready as I'll ever be," she said, gripping the door handle.

Before locking the car, Molly opened the back door, reached in and grabbed her laptop. "I'm not leaving this anywhere," she stated, closing the door. "You should grab yours, too."

"Mine is buried, no one'll find it." She glanced up and down the street. "I don't think there's a car theft problem in this town."

"Well, I'm not taking any chances," Molly replied defiantly, closing the car door.

Standing next to the car waiting for Stacey to leash Henry, Molly did a 360, taking in her surroundings. "This is such a charming little town. Much prettier than I imagined," she said, looking down Creek Drive where she saw a few more cottages that were now businesses, as well as a fire station. She noticed before turning onto Creek Drive that they were near the top of Main Street where there were less businesses and more residential cottages, as well as a few hotels.

"I'm ready now," Stacey told her, holding onto Henry who'd stopped to take a bathroom break next to a tree.

The street was quiet with few parked cars, and the only sign of life was a middle-aged woman walking her Terrier.

"It's so quiet here," Molly said, walking around the car towards the gate of the realty office. Before they reached the front door it opened. They were greeted by an attractive, slender, middle-aged woman dressed in a beige business suit, white blouse and beige flats. Her hair was silver-grey, layered and flowing onto her shoulders. She wore little makeup, just a touch of rouge to accentuate her cheeks and light pink lipstick, but even at her age Molly felt she didn't need it. Her warm, friendly smile immediately made them both feel welcomed, easing their unsettled nerves.

"Hi there, I heard you pull up. It's so nice to finally meet you," Vera said, holding out her hand, her voice calm and friendly just like her smile.

Feeling underdressed and fatigued from her journey, Molly brushed her hair away from her face and climbed the steps to meet her in a handshake. "Hi, it's great to meet you too," she said, shaking her hand. "This is my friend Stacey."

Stacey shook Vera's hand and smiled. "And this is Henry," Stacey said as she looked down at him and smiling. "Is it okay if I bring him inside?"

Vera smiled again. "Yes, of course. I have two dogs that hang out with me here all the time. We're a dog-loving town, and you'll be happy to know that most folks allow dogs into their stores."

"That's awesome. Henry'll like that," Stacey replied.

Vera turned and led the way. "Well, let's go inside. I was so worried when you called and told me about your car. I'm so sorry that happened to you." She stood by the door, allowing Molly and Stacey to walk inside. "There's so much crime in the city nowadays. You won't find any of that in our town, I can assure you."

"That's good to hear," Molly said, looking around the office from where she stood, taking in the rustic, country vibe. "I love all your decorations," she said, looking at the antique signs, farming tools and lamps.

Vera smiled as she walked over to her oak desk. "Thanks, many of them were my father's and I continued with the collection after he passed ten years ago. He's now with Mom who died when I was young."

"I'm so sorry," Molly said. "It's a beautiful collection."

"No need to be sorry, he lived a good, full and long life." She pointed to a green velvet couch against the wall. "Why don't you both have a seat while I grab the keys and a copy of the lease, then you can follow me over to the apartment."

"Thanks, that'll be great," Molly said, taking a seat, followed by Stacey and Henry who sat at Stacey's feet, as usual.

Stacey turned her head and looked at the old black-and-white framed photographs hanging on the wall. "I love these pictures, were they all taken here?" she asked Vera who was now at the printer.

Vera turned her head, holding printer paper. "Yes, they are, and as you can see, the town hasn't changed much."

"I noticed that, and I recognize some of the buildings from driving down Main Street. From what I've seen so far, I really like this town," Stacey said as she pet Henry who had jumped on her lap.

"I have a few more documents to print and then we'll be on our way," Vera informed them, leaning over the printer.

"Take your time, there's no rush," Molly replied. "It feels good to be still and not driving."

"I'm sure you're both extremely tired after traveling for five days."

"That's an understatement," Molly joked. "I don't want to see the inside of a car for a while."

A few minutes later Vera shuffled some papers in her hand, grabbed some keys off her desk, and threw on her black coat from the wooden coat stand before grabbing her purse. "Okay, I'm all set, my blue Subaru is parked out front. The apartment is at the top of Main Street and two blocks over on the right."

"Great! That's really close to town," Stacey said, standing first. "I'll be able to walk everywhere while I'm looking for a waitress job, and I'm happy to see that there's plenty of restaurants to check out."

"You shouldn't have any trouble finding work, there's always a few places that are looking for help. I'll put the word out, too," Vera told her.

"Thank you so much!" Stacey said with a huge smile. "I was a waitress in Texas, so I have experience."

Vera nodded. "I may know of a couple of places." She walked over to the front door and opened it. "Go ahead, get in your car and wait for me, I have to lock up."

"She seems really nice," Stacey said, stepping into the car after getting Henry settled in the back.

"Yes, she does. I hope Caroline is just as nice."

"Are you nervous about meeting her?"

"Of course, I am. It's all I've been thinking about for the past three years. My biggest fear is that she'll hate me. I'm going to do everything in my power to make sure that doesn't happen."

"I can't see that happening, how can anyone hate you?" Stacey reassured her. "You don't have a mean bone in your body. I'm sure everything is going to work out fine."

"I hope you're right," Molly said. She started the car when she saw Vera walking down the steps from her office and proceeded to wait for her to pull away from the curb before following her.

They followed Vera a few blocks up Main Street, passing more shops, restaurants and a museum on the left. When they reached the top, they came to an area that seemed to be only hotels and lodges.

"Looks like this is the tourist part of town," Stacey said. "There's a lot of hotels here."

"Yep, Yellowstone National Park is less than an hour away, and apparently this town is a popular ski resort in the winter."

Molly followed Vera, turned right onto Birch Drive, then made a left after a church onto Aspen Lane. "This is the street," Molly said. "I remember the street name from the listing."

Stacey rubbed her hands together and squealed. "Ooh, we're almost home."

They passed numerous single-family cottage-style homes, all with immaculate front gardens decorated with various lawn ornaments, bird feeders, bushes and shade trees. When they reached the middle of the road, they made a left into a large driveway, passing the *Madison Creek Courtyard* sign. Ahead of them were a dozen single detached log-style units, all with brown wooden doors and a window on either side. The first thing Molly noticed was that there were no stairs or elevators. Each unit had a single driveway and a carport on the right. The main driveway curved around, passing each unit. It was quiet and only a few lights were on in the homes. Surrounding the property were tall pine trees and evergreen bushes planted in front of each unit below the windows. Wooden benches were scattered along the pathway paralleling the driveway, and in the center was a flower garden surrounding a flagpole which proudly displayed the American flag.

"This is really cute," Stacey said, taking it all in.

"It sure is, and it's so quiet. Vera called them apartments, but they're like little single log homes," Molly replied, following Vera closely.

After passing four of the units, Vera came to a stop before the driveway and veered to the left.

"This must be it," Molly said, pulling up behind Vera and turning off the engine.

"I hope so, I love that it's in the back, tucked away," she said, staring out the window.

"Me too," Molly said, stepping out of the car.

A few seconds later Vera stepped out smiling, holding the lease and keys. "Well, here we are."

"This is really nice," Molly said, following Vera to the front door with Stacey and Henry close behind.

"I think you're going to love it here," Vera said, unlocking the door. "It's close to town, super quiet, and I know everyone that lives here; you couldn't ask for better neighbors. Most are older than you, probably more in my age group, but everyone looks out for each other and are always willing to help with anything."

Molly and Stacey anxiously followed Vera into their new home and waited while she turned on the lights.

Vera smiled after the lights illuminated the living area where they stood, as well as the small adjoining kitchen. "Welcome ladies!" she said with open arms. "What do you think?"

Molly looked over the space, loving the country vibe that she'd felt in Vera's office. The brown faux leather couch and matching armchair filled up quite a bit of the small living room, and the wooden coffee table in the middle left little room to walk around in, but it felt cozy and warm, and the pictures of mountain peaks and wildlife just added to the country charm. Between the couch and armchair was a small end table that matched the coffee table, and on it sat a lamp with a green glass shade. Molly pictured herself curled up with a blanket reading a book in the armchair on a winter night with snow falling outside.

"This is perfect!" she said with a huge smile as she walked through the living area to check out the kitchen and opened one of the wooden cabinets. She was shocked by what she saw. "Wait - there're dishes in here!"

Vera chuckled. "Yes, and saucepans in the lower cabinets, and linens and towels in the hallway closet."

"What?" Molly gasped. "When you said it was furnished, I figured it was just basic furniture, not all of this."

"This is what furnished in our town means. They may do it differently in the city, but you get the full package here."

"This is fantastic!" Stacey squealed, racing to the kitchen to see what other treasures were hidden in the cupboards.

"I can't believe this," Molly cried, holding a frying pan. "I've been so worried since my car got stolen. It had everything we owned in it, including all of our bedding and essentials to get us by until we could get more." She chuckled to herself. "God knows where we'd buy all that stuff though, I didn't see a Walmart anywhere in town." Molly looked at Vera. "Where do people here buy things like that, anyway?"

"Well, there's no need to worry, you have everything you need here. As for shopping, we have a small market here in town, and Billings is just under an hour away where you'll find many of the big stores like Walmart."

"Oh, that's good to know." Molly turned around and looked at

Stacey who was checking out the drinking glasses in one of the kitchen cupboards. "We can drive to Walmart and buy more clothes, and maybe some shoes. I'm so tired of wearing these tennis shoes," Molly said as she looked down at her feet. "These are the only pair of shoes I own. How sad is that?"

"That's a great idea, let's go tomorrow," Stacey said enthusiastically, taking a seat at the bistro table. "I really like this space," she said, running her hand across the wooden top of the small table.

Molly laughed aloud. "Are you nuts? I'm exhausted. I don't plan on doing anything tomorrow except maybe checking out the town. I'll call Caroline's assistant Lucy in the morning to tell her we've arrived and find out when she'd like to meet."

Stacey leaned back in her chair. "Yeah, you're right. I'm just excited, I want to see and do it all now," she joked.

Molly joined her at the table, taking a seat across from her. "This is where we'll be having our morning coffee every day."

"Yes, it's perfect, and I love this window we can look out of."

"You'll get the sun coming in from that window," Vera told them. "It's nice and bright in the morning."

"This just keeps getting better and better," Molly said. "My patio in Texas never got any sun."

"Let me show you the bedroom and the bathroom, then we'll go over the lease before I let you two get settled. I'm sure you're both exhausted."

"That'd be great," Molly replied. "Hey, I looked for the bookstore while driving through town but didn't see it. Can you tell me where it is?"

"Sure. When we reached the top of Main Street we made a right onto Birch Street; you want to make a left from Main Street, and it's the second store on the left, on Birch Street."

"Oh great, thanks,"

"It's an amazing store, but it's a lot of work for Caroline at the moment. I'm glad you're here to help her, she needs it."

Molly had the urge to ask Vera about the issues Caroline was having in her private life that prompted her to hire her, but felt it wasn't Vera's place to tell her, and didn't want to put her on the spot, so she smiled instead. "I'll do whatever I can to help."

Vera left after she'd given them a tour of their new home and answered all their questions, Molly and Stacey wasted no time breaking out into a dance and cheering with Henry barking at their feet, who was unsure what the outburst was about.

"We made it, we're home!" Molly squealed. "I can't believe we're here, and this place is so cute."

"I can't believe it either. This is so much nicer than our dreary apartments back in Texas, and its *ours*," Stacey said, picking Henry up and hugging him. "How do you like your new home, buddy?" Henry replied with a bark and both girls laughed.

Molly smiled, pets Henry on the head and looked at Stacey, "I'm feeling really good about this place, and it's a new start for both of us. Welcome home, Stacey."

Stacey smiled, leaning in to give Molly a hug with Henry nestled between them. "Welcome home, friend."

CHAPTER 31

Even though Molly was exhausted from the five-day road trip and the stress of having her car stolen, she still had trouble falling asleep, tossing and turning for a few hours after collapsing on the bed. No matter how hard she tried, she couldn't turn her brain off. Not only was the excitement of sleeping in her new home keeping her awake but being in a small town she thought she was probably just a few miles away from wherever Caroline lived, and that blew her mind. Lying awake and looking at the white ceiling, Molly wondered what she was like? What her husband and home were like? Would they like each other? She had so many questions, and in a few days hopefully all of them would be answered.

MOLLY HAD no idea when she eventually fell asleep, but knew it had to be in the early hours of the morning. A gentle knock on her bedroom door woke her. "Come in," she said, rubbing her eyes.

Stacey opened the door slowly and peeked her head into the dark room. "Hey, are you still alive in here, it's almost noon."

Molly opened her eyes wide and sat up, looking around the room, remembering where she was. "What? You're kidding me! I can't believe I've slept half the day away," she yawned. "Hey, how was it, sleeping on the couch?"

"It's so comfortable, even better than my bed in Texas," she laughed. "You're not the only one that slept in, so don't feel guilty. I didn't get up until 10:00 and that's late for me. I figured you were tired, but when it got to be noon, I started getting worried," Stacey said as she sat down on the edge of the bed. "I took Henry for a walk around the grounds - this place is *amazing*. I met two of our neighbors, Jake and Maria, an older couple who've lived here for over ten years, and a nice lady named Audrey, probably in her 50's, who lives alone with her dog, a Terrier named Chester. She told me her husband died last year, which I thought was sad because she's not that old. We talked for a while and watched Henry and Chester play which was awesome. Henry hasn't been around many dogs," Stacey chuckled. "I think Henry likes it here too."

Molly yawned again in the middle of a stretch. "That's great! I'm sorry I didn't go with you; I would have loved to meet them."

"Oh, you will. In fact, I invited Audrey over for dinner one night after we get settled. I hope that's okay, she just seems so lonely."

"Yes, of course, that's fine. This is our home now, and we should get to know our neighbors." Her stomach rumbled and she quickly changed the subject. "Hey, have you eaten? We don't have any food here and I'm dying for a cup of coffee."

Stacey shook her head, "No I haven't, and I'm famished too. Coffee sounds great."

"Let's go eat at one of the restaurants in town, then we can check out the local market."

"Sounds like a plan," Stacey said, standing up from her bed. "I'll go check on Henry while you get dressed, I also need to freshen up and do something with my hair."

After Stacey left the room, Molly sorted through the few clothes she had and threw on a pair of jeans, a black t-shirt, and the tennis shoes she'd been wearing all week. On her way out she grabbed the only jacket she owned, a black hooded sweatshirt. After brushing her teeth and combing her hair in the bathroom located in the hallway that she shared with Stacey, she went back to her bedroom and grabbed her purse and phone. When she entered the living room, she found Stacey lying on the couch scrolling on her phone with Henry on her chest.

"We need to buy a TV," Stacey remarked, petting Henry. "It's too quiet in here, and I miss the morning news."

Molly laughed. "There're quite a few things we need and yes, that's at the top of my list. We can get one at the Walmart in Billings. But right now, I'm starving. Are you ready to go?"

"Yep," Stacey said, tapping on Henry so he'd move. "I put Henry's bed and water dish in the kitchen by the bistro table. I hope he's going to be okay; this is all new for him."

"He'll be fine. I hear dogs adapt quickly." She nudged Stacey's leg, still lying on the couch. "Come on, let's go. I need some coffee."

After exiting the driveway, Molly remembered how to get to Main Street, then made a left into town.

"Keep your eyes peeled for a good restaurant. I'm in the mood for a big breakfast," Molly told her.

"Me too," Stacey replied, looking out the window.

After driving for a few minutes, Molly spotted a diner on her left. "That place looks good," she said, pointing at the wooden sign and reading "*Angie's Diner, Breakfast All Day.*"

"Looks good to me," Stacey agreed.

"Don't let me forget to call Lucy after we get a table. I should have called her before we left," Molly said, turning into the parking lot. Molly scanned the packed parking lot after exiting the car. "This is a popular place, it must be good."

Stacey stood next to the car and looked at the rustic wooden building with red trim around the windows with wooden tables and benches in front, all of which were occupied. "Looks like a regular hangout for the entire town."

When they entered the busy restaurant, they were instantly

greeted by a young, blonde waitress, her hair pulled back in a pony-tail wearing blue jeans, cowboy boots, and a red-and-white short-sleeved cotton checkered shirt. "Hello ladies, welcome! Table for two?"

"Yes please," Molly replied, admiring the western theme décor of the restaurant and enjoying the country music playing in the background.

The waitress led them to the back of the restaurant to what seemed to be the only available table which was decorated with red-and-white checkered tablecloth.

Molly took a seat and smiled at the waitress as she placed two menus in front of them. "This place is busy."

"Yeah, it's the lunch rush right now. It will quiet down in about an hour." She smiled. "My name is Julie and I'll be your waitress. Can I get you ladies something to drink?"

In unison Molly and Stacey said, "coffee, please."

"You got it, I'll be back in a jiffy," the waitress said.

Molly immediately pulled out her phone from her jacket pocket. "I need to call Lucy and let her know we're here."

After a few rings Lucy answered. "Molly, it's so good to hear from you. Did you make it?"

"Yes, we did. We're having breakfast at Angie's Diner right now."

"You picked one of the best restaurants in town. Is Angie there?"

Molly looked around. "I'm not sure, Julie's our waitress."

"Oh, that's her daughter. Tell her I said hi, and I'm so sorry to hear about your car. That's terrible."

"Thanks, yeah, I don't think I'll ever get it back, but the insurance company has been great, and I have a rental for 30 days."

"Oh good! I'm happy to hear your insurance company is treating you right."

"We just got into town yesterday and I wanted to see when you'd like to meet. I'm anxious to see the bookstore and meet Caroline."

There was a moment of silence before Lucy spoke again. "Molly, it's been a rough week. Why don't we plan on meeting at the book-store on Monday morning, say 9:00?"

"That'd be great, I'll be rested up by then and ready to work. I really appreciate this opportunity, and I won't let you down."

"I know you won't, Molly."

"Will Caroline be there on Monday?"

Again, there was a moment of silence. "I'm afraid not, her husband passed away three days ago."

CHAPTER 32

Molly gasped, covering her mouth with her hand, causing Stacey to look up from the menu and whisper, "is everything okay?"

Molly shook her head, raising her hand to silence Stacey. "Oh, my goodness, I'm so sorry to hear that. Please give her my condolences," Molly said into the phone.

"Thank you. Understandably she's not doing too well and needs some time alone with family. In the meantime, I'll be working with you and getting you started at the bookstore," Lucy told her.

Molly rubbed her brow, stunned by the devastating news. "Yes, yes, that's fine. I completely understand. Please tell Caroline that I'm deeply sorry for her loss and I'll see you on Monday."

"What's going on?" Stacey asked as soon as Molly ended the call. "You said condolences?"

Molly looked at Stacey, her eyes sad. "Caroline's husband died three days ago. That poor woman."

"Oh no, that's terrible. How did he die?"

"I don't know, I didn't want to ask." Molly leaned back in the booth. "What a terrible time to arrive. I feel awful."

"Why? She hired you." Stacey leaned back in her seat and folded her arms. "Come to think of it, didn't Lucy tell you that the reason they were looking for a manager was because Caroline was dealing with some personal issues?"

Before Molly could reply, Julie returned with two large mugs of steaming coffee. "Here you go. Are you ready to order?" she asked, setting the mugs on the table.

After placing their orders of bacon and eggs with hash browns, Molly took a sip of her coffee before picking up their conversation. "Yes, she did tell me that." She thought for a moment and took another sip of coffee. "Maybe Caroline knew her husband was dying. How awful..." Molly looked up, her brow creased. "This is such bad timing on my part, to show up here with everything she's dealing with - I feel so selfish." She sighed heavily. "Now, how am I going to tell her the real reason why I'm here? She'll definitely hate me."

Stacey sat up, her back straight, her tone sharp. "Now, just stop it and don't be talking like that. After all, you're not planning on telling her right away anyway. You told me yourself that you needed some time to prove yourself to her and turn the bookstore around so she couldn't help but like you."

"I know, but that's all changed now. I feel really uncomfortable with everything that's going on."

Seeing the worry in Molly's eyes, Stacey tried her best to reassure her. "Look Molly, you've traveled a long way to get here. You've given up everything you ever owned; you even lost your car. You can't give up now, you've worked too hard for this. No, you weren't expecting this, but you'll get through it. Let Caroline mourn her husband. In the meantime, focus on why you're here and turn that bookstore around. Do whatever it takes to make everything turn out the way you hope it will."

Molly gave her a weak smile. "You're right, I'm not going to rush anything. I'll focus on the bookstore and let Caroline take all the time she needs; I'm not going anywhere."

"That a girl," Stacey said, giving her an encouraging smile. "Do you still want to go shopping after we eat?"

"Yes, we have nothing at home. Let's just go into Billings and find a Walmart. We can buy everything there. Food, clothes, and a TV."

"Sounds like a great plan." Stacey chuckled.

Molly creased her brow, "what's funny?"

"This is our first day in a remote town in the mountains, and where are we going? The nearest city! Do you think we'll survive out here?" she said, laughing even louder.

Molly matched her laugh. "This is an exception, we own nothing, remember?!"

AFTER AN EVENTFUL DAY OF SHOPPING, they returned home by 6:00, Walmart being the only store they shopped at, anxious about Henry being left alone in a strange place. Their car was full of groceries, clothes, toiletries, and a small TV that fit in the car and would get them by until the larger one they'd ordered was delivered in a few days.

"I hate this part of shopping," Stacey said, grabbing a few bags from the back seat. "Now we have to unpack it all."

"Take those in and then tend to Henry, I'm sure he's hungry," Molly said, grabbing more bags. "He's barking up a storm inside. I can get the rest."

"No argument from me," Stacey replied, heading to the front door. "Mommy's home, baby," she called, setting down the bags so she could open the door. Henry barged outside, found the nearest bush and relieved himself.

"I hope he didn't have any accidents inside," Molly hollered, walking to the front door.

"I'll do a quick check," Stacey said, walking inside. "All clear in here. He was a good boy," she said, smiling.

It took three trips to unload the car, and Molly was thankful they didn't need the elevators or stairs. "After you've fed Henry, do you want to set up the TV? We have internet thanks to Vera, and I'll put the groceries away."

Stacey joined her in the kitchen." Sure, I can do that," she said, grabbing Henry's bowl from the dish rack. "Tomorrow's Sunday, what do you want to do?" she asked.

"Not much. In fact, I want to tuck in early tonight and tomorrow I want to take it easy and relax around here, if you don't mind. Monday's a big day for me, and I want to be fully rested."

Stacey poured some dry kibbles in Henry's bowl and placed it on the floor next to his water. "That's a good idea."

"Hey, I'll be gone all day; it'd be a good day for you to take a walk into town and maybe start looking for a job, what do you think?" Molly suggested.

Stacey smiled. "I was thinking the same thing. I told you I'd start looking for a job straight away, and I meant it. I'm not going to let you down, Molly. I don't want you to ever regret bringing me here."

"I know you won't let me down. I have faith in you and that you'll find work soon and have a paycheck by the time rent is due next month, because if you don't, you'll have to find another place to live."

Stacey wasn't sure if she was joking or being serious and gave her a weak smile. "Like I said, you have nothing to worry about, but man, talk about pressure!"

"I've always worked my best under pressure, don't most people?"

"Not me, but it doesn't look like I have a choice."

CHAPTER 33

Molly woke up Monday morning feeling rested after spending the entire day at home Sunday organizing the items they'd bought from Walmart. Their place was beginning to feel more like a home with the personal touches they'd added with new knick-knacks, pictures, a couple of lamps, candles, and throw pillows for the couch and her bed.

But what Molly couldn't control were her nerves which were peaked, even after two cups of coffee. She spent an hour taking a shower and getting dressed in a navy-blue skirt and white blouse that Stacey had helped her pick out at Walmart. After applying makeup, which she hadn't done in months, and blow drying her hair, she tried to calm her nerves with another cup of coffee.

"Look at me, my hands are shaking," she said, sitting at the bistro table with Stacey.

"You look fabulous, and very professional. You'll be fine, it's okay to be nervous. How can you not be? This is a huge milestone for you. Everything is slowly coming together."

"I must admit that I'm kind of relieved Caroline won't be there. I know that's a horrible thing to say, but I just don't think I'm ready. So why am I so nervous?"

"You're under a lot of pressure right now. And aren't you forgetting that you also need to impress Lucy? After all, she's the one that hired you, and she can fire you just as quickly."

"Yeah, you're probably right. Imagine what a mess I'd be if Caroline was going to be there? I'd probably run the other way."

"Hey, weren't you telling me last night that you work best under pressure?"

"Yes, but this is a different kind of pressure, one I've never experienced before." Molly picked up her phone and checked the time. "I need to get going. I've decided I'm going to walk there; it's only a few blocks away, it's a beautiful morning, and I'll get to see more of the town."

"That's a great idea!"

"I'd let you drive my car, but you're not insured, sorry."

"That's fine, I'm looking forward to walking and exploring the town while I'm looking for a job."

"Good luck with your job hunting," Molly said, grabbing her jacket from the couch as she headed out the door.

MOLLY HAD no trouble finding the bookstore. Vera's directions were spot on, and she arrived ten minutes early. Her first thoughts of the store were that it desperately needed a coat of paint. The store blended in with the red brick building, but there was no curb appeal or anything that made it pop or stand out. The *Read More Books* sign was peeling and faded, and the lettering was far too small. If she was driving by and didn't know the store was there, she'd more than likely miss it. It needed bright colors, a large sign with bright letters, and definitely some tables outside letting people know it's a place to relax and hang out. Molly wondered if they served any kind of baked goods or coffee; if not, then that would have to change soon enough.

Standing outside the store waiting for Lucy, Molly scanned the neighboring businesses; to the left was an antique store, and to the right a clothing boutique. She was happy to see neither carried food nor beverages of any kind, and she didn't see any food establishments nearby, concluding that most of the restaurants in town were on Main Street. *That's good, no competition*, she thought to herself, watching every car go by, which were few and far between.

The store was located on a two-lane road where most of the buildings were red brick and had flat roofs except for a log cabin style building across the street which was a real estate office. Molly checked the other businesses close by, and from where she stood, she spotted a nail salon, a bank, another boutique, a thrift store, and a sporting goods store.

Molly turned and looked through one of the large windows on either side of the faded, blue-painted door of the bookstore, noticing immediately that the windows needed a good cleaning. Some sort of illumination was also needed to brighten up the place. She pressed her face against the chilled glass and squinted to block out the shadows obscuring her view. There were no lights on inside, making it dark and dingy, but it seemed to be of a good size with rows of bookshelves in the middle of the store as well as bookshelves on every wall. There were no books in the windows, which Molly would soon change, and she didn't notice any kind of seating inside where customers could sit and browse through the books. "I'm going to do wonders with this place," Molly said aloud, her nose still pressed against the glass. "My head is spinning with all kinds of ideas. Caroline is going to love me," she added, feeling confident all of a sudden.

After inspecting the inside through the windows, she stood back and looked at the store from the curb, focusing on the aged wooden sign and the faded paint on the trim and door. "This place needs some bright colors to make it stand out so people can't miss it as they drive by," she said, excited about her ideas. Lost in her thoughts and ideas, Molly didn't hear a car pull up alongside the curb behind her. A female voice caught her attention.

"Are you Molly?"

Molly turned and looked through the open window of a white Dodge Durango and recognized Lucy from their video chat. She released a nervous smile. "Yes, and you must be Lucy."

The woman nodded, "I am. Sorry I'm a little late, I hope you haven't been waiting too long?"

Molly stood back from the curb and shook her head. "No, I've only been here a few minutes."

Lucy stepped out of the car. Molly was surprised by her casual dress of blue jeans and a red, long-sleeved, untucked cotton shirt and black, low-heeled boots. Her short auburn hair was complimented by her medium hoop earring. After stepping out of her car, Lucy opened the back door. "Let me just grab my laptop and briefcase and I'll be right with you," she said.

"Take your time," Molly replied, suddenly feeling overdressed.

Holding her briefcase in one hand and her laptop bag hanging from her shoulder in the other, Lucy approached Molly and held out her hand. "It's so good to finally meet you. I'm so sorry Caroline couldn't be here."

Molly took her hand. "It's good to meet you, too. I'm so sorry to hear about her husband. I can't imagine the pain she must be going through; my heart goes out to her."

"Thank you, I'll let her know. She plans on being here next Monday to meet you. She just needs a week to get her affairs in order. I'll let her tell you anything she wishes to share in person. It's not my place to discuss her family and what they're going through, but in the meantime, she wants me to work with you and get you settled, which I'm more than happy to do." Lucy walked towards the front door and opened it with the keys dangling in her hand. "Let's go inside and I'll give you a tour."

"Sounds good."

Once they were inside the store, Lucy left her standing by the front door as she walked over to the wooden counter against the wall and turned on the overhead lights. "There, that's better."

Molly remained standing in front of the door, surprised by the size of the store. With no lighting, she couldn't see the back of it from outside but then saw that it was clearly much bigger than she'd expected. Every wall was covered with brown wooden bookshelves, all of them six shelves high. Additional aisles of bookshelves were scattered throughout the store, each categorized by genre, and non-fiction books by subject.

"Normally Albert and Hailey would be here to open the store, but Caroline decided to close it for a week after her husband Pete passed away. She also wanted you to have some time to go through every-thing and familiarize yourself with the store and get organized. Albert and Hailey will be here next Monday, along with Caroline."

"Oh, good. I'm excited to meet them."

"They are wonderful and have been working for Caroline for a few years. They are young like you, in their late twenties and have all that energy," Lucy, laughed. "Come on, let me show you around," Lucy said, leading the way. "With everything that's been going on in Caroline's life, you can see the store has been somewhat neglected." She turned to me and smiled, "which is why *you're* here."

"It's a lot bigger than I imagined and there's great potential," Molly admitted.

Lucy stopped in the middle of the store and began pointing at bookshelves. "All of the books in the middle of the store are works of fiction," she said. Pointing to the shelves on the left wall, she said, "along that wall are non-fiction books; mainly outdoors, sports, and motor vehicles," she informed Molly. "On the other wall are crafts, cooking, hobbies, and gardening books. Over in the far corner, in the back where the round red tables and chairs are, is the Children's section."

Molly glanced around and appreciated the soft beige carpet below her feet. It seemed to be in good shape, softening the noise in the store. The store definitely needed more lighting. Posters of book covers hung around the store, which she noticed were from books released a few years ago. Molly's first thought was that they needed to be illuminated and hung in prominent places where they would be noticed. Along one of the back walls to the right of the Children's section she noticed a tan couch that blended in with the light brown wall behind it, and a black metal coffee table in front of it. "Is that the only seating area?" Molly asked.

"Yes, that's it. More seating would be nice," Lucy said, walking over to the only counter in the store. Behind the counter was a large, framed picture of Mark Twain standing in front of a small log cabin with a collection of his books beneath it on a glass shelf.

"I love Mark Twain," Molly commented, walking up to the counter. "Is that his cabin?"

"I believe so," Lucy replied, setting her laptop and briefcase on the wooden surface of the counter next to a selection of candles and incense that the store sold.

Molly admired the vintage books on the shelf below the picture. "Do you have any more vintage books in the store, or a vintage book section?"

"We have a few, maybe a dozen, but not enough for them to have their own section."

"Well, we'll have to change that. Locals can bring their books in to sell, and I'm sure I can find some decent ones on Ebay that we can carry in the store and make a profit off of."

Lucy smiled, "that's a wonderful idea."

"Adding to the list," Molly chuckled, feeling pleased with herself as she rested her hands on the small counter which she noticed had limited space for customers to place their purchases. On the front panels of the counter were two more book posters, again of older books. She scanned the bookstore and had so many questions.

"Lucy, this is a wonderful store with a great selection of books, but it's lacking in so many areas. If I was a customer, I'd see no reason to stay or come into the store unless I'm looking for a specific book. There's no comfortable lounging area, or even a place to buy beverages and snacks which would entice me to stay longer, and adding areas to relax and browse other books would help as well. Does the store hold monthly events or have any kind of book club or groups to entice readers to come to the store?"

Lucy shook her head. "Not currently. It's something Caroline has been wanting to do, but her life's been consumed with taking care of her husband for the past two years."

"I can understand that. How has she managed to stay open?"

"It's the only bookstore in town, so there's no competition, but

Caroline doesn't want it to be just another local store for the residents, she wants it to be an attraction for the town. A store that's known beyond Riverbanks and may help in putting the town on the map." Lucy folded her arms and looked around the store. "She's always had big dreams for this place but has never been able to get it off the ground or even know where to start. She knows it's a tall order, but it's her future and her life, one she must feel secure in without her husband. With her husband being sick, she's not had the time, and admits it's been neglected."

"I need to ask as there's so much you can do with this place; I'm excited to get started, but what kind of budget are we looking at? With everything Caroline is going through, is she going to be able to afford anything I propose? You mentioned that the store is struggling, and you'd like me to try and turn it around, but that will cost money. You need to spend money to make money, and if the store is barely making it, how can she afford to make any improvements? I just need to know where I stand budget wise - I'm sorry if I'm being too forward."

"No, you're not being forward at all, it's a good question, and you have every right to ask. In anticipation of hiring someone to save and turn this store around, she took out a business loan and has the budget to invest."

Molly smiled. "That's good to know. I think with some of the ideas I have we should be seeing some profitable results within six months. I'm going to get this store back on track as soon as I can."

Lucy reached across the counter, smiled, and squeezed Molly's arm. "I have a good feeling about you. I know we made the right decision when we hired you. Your enthusiasm is encouraging, and I can't wait to see what you do with this place."

"Well, there's no time like the present. The first thing I'd like to start on immediately is giving this place a new paint job inside and out. We need to brighten it up, make it pop, and have people notice it when they drive by. To achieve that, I think we should remain closed for two weeks rather than one. I need time to choose a color scheme and hire painters. Are there some local artists that would enjoy painting murals? I have a vision of large, bold inspiring words related to books, such as *Read, Joy, Imagine and Escape,* to name just a few, painted on the walls along with well-known fictitious characters and famous excerpts from authors." Molly spoke quickly, her eyes shining and arms dancing. "And I could use all the help I can get; this is a huge project. Can we have Albert and Hailey come in and *not* take the two weeks off while the store is closed? They would be a tremendous help prepping this place for paint and moving books around."

"I like that idea!" Lucy said, smiling. "Yes, I know of a few local artists, they're very good, and yes, I'll call Albert and Hailey and tell them to come in tomorrow. Let me show you the storage room and office in the back next to the bathroom, and you can take inventory of what we have as well as seeing what you'll need to get started."

With a large smile, Molly stood and clapped her hands. "Great, let's do this!"

CHAPTER 34

Molly and Lucy spent the next few hours in the office going over the accounting ledgers, suppliers, inventory, and office equipment. It was a spacious office, bigger than she'd thought, with three desks, two printers, three desktop computers, and a wall of file cabinets. In a separate area was a coffee station, a small fridge, and a microwave. Sitting at one of the desks going over the software, Molly discussed with Lucy some of her ideas, quickly jotting down notes as she spoke, and smiling each time Lucy showed excitement and gave her approval.

Giving her eyes a break from the glare of the computer screen and her voice a rest from talking so much, Molly leaned back in her chair and grinned, looking up at the ceiling, "Oh, I wish it was six months from now so we could see how much this place has shaped up. It's going to be fantastic; I just know it. There's so much to work with."

"It'll be here faster than you know it," Lucy said, sitting at one of the other desks. "Hey, will you be okay here on your own for the rest of the day? I have a set of keys for you," she said, reaching into her purse. "I really should get back to Caroline and give her a hand. She's feeling overwhelmed and at a loss right now."

"Yes, I'll be fine, I'm sure Caroline needs you. I'm going to spend the afternoon choosing paint colors for the inside and outside of the store, as well as calling some contractors if there's time. You go right ahead."

"Great! Do you have any questions before I leave?" Lucy asked, standing.

Molly shook her head. "Nope, I think you've covered everything."

"Okay then, but if you need anything you have my cell phone number."

After Lucy left, Molly sat silently in the office, taking it all in, feeling proud of herself for garnering the responsibilities Caroline and Lucy had entrusted to her. She felt honored to have such a role and knew she would do an outstanding job: Anything less would be unacceptable. She had set her expectations and her performance bar extremely high, and, like she'd told Stacey, she worked best under pressure.

Left alone in the bookstore, the silence was deafening. Molly added *background music in the store* to her list with the keywords *relaxing, soothing* and *calming*. Molly immersed herself for hours in her work, losing complete track of time. When she finally arose from her pages of notes and the long list of tasks, she checked her phone and was surprised to see it was 7:00 in the evening. "Shit! I've been at this for hours," she said aloud, shocked at how the day had escaped her. "Clocks! We need clocks in this place," she shouted, grabbing her list.

Feeling pleased with how much she'd accomplished in just her first day, she smiled at her calendar. She had two local artists coming by the store tomorrow, as well as a sign maker. She had found a local contractor whose prices she thought reasonable. He would be coming by in the morning to discuss paint colors for the store and hopefully start painting the following day.

Excited for tomorrow to begin, Molly decided to call it a day. She grabbed her jacket and notepad before turning off the lights, locked up the store and began the short walk home, suddenly realizing she hadn't talked to Stacey all day. She was anxious to hear how her day went, and if she found a job.

It was already dark when Molly left the store, and the temperature had dropped drastically to a chilly 42 degrees. The streets were quiet, illuminated by ornate streetlamps with the occasional car or truck driving by. Molly zipped up her jacket to block the slight breeze and quickened her pace, anxious to get home and out of the cold.

Ten minutes later she opened the front door to her home and welcomed the rush of warm air as she stepped inside and found Stacey and Henry curled up on the couch watching a movie.

"Hey, how's it going?" Molly asked, closing the door behind her and setting her things on the bistro table in the kitchen.

"There you are," Stacey said, without pulling her eyes away from the TV. "Have you been at work all day? You left almost ten hours ago."

"Yes, I have. It's a much bigger job than I anticipated, and the store is a lot larger than I imagined, too. It needs a lot of TLC and a face lift; the poor place has been neglected, and the way it is now I'm surprised they're even in business."

Stacey sat up and looked at Molly. "Really? That bad, eh? Do you think you've taken on more than you can chew?"

Molly shook her head. "Oh, hell no. I've got this, but I'll be working long hours every day until I can turn the store around and make a decent profit for Caroline."

"And you're okay with that?"

"Sure, why wouldn't I be?" Molly rubbed her hands together, still chilled from the walk home, changing the subject. "Anyway, enough about me, tell me how your day went. Did you find a job?"

Stacey shook her head and frowned. "No, and my feet are killing me. I walked from one end of Main Street to the other, stopping at every restaurant. I must have asked over 15 places if they were hiring, and all of them said no and to come back in the spring."

"In the spring?" Molly screeched. "That's months away!"

"I know, but apparently all of the restaurants have a skeleton crew working during the winter months which are right around the corner."

"But what about all the skiers that come here?"

"It's still not as busy as the spring and summer months. They get a lot of tourists from Yellowstone." Stacey leaned back on the couch and threw her head back into the cushions. "This really sucks, I need a job now."

"Yes, you do, but it's only your first day of looking. Maybe you'll find something tomorrow," Molly said with a caring smile, trying to boost her morale.

"But I don't know where else to look. I'm sure I've hit up every restaurant in town. God, I wish I had my website business up and running. I could work from home if I did. I know I could do really well with it once I get it off the ground." She turned and looked at Molly. "Speaking of which, I have some classes to do online tomorrow, so there goes half my day."

Wide-eyed, Molly joined Stacey on the couch. "Wait a minute, I think I may have a job for you."

"You do?" Stacey questioned, her brow furrowed.

"Yes. The bookstore needs a website. I was surprised when Lucy told me, I guess they've never had one."

"You're kidding! All businesses need a website."

"That's what I thought, and I'm going to hire you to do one for the store. I'd also want you to maintain it once it's up and running. I plan on having a monthly Calendar of Events at the bookstore, a book club, author signings, featured books on sale, new releases, and so much more, all of which can be listed on the website. I've even thought about selling books on the site, too." Molly gave Stacey a large smile. "What do you think? Is that something you think you can put together and manage?"

"Heck ya! I can do all of that. Really, you're giving me a job? I don't have to look anymore?"

"Well, it's a start and yes, it's a paying job. The bookstore can be your first client for your website design business."

Stacey leaned in and hugged Molly. "I can't believe this. Thank you!" She quickly stood and paced the room, unable to control her excitement. "Forget about waitressing, I'm going to officially start my own business. She pointed to the small space in the back of the room. "I can put a desk right against that wall for a workstation. I need to think of a name, then I can put an ad in the local paper, distribute flyers around town, and create a website for the business." Stacey skipped across the room, clasping her hands together. "Oh Molly, I'm so excited. I only have a few more classes left and then I can go full steam ahead with my business plan."

"I think that's a great idea. Do you want to come into the store tomorrow after your classes and get started? We have three desks in the office," Molly smiled. "Give me your rates and I'll forward them to Lucy."

"Wow! I went from lying on the couch feeling depressed to being hired for doing what I love best *and* starting a new business. Yes! Of course I'll come in, is noon okay?"

"Whatever time works for you. It's your business, you're your own boss now."

Stacey smiled. "That's right, I am."

CHAPTER 35

For the rest of the week everything went according to plan, and renovations for the bookstore were moving fast. Molly was pleased with the progress - working long days and well into the early evenings had paid off. She wanted to see significant changes before her meeting with Caroline and felt she'd definitely achieved that.

The bookstore had been bustling with painters, contractors, and an extremely talented artist all week. The store now popped with a bright red front door, sparkling clean windows framed with red trim, and a new wooden sign with red letters and black edging, much larger than the old one. It was due to be delivered this morning and installed before Caroline's arrival at noon. Thankfully Caroline couldn't make it to the store until later in the day, giving Molly more time to put on some last-minute touches, which included hanging the sign.

Molly arrived early at 7:00 am, and just as she did every day, enjoyed her morning stroll through the quiet streets, sipping on her coffee to go. Standing outside the store, she smiled as she looked at the fresh new paint job before unlocking the door. It definitely caught your eye and was the most prominent business on the street.

Since the outside of the store had been given a fresh new look, people had stopped by and knocked on the door asking if it was open, which pleased Molly greatly. She introduced herself and told them the plans for the store, and that a grand re-opening would take place in the near future. It was gratifying to see the excitement in their eyes when she told them the news. She handed out business cards with the new website Stacey had diligently been working on.

Molly smiled again when she entered the store; so much had changed in just one week. Brand new custom-built wooden shelves lined every wall. Painted above the shelves on the calming beige walls with white trim were beautifully bright, colorful murals of pictures related to reading which included stacks of books, pages of books with famous quotes, paintings of children, and families reading books together. In between the murals were large, encouraging words painted in gold and italicized, including, *"Get Lost in a Book," "Relax," "Read," "Love Books,"* and *"Lose Yourself in a Book."*

Molly walked across the plush beige carpet that she'd shampooed which was now stain-free with a fresh smell. She got to the Children's section at the back of the store which was separated by a wall with a large archway at the entrance built by the contractor. An amazing young artist named Emily did an incredible job painting a mural with blue skies, puffy white clouds, colorful trees, and many children's favorite books, including, *Dr. Seuss, Big Bird, Cookie Monster, Clifford the Big Red Dog and Winnie the Pooh.* Molly was pleased to see that the contractor had finished building all the low white bookshelves which lined the walls in the Children's section and had also installed the multi-colored carpet tiles. "This looks really good!" Molly said to herself. "I can't wait until the red bean bags and small reading tables and chairs arrive."

Standing in the archway of the Children's section, Molly turned around and looked at the new large glass counter framed in oak with glass shelves she planned on filling with vintage books, magazines, fountain pens, ink bottles, an antique typewriter, and beautiful time-pieces. Behind the counter were the original glass shelves where she planned to hang the Mark Twain picture.

Still carrying her laptop, Molly walked over to the counter, set it down and pulled out her cell phone from her jacket pocket to check the time. It was almost 7:30 am. In half an hour the sign maker should be arriving to install the new sign outside as well as the small wooden signs he'd made for the bookshelves, labeling each section. She also planned to have Albert and Hailey, who would be arriving at eight, put as many books as they could back on the shelves before Caroline arrived.

Molly brushed her hand across the glass surface of the counter. She was finally comfortable with the way she'd arranged the book-store and felt assured that Caroline would also be pleased with the changes and vast improvements she'd made so far. But she knew she was just getting started and couldn't wait to see how the store would look a week from now. Caroline's assistant Lucy had been stopping by every day for a few hours, pleased with the daily improvements she'd seen, and had kept Caroline in the loop, expressing her utmost approval of Molly's work.

If everything went according to plan, next week they'd begin construction at the beverage and pastry corner, adding three new red couches, a few dark wooden coffee tables, six bistro tables and chairs, and four matching red armchairs.

Molly walked behind the counter and sat on the wooden stool. Taking a sip of her coffee, she scanned the space of the new improved store, smiling. She whispered, "how could Caroline *not* like me after what I've done to this place?"

For the next few hours Molly didn't have time to think about her meeting with Caroline. She was too busy adding last minute touches for her grand arrival and directing Albert and Hailey on where to shelve the books. What pleased her the most was the beautiful bold red sign on the storefront. It definitely popped and got your attention, even if you were standing across the street, which Molly verified for herself. It was bright, bold and beautiful. And finally, the store was inviting from the outside. Once she'd added tables and chairs in front of the two large windows, Molly hoped no one could resist coming into the store.

By 11:30 Molly's workload began to slow down, and with time to think about Caroline's arrival, her demeanor quickly changed from excited and proud to extreme nervousness and intense anxiety. Wanting to be alone with Caroline, she told Albert and Hailey to take an early lunch.

Molly embraced the silence once they'd left and rubbed her sweaty palms on her jeans. "God, I can't believe how nervous I am," she whispered under her breath, walking to the office. For over three years she had thought about this day, and now it was finally here. So many scenarios had played out in her mind on how their first meeting would be. She prayed the actual meeting, just minutes away, would be one of the good scenarios she had acted out in her mind, and not those full of disappointment and heartbreak that had haunted her for years.

Molly had contemplated having Stacey in the store for this momentous occasion for moral support but decided against it, fearing that everything may fall apart. This was something she had always pictured doing on her own. It was personal, and only between her and Caroline. Molly wasn't about to change that now and asked Stacey if she wouldn't mind working from home. At first, she protested, wanting to show her support, but after Molly explained her reasoning, Stacey soon conceded and reminded her that she was just a phone call away.

Sitting at her desk, Molly checked the time on her phone for the third time in ten minutes, having done nothing but stare at the blank screen of her laptop since she entered the office. She wasn't sure how she should be feeling right now. Her emotions were all over the place, with fear dominating her and a sudden urge to run as far away as possible, thinking this was all a terrible mistake. Feeling beads of nervous sweat form on her brow, Molly left her seat and went to the ladies' room to moisten her face with a damp washcloth. It brought instant relief and calmed her nerves substantially. She looked at her reflection in the mirror, her face still damp and red, and told herself aloud, "you've got this Molly. You've waited so long for this moment. Everything is going to be okay."

While trying to calm her nerves, she heard the new brass bell ring on the front door of the store and gasped. "She's here!" she whispered, fluffing her hair with her fingers. Molly stood up straight and took one last look in the mirror. "It's time to meet Caroline."

CHAPTER 36

Closing the bathroom door behind her, Molly heard the now familiar voice coming from the front of the store. "Hello Molly, are you here?" said Lucy.

"Yes! I'm here," Molly called out, walking through the store to greet them, her nerves peaked. "Come on Molly, calm down," she whispered under her breath as she rubbed her sweaty palms on her jeans once more. Molly came to an abrupt stop when she passed the counter, her heart pounding beneath her chest, her breaths short and deep. She had pictured this moment a million times in her head, but what she saw before her had never crossed her mind. In front of her stood Lucy whom she knew, and next to her wearing black slacks and a white wool sweater was Caroline, but what took Molly by surprise was the little girl dressed in a red coat, jeans and red tennis shoes, with blonde, curly hair framing her face and holding Caroline's hand.

Lucy smiled, "Molly, there you are." She glanced around the store and smiled again. "The store looks fabulous."

"Oh, we have a long way to go, but we're getting there," Molly said nervously.

"Well, this is your estranged boss, Caroline," Lucy joked.

Caroline held out her hand and gave Molly a friendly smile. "Hi

Molly, it's so nice to finally meet you. I'm sorry I've been absent since you arrived, but I've been trying to sort out my life since my husband passed away. It's been a very trying week."

Molly took her hand and gave it a gentle squeeze, surprised how chilly her skin was. She looked much older than the pictures she'd seen of her online. Her skin was pale, and she looked tired. But that was understandable after what she'd been through. She wore no makeup to conceal the crow's feet framing her eyes and had a few light wrinkles around her lips. Her shoulder-length dusty blonde hair with visible grey streaks was feathered and layered away from her face. She was a good four inches taller than Molly's five-foot five-inch frame and physically looked to be in good shape. Molly took in every detail, not believing she was standing before her and holding her hand. "It's okay. I'm so sorry for your loss. I had no idea your husband was sick."

"Not many people did which wasn't easy to achieve living in such a small town."

"And who is this?" Molly asked, smiling as she looked down at the little girl holding Caroline's hand.

Pride filled Caroline's eyes. "This is my daughter, Emma."

Flooded with mixed emotions, Molly wasn't sure how to react and fought to hold back the tears she felt forming. "I had no idea you had a daughter either," and instantly regretted saying what she said next. "There's no mention of her anywhere online. How old is she?"

Caroline pulled away her hand and creased her brow. "You looked me up online?" she asked, her eyes narrowed, her lips tight. "Have you been stalking me?" she asked, followed by a nervous laugh.

Molly lied. "No! That *does* sound bad though, doesn't it? When I found out I had the job, I admit, I did look you up, but only to see who my new boss would be, that's all. I wouldn't call that stalking, would you?"

Caroline's body relaxed. "I was just making a joke; I would have done the same thing. I do try to keep much of my life as private as possible, including my daughter's, who is only four."

Molly had so many questions, but knew they had to wait. Now

wasn't the right time, especially with her daughter present. She then wondered if there ever would be a right time? Instead, she nodded. "That's understandable. Some people put their entire lives out there which I personally don't think is a good idea." Still stunned to learn of Emma and trying to keep her emotions in check Molly shifted the conversation. "Well, let me show you around so you can see all of the improvements I've made."

"I've already seen what you've done to the outside when we pulled up. I spotted the new sign from a distance, it looks fabulous. I can't believe what you've accomplished already in such a short time. You've truly outdone yourself, thank you *so* much."

"You're welcome. I can't tell you what a relief it is to hear that you're happy with my work." Molly smiled. "Honestly, it's a labor of love. I really enjoy what I do." Molly clasped her hands together, locked her fingers and raised them to her chin. "I've been so nervous and worried you'd hate everything I've done so far."

Caroline reached out and gently rested her hand on Molly's shoulder. "Oh Molly, you have absolutely nothing to worry about. The visions you have for this place are beyond anything I could have ever imagined. Lucy and I agree, hiring you was definitely the right decision."

Feeling at ease and relieved that she and Caroline were off to a good start, Molly spent the next hour walking with her through the store and discussing changes and her plans, while Lucy entertained Emma in the Children's section, reading to her from a variety of books.

"I'm sorry there aren't any chairs here yet," Molly told Lucy in the Children's section. "They should be arriving next week."

"Oh, we're fine. I grabbed one of the office chairs, and Emma's comfortable sitting in my lap."

Before heading to the office 30 minutes later, Caroline checked in with Lucy and smiled when she found her daughter sound asleep on Lucy's lap.

"She's worn out," Lucy whispered.

"I'll be in the office if you need me," Caroline whispered back.

"I haven't made any changes to the office, it functions fine just how it is at the moment," Molly told Caroline as they walked to the back of the store. "But I wanted to show you the website Stacey's been working on. She's done a fantastic job and will continue to maintain it with a calendar of events as well as updating books that can be ordered from the site."

Sitting next to Caroline at the desk, Molly spent the next half hour showing her the features of the site and explaining how it would benefit the store. While they talked, Molly questioned herself; was it a good time to have that serious conversation that initially brought her to Riverbanks? They were alone and Molly had her undivided attention, but she refrained, afraid of ruffling any feathers.

"This is amazing, Molly. I know absolutely nothing about this stuff, it goes way over my head," Caroline chuckled, holding her hand up to her mouth. "When it comes to technology, I think I got left behind," she joked and then smiled, "Molly, I want to tell you this; because of what you have done to this store and your ongoing plans, I can honestly say that I believe Emma and I are going to be okay moving forward without Pete, something I've been unsure of until today and seeing the store."

"I'm sure it's been difficult for you."

"It has and still is, and will most likely continue to be for quite a while. We bought this store shortly after Pete and I got married. We didn't need it for the money back then, Pete made a good salary, this was something for me. I love to read, and ever since I can remember, I've wanted to own a bookstore, and thanks to Pete, he made it happen. I had so many plans for this place, but for whatever reason I couldn't get it off the ground, and I was literally overwhelmed when I started to think about making improvements and have the store provide us with a second income. I'm astounded by what you've done in a week," Caroline chuckled, raising her hand to her mouth again. "You know, the store still looks the same as it did the day I bought it, I've not done a thing to it. I can't even keep up with new releases, and this store soon taught me that I'm a terrible business manager, but I wasn't about to give up."

"I'm glad you didn't. You have a wonderful place here; it just needs some TLC."

"And someone who knows what they're doing, and you certainly do. As you know the store has been barely hanging on by a thread, but I was okay with that. It was more of a hobby for me and got me out of the house. But when Emma was born four years ago, I wanted to make it work and told myself that when she got a little bit older, I'd devote all my time to turning the store around and making it a successful business. However, two years ago we got the devastating news that Pete had terminal cancer."

"I'm so sorry," Molly replied, pity in her eyes.

Caroline wiped her moist eyes. "Thank you. We were told he had a life expectancy of six months; it's a miracle he lived for another 18. I'm thankful that Emma and I were able to spend that extra time with him."

Molly reached across the desk and handed her a tissue. "Here you go."

Caroline dabbed her eyes. "Thank you. It's so hard, I can't believe he's gone, and it hurts every time I think of Emma growing up not knowing her father and what an amazing man he was. Pete had to quit his job last year, he was just too sick and weak to continue. I stayed home to take care of him, which wasn't easy when you have a toddler, but I never told Pete how exhausted I was and that we were quickly going through our savings." Caroline abruptly stopped talking and looked at Molly. "I'm sorry, do you mind me telling you all this? I wanted to give you some history of the store and it looks like I'm defending myself on why I've never done anything to it, but taking care of my husband and daughter took a toll on me and left me with no time for the store."

"It's fine, I'm just sorry to hear about all of the heartache you've been through."

"Thank you. I've not talked about Pete's sickness to many people, or my struggles. Lucy knows everything. We've been best friends for years, and she helps me whenever she can even though she has a full-time job and a family of her own. I don't know what I would do without her. I knew six months ago, as our savings continued to drain, that I had to think of my future and how I would be able to provide for my daughter." Caroline looked around the office and managed a smile. "This store is all I have."

Molly remained quiet, stunned by how much Caroline was opening up to her. She hadn't expected her to pour her heart out to her and was unsure how to react. Her heart went out to Caroline and her daughter Emma. With everything going on in *her* life, Molly was beginning to think that coming to Riverbanks was a bad idea. How could she even begin to tell Caroline the real reason she was here? Yes, the job was fantastic, and she loved every minute of it, but it was secondary to her true intentions. How could there ever be a right time to tell her? Molly wondered, looking at Caroline's face, whose eyes expressed only sadness.

CHAPTER 37

After Caroline left, Molly found it difficult to concentrate on her work. Albert and Hailey returned from lunch and spent the rest of their shifts stocking the books on shelves, while Molly remained in the office, uncertain of her future with the bookstore.

Meeting Caroline in person and discovering she had a daughter put everything in a different perspective. Caroline was not only mourning the death of her husband, but also raising her young daughter alone as she tried to get her life back together. Molly felt like a thorn in the midst of Caroline's troubles and believed she would only add additional pain and stress to the challenges Caroline was currently facing once she confronted her with the truth.

"How the hell am I supposed to carry out my plans?" Molly hissed, tossing her head back against the chair and continuing to speak aloud, letting go of her frustrations. "Meeting her went okay, but now I've been thrown not one but two curve balls, her daughter and the passing of her husband. I didn't anticipate any of this, and I don't know if I can carry out my ideas. Am I being selfish by pursuing my plans?" Frustrated and unsure of what to do, Molly leaned forward, rested her elbows on the desk, and raked her fingers through her hair. "Shit! I don't know what to do." She picked her phone up off the desk and saw that it was almost 6:00. Realizing Albert and Hailey would be leaving soon, she decided to call it a night herself and shut down the computer before grabbing her jacket, purse and laptop.

"Hey, I just wanted to let you know that we're leaving," Hailey hollered from across the store as Molly approached the counter.

Molly forced a smile. "Thanks for everything, I'll see you both in the morning."

"See you then," Hailey called out as they walked towards the front door and left.

As SOON AS Molly opened the door to her home, she was greeted with a sharp bark from Henry who instantly jumped off the couch and ran over to her.

"Hey buddy," Molly said, petting the top of his head before placing her laptop and purse on the couch.

Stacey turned her head from where she sat at her desk. "Hey, how'd it go?" she asked, pushing her chair back and standing. "I want to hear all about your day. How was Caroline? Was she everything you imagined?"

Molly dragged her feet to the other side of the couch and flopped down. "It went okay, but I feel terrible."

Stacey joined her on the couch, her brow furrowed. "What, why? You just said everything went okay? I don't understand."

"Everything is such a mess. There's no way I can ever tell Caroline why I'm here. She's so nice and we get along great. She loves what I've done to the store, and she loves the website, by the way."

"Oh, great! I was a bit nervous about what she would think. I'm so pleased she likes it, and I'm not even finished with it yet. But if she's so nice, what's the problem? I thought that would make everything easier."

"It's because of all the stuff she's going through. I mean, she just lost her husband and then I show up and not only that, she also has a daughter."

Stacey gasped. "What? Oh, my god, then that makes…"

Molly quickly interrupted, waving her hand to hush her. "Yes, I know. It changes everything."

"How did you not know this with all of the research you've done?"

"She's very protective of her daughter and has led a private life with her husband. Most of what I found online was before her daughter was born."

"Well, you still have to tell her, it's why we left our lives in Texas and came here."

"It's why I came here; you came here to start a new life after a bad breakup," Molly corrected her.

Stacey shrugged her shoulders. "Well, true, and it was the best decision I've ever made." She grinned. "I got a new client today. He's really cute."

Molly chuckled. "Wow! Sounds like you're over your bad breakup. Who's the guy and how did he find you?"

"Riverbanks has a group on Facebook, so I posted my services on there, and within the hour this guy named Craig messaged me; he wants me to design a website for his rustic furniture business. He makes log furniture and wall decor."

"Have you met him in person?"

"No, but we're going to meet tomorrow and discuss it over lunch. I sent him my rates and he said they were reasonable."

"If you've never met him, how do you know he's cute?"

Stacey giggled. "I looked up his profile on Facebook. He looks like a real cowboy; he's got the hat, the big belt buckle and the boots," she smirked. "It also says that he's single."

"Cowboy seems to be the stereotype around here," Molly joked. "Congratulations, it seems as though the word is getting out about your business. You're going to do just fine."

"I had a woman that owns one of the restaurants reach out to me, too. She said she'd get back with me tomorrow after speaking with her husband. This sure beats waiting tables." She leaned back, folded her arms and emitted a triumphant smile. "I've also thought of a name for my business, I've designed some business cards, and filled out all the necessary documents for a new business start-up."

"Wow! You *have* been busy - I'm impressed. So, what name did you come up with?"

Stacey raised her hands and beamed. "Endless Web Creations and SEO."

Molly nodded. "I like that, and you know SEO?"

Stacey lowered her hands and said excitedly, "yes, we covered it in class, so it's an added service I can offer to those that already have a website but need help with the back end of the site. All the technical stuff that most people hate."

"I didn't know you were so smart," Molly joked.

"Hey! I'm not just a pretty face, you know. So, you like the name? Be honest with me, I can take it."

"Yes, I do. It doesn't limit you to one or two fields, the word *endless* tells potential customers that you can do web designs for anything."

"Exactly!" Stacey said, clapping her hands. "Oh, I'm so excited!" She patted Molly's knee. "But enough about me, what about you? If it makes you feel any better, you've just met Caroline, and you said she's nice. Give it some time, build your friendship with her and let some time pass so that she can grieve her husband. She's extremely emotional and scared right now. Let her gain her strength back, and in the meantime continue to build her confidence and trust in you."

"Yeah, you're right, but damn, she has a daughter. I can't wrap my head around that."

"You need to just focus on the bookstore and put all of this emotional stuff aside for now." Stacey grinned. "You also need a social life - in fact, we *both* need one," Stacey laughed. She looked at Molly, her eyes big and bright. "Hey, you should join the Riverbanks Group on Facebook. Introduce yourself and tell the people of this town about your plans for the store. It seems like the whole town is in that group posting events, services needed, and services offered. Quite a few people have added me as a friend, and this weekend a local band is playing at one of the restaurants in town. We should go!" she said excitedly. "It would be a great way to meet some of the locals."

"That's not a bad idea. I want to support local businesses by selling their merchandise in the store. Crafty things, like candles, incense, jewelry, and books, of course, by local authors. I could make a post in the group, and it'd be great to have authors come in and do book signings. I'll join tomorrow." Molly smiled. "Thank you, and yes, I think we both need a night out. Let's go check out that band this weekend."

CHAPTER 38

Sharing her concerns last night with Stacey with regard to Caroline helped Molly immensely. She woke up feeling refreshed and energized after finally getting a good night's sleep, not getting out of bed until after 8:00 am. Determined to have a more positive attitude, Molly told herself that she was not going to think about anything but the store, everything else would have to wait. Now wasn't the time to be wasting energy and negative thoughts that wouldn't solve anything, it would just interfere with her progress on the store.

Standing in the kitchen, she poured herself a cup of coffee to go, to enjoy on her morning walk to work. Molly let out a loud wolf whistle as Stacey entered the room. "Wow! Look at you, girl, are you hoping to get a date or a new client?"

Stacey nervously rubbed her thigh with her left hand. She was dressed in tight-fitting Levis, a low-cut white shirt revealing the top of her breast line, and brown-heeled cowboy boots.

Her blonde hair cascaded down her back, beautifully styled with large, enhanced curls. She wore more makeup than Molly had ever seen her wear in weeks. Jet black eyeliner framed her eyes, and ruby red lipstick shone on her lips. Molly also noticed she'd done her nails, painting them a shiny red, as well as a delicate silver horseshoe on a silver chain that hung around her neck.

"Do you think it's a little much?" Stacey asked, looking down at her attire.

"You look fantastic. I've just not seen you so dressed up and manicured since we left Texas."

"It does feel a little weird. It took me hours to get ready," Stacey laughed. "I'm out of practice. I've been up since the crack of dawn worrying about what I should wear," she confessed, smoothing her long shirt sleeves down her arm. "Maybe I should go change?"

Molly placed her mug on the counter and joined her. "No, don't you dare! I'm sorry, I was just making a silly joke."

"Well, I do like the guy, and yes, if I'm going to be honest, I *am* dressing to impress, but I certainly don't want to scare him away."

Molly chuckled. "You're not going to scare him away. You look beautiful. Now go on and get out of here, and *stop* worrying. Call me later and let me know how it went. I'll be thinking of you."

"Thanks, I will. We're meeting for breakfast; I just have to feed Henry and grab my laptop and jacket, then I'm out of here," Stacey said, picking up Henry's bowl from the floor.

MOLLY ARRIVED at the store shortly after 9:00, finding Albert and Hailey waiting outside.

"I'm so sorry guys, I slept in. I hope you haven't been waiting too long," Molly said, fumbling for the keys in her purse.

"No, it's only been a few minutes," Hailey told her. "I'm just glad you're okay. I was worried when I got here and the door was locked. You've always been here around 7:00."

"Yeah, I've been working non-stop and it finally caught up with me, so I decided to have a lie-in this morning."

Albert smiled. "I'm glad you did; you've been working your ass off."

Inside the store, Molly set her things down on the counter and turned on the lights. "I'm going to do some work in the office this morning, and I'd like both of you to continue getting the books on the shelves from the boxes in the storeroom. After you've finished with that, I'd like you to get the inside of the front windows clean so that we can showcase our new releases in the left window, as there's a shipment arriving later today. And I'd like to showcase the local authors in the window to the right."

"Fantastic!" Hailey squealed. "It's going to be fun organizing the displays."

"Yes, we'll do it together," Molly told her, grabbing her laptop and coffee from the counter and heading for the office.

Molly closed the office door behind her, enjoying the solitude and silence. It was taking all of her willpower to stay focused on the job. Her mind kept wandering back to Caroline. "Focus, Molly," she said aloud, shaking her head before taking a seat at her desk.

After Molly joined the Riverbanks Facebook group, she spent the next hour scrolling through many of the posts. She wrote a long, detailed post introducing herself and her plans for the bookstore. She expressed how much she wanted to support local authors and merchants, and also to tell everyone to reach out to her if they'd like to have their books or products showcased in the store. To enhance the post, Molly added a picture of the store showing the freshly painted storefront and its bold new sign. After making her post she continued to scroll through the group, surprised by how active it was for a small town. "Stacey was right, it seems as though the entire town is here and everyone wants to help each other. I love this small-town vibe," she grinned.

Within minutes of posting about the bookstore, comments were left and messages started coming in, along with friend requests. Molly smiled as she read the positive comments welcoming her to Riverbanks and how excited they all were for the re-opening of the bookstore. Some even made their own posts, spreading the news that Riverbanks would be getting a new and improved bookstore, and still others posted about the beautiful new paint job the store had recently received.

"This is amazing!" Molly shrieked, leaning back in her seat and grinning like the Cheshire Cat.

Molly soon lost track of time as she got busy scheduling merchants and local authors who had messaged her that they'd like to bring in their products and books to the store. She had been engrossed in her work for hours and had no idea it was already noon until she heard a knock at the door. Hailey opened her door and peeked around it. "We're going to grab some lunch, do you want us to bring you back anything?"

"It's noon already?" Molly replied, shocked. "Yes! Would you mind?" she said, grabbing her wallet from her purse and handing her a twenty. "Surprise me, whatever sounds good," she laughed. "I'll eat anything at this point, I've not eaten a thing all day."

After Hailey left Molly looked at her calendar and couldn't believe she had booked six authors and 15 merchants to come by the store next week. "This is brilliant, I had no idea this small town held so much talent. We're definitely going to put Riverbanks and this bookstore on the map."

Molly continued to peruse through the Facebook group, answering questions people asked about the bookstore. She made a note to join the Billings, Montana Group, excited about the response she might get, as it was a large city. In the midst of scrolling, her phone rang. When she saw it was Stacey she answered right away. "So, how did it go?"

"It went great! He's even cuter than his picture," Stacey giggled. "He was so polite, calling me Ma'am. I don't think anyone has ever called me that before, and he's a *real* cowboy, tall, handsome, short dark hair and muscular arms. Oh, and his hands looked strong too, you can tell he works with his hands."

"What about the job? Did you get it?" Molly laughed.

"Oh, yes, sorry. Yes, he hired me on the spot. I'll be starting work on his website next week after he's sent me the files."

"And, did he ask you out on a date?"

"No silly, not on our first meeting. He's too much of a gentleman to do that, but I did feel the chemistry between us, it was amazing! I wanted to lean over the table and kiss him right there," Stacey confessed.

"Stacey, slow down! I've never seen you so eager to hook up with a guy."

"Well, after being with that idiot Doug, I feel just like a butterfly that's sprung out of its cocoon. There's no stopping me now."

"Well, I'm happy for you, but take it slow with this guy. Get to know him first. He may be super handsome, but he might end up being a jerk. I'm saying this because I'm just looking out for you. You thought Doug was amazing, you even thought you'd marry him someday, and looked how that turned out."

Stacey didn't respond to her comments about Doug. "Craig is too nice to be a jerk. Wait until you meet him, then you'll see what I mean."

"Well, I hope you're right. Listen, I gotta get back to work and I just heard the bell on the front door. I think my lunch is here. I'll see you tonight."

After ending the call, Molly left the office and headed to the front door, shocked to see Caroline walking towards her.

CHAPTER 39

Stunned by her presence and noticing how tired she looked, Molly knew she had been crying just by looking at her swollen, red eyes. Molly spoke softly, trying to hide her nervousness. "Caroline, I wasn't expecting to see you today. Did we schedule a meeting? If so, I'm so sorry I forgot, I've been extremely busy."

Casually dressed in blue jeans and a red sweater, Caroline raised her hand. "No, we didn't have a meeting. I just dropped Emma off at daycare for a few hours and wanted to see the store again. I want to thank you once more for all the work you're doing." She paused, diverting her stare to the floor. "And, if I can be truly honest, I didn't want to go home."

Molly approached her, unsure of what to do with her hands - now sticky with sweat - and quickly folded her arms. "You didn't want to go home? But why?" Molly asked, her voice soft. "Did something happen?"

"No, nothing happened. When Emma is home I'm fine, she keeps me busy, but when I'm alone it's really difficult. I see Pete everywhere. He died in that house, in our bed, and I can't turn off the movie in my head. I sit numbly in that house and just cry." Tears rolled down her cheeks. "I'm sorry, I don't know why I'm telling you this. I just didn't know where else to go, Lucy's at work."

Molly unfolded her arms and reached out to Caroline, taking her hand. "It's okay. I can only imagine how difficult this is for you. I wish there was something I could do to take away the pain you're going through."

"Thank you. Just having someone to talk to really helps. When Pete got sick two years ago, I became a recluse. I wanted his illness to only be known within the family, and Lucy of course, who I consider family. The thought of people coming and going from my home while I was dealing with my husband dying was something I just couldn't bear."

"I can understand that. Would you like a cup of tea? I have some in the office."

Caroline sniffed back her tears. "I don't want to be a bother, you're so busy."

"It's no bother. Please, let me make you some tea. It's lunch time anyway, and I'm waiting for Albert and Hailey to return with mine." She wrapped her arm around Caroline's shoulder and gave her a gentle squeeze. "Come on, let's get you a cup of tea."

Inside the office Molly pulled out one of the chairs. "Here you go."

Caroline took a seat, setting her purse on the desk in front of her. "Some days I feel like I'm losing my mind. I used to be so good around people, involved with the community, but for the last few years I've completely shut the world out. I wanted to spend my last two years with just Pete and our daughter, and I honestly don't know how to pick myself back up."

Molly handed her a cup of hot tea. "Well, you've made a good start by hiring me. This store is going to support you and Emma. It's a gift from Pete that will keep on giving. I've been posting about the store on Facebook and it's created a real buzz. This town is excited to see what comes next."

"Really? I thought the town had forgotten about my store."

"To be honest, they probably had. You yourself said it's been neglected, but now we're bringing it back to life. I'm going to make this store successful, and everyone will know about it. It'll be a major part of the community - a gathering place for the town. I'm sure it's going to take some time for you. I know you're still healing right now, but as time goes on and when you're ready, I'm sure you'll be spending more of your time here at the store. When you do, I know the community will welcome you back with open arms."

"But what if they ask about Pete? Many people knew him, but they don't know that he's passed."

"Be honest with them. Tell them he passed away and how hard it's been for you and Emma, but you're both doing okay. They'll probably give you their condolences, then you can steer the conversation towards the bookstore. Just stay in control of the conversation."

"That's good advice, thank you. I really think I should be helping you more with this place, but I just can't do it right now. I honestly think I'd be more of a burden than an asset."

"I'm doing fine, and Lucy has been a tremendous help, along with Albert and Hailey. Don't rush it, you'll know when you're ready. Your job right now is to be there for Emma." Molly gave Caroline a caring smile. "How's Emma doing by the way?"

"She's doing okay. She's young, so I don't think she understands that her Daddy is never coming back. We talk about him every day, we look at photos, and I also try to explain his illness to her. When she finally does understand I will be there for her."

A knock at the door interrupted them and Hailey entered the office. "Oh, sorry, I didn't know you had a meeting." She looked over at Caroline, "Hi Caroline," then looked back at Molly. "Here's your lunch - Tuna Fish on Rye. I hope that's okay," she said, handing it to Molly.

"That's great! Thanks. I'll be out in a bit."

"I don't want to keep you from your lunch," Caroline said, quickly standing.

"No, please stay. You haven't even touched your tea."

Caroline returned to her seat. "Okay," she said, taking a sip of her hot beverage before speaking. "Do you still plan on opening the store next week? You've said you wanted to keep it closed for a couple of weeks."

"I do, but it will be a soft opening. We still have a lot to do, but the longer it stays closed the longer it's not making any money, and you and Emma need that income."

"What do you mean by a soft opening?" Caroline asked.

"We're going to open it as stands at the moment; no big announcement. I'll post on Facebook and in the local paper that the store has reopened after some remodeling, but..." Molly paused and smiled. "I'm glad you brought this up, because I'd like to do a grand opening in a few months. Then we can have guest authors, book discounts, children readings, coloring, games, cake and beverages of course, but I do have one concern."

"That all sounds fabulous; by then I hope to be feeling better and able to attend."

"And maybe do a speech?" Molly asked nervously.

"Oh, I don't know, Molly, I'll think about it." She paused and shook her head. "No, I shouldn't have to think about it, I'll do it. I need to get back into the swing of things with the community and that'd be a great start." She smiled. "Yes, I'll definitely do it. Now what was your concern?"

"Great! The people of this town would love to hear from you. My concern is the weather; I was thinking of having the Grand Opening during the holidays as Christmas is just a few months away, and I thought this could be your holiday gift to Riverbanks. A new and improved bookstore. But the timing would put us in the middle of winter. What if we have frigid temperatures and a lot of snow? No one will show up?"

"What a beautiful gesture. I think it's a wonderful idea, but you're right, there's a fair chance we may have snow, but to be honest I'm really not worried."

"You're not?" Molly was surprised.

Caroline shook her head and chuckled. "No, it'll just add to the festive season. I can see it now; holiday lights inside and outside the store, a large Christmas tree standing tall inside, and Christmas carols playing softly in the background. The sweet aroma of hot chocolate and apple cider lingering in the air, Santa Claus reading to the children, and local musicians playing holiday tunes for the event will make it ever so delightful."

Molly smiled. "I have the same vision, but like I said, what if it's too cold and we get a lot of snow?"

Caroline leaned back in her seat. "One thing you'll learn about small town living is how supportive the people are of one another, *especially* small businesses. Life here goes on in all types of weather, including snow. If they can't drive they'll bundle up and walk across town to support you."

Molly was shocked. "Really? That would *never* happen in Texas. We always stayed at home buried under our big blankets waiting for the ice storm to pass," she laughed.

Caroline chuckled. "Trust me, they will come. I may be out of touch with the community, but I know how folks are around here. Like you said, they're excited about this place and they want this store for themselves, their families and their children. I wouldn't be surprised if most of the town showed up."

"Okay then! Well, you certainly eased my mind, thank you. A Christmas Grand Opening it is," Molly smiled, rubbing her hands together.

Caroline took another sip of her tea and gently smiled. "I'm glad I stopped by. This really helped, and thank you so much for listening to me." She smiled again. "I *do* feel better because of it."

Molly matched her smile, pleased they were getting along so well. She was not expecting to be the person Caroline came to for support, someone to lean on and talk to; why would she risk destroying all that? Molly feared that that may be what might happen when she told her the truth. "You're welcome, and please come by any time you need to talk," she said quietly, not knowing what else to say.

CHAPTER 40

After Caroline left, Molly tried to focus on her work but found it to be a challenge. She joined Albert and Hailey in the front of the store as they spent the rest of the day designing the front window with newly released books that arrived while Molly was in the office. The friendship between her and Caroline was blossoming. Caroline had entrusted her with details of her personal life, things she hadn't shared with anyone, and Molly did not want to jeopardize that bond or trust, but feared it would soon be inevitable.

Molly stood alone on the sidewalk in front of the store watching Albert arrange small, rustic wooden bookshelves and stands in the window. She nodded her approval when she was satisfied with the layout.

As she gave Albert directions from the street, Molly struggled to stay focused as she had a conversation with herself. "I can't tell Caroline," Molly whispered to herself as she directed Albert to move one of the shelves once more. "But if I don't, I'll be cheating myself," she sighed. Continuing on with her solo conversation with force and determination she said, "I need to accept the consequences no matter what. And I must stay strong." Molly nodded at Albert, approving the positioning of the shelf in the window. Albert smiled, giving her a thumbs up. Still distracted, Molly spoke aloud to herself again. "I'll find the right time to tell Caroline soon enough. I can't go on like this much longer, keeping all this inside of me. The sooner I tell her the sooner I can move on."

As she was lost in thought and frustrated with herself, a tap on the window startled her. She looked up and saw that it was Hailey. Unable to hear her, Molly walked back inside. "I'm sorry, I couldn't hear you; what did you say?"

"Do you want us to start putting the books on the shelves now?" Hailey asked.

"Yes please, and make sure the covers are visible from the outside, I have more metal bookstands in a box on the counter if you need them." Molly walked towards the front door. "I'll go outside and see how they look while you and Albert put them on the shelves," Molly said to her before returning to the street, still fighting with her demons about what to say to Caroline.

Twenty minutes later as she stood in front of the store giving Albert and Hailey directions, Molly felt something brush up against her leg. Startled, she quickly jumped back and looked down at her feet, surprised to see a friendly Calico cat with Tabby markings and an off-white belly purring up at her. Not wanting to scare the cat, Molly slowly reached out her hand to hold near the cat's nose. "Well hello there, and what's your name?" Surprising Molly, the cat didn't bolt but instead continued to purr, rubbing its face against her hand. Molly stroked the top of its head, smiling as the cat purred louder. She bent down and rubbed its back and laughed when the cat rolled over. "Oh, you want me to pet your belly, and I see you're a girl," she said, giving the cat a good belly rub. "There you go, how does that feel?" Molly said in a sweet voice, noticing her gorgeous emerald eyes. "You're beautiful."

A few minutes later as Molly got acquainted with her new friend, Hailey joined her. "Whose cat is that? It's so cute," she said, watching Molly pet her. "Is it a boy or a girl?"

Molly continued to stroke the cat's back. "I have no idea whose cat it is, but it's a female." Molly glanced down the street. "She's super friendly, and just showed up out of nowhere, but there's no collar on her." Molly continued petting the cat. "I wonder where she came from?"

Molly stood up and immediately the cat did the same, not taking her eyes off her. "I wonder if she's hungry?" Molly said, smiling down at the cat. "Hey sweet girl, do you want some milk?" Molly turned and looked at Hailey. "Watch her for a minute, I'll go grab some milk from the fridge."

Hailey laughed. "I don't think I need to watch her; look, she's following you."

Molly turned her head and saw the cat following close behind. She took a few steps, and the cat followed. "Oh my goodness, she is!" She clicked her fingers and continued to walk to the office. "Come on girl, come with me," Molly said, quickening her pace. Not missing a step, the cat followed closely and kept up with her. She waited patiently and sat in the middle of the office as Molly placed a bowl of milk in front of her. Molly sat in one of the office chairs and watched her quickly lap up the milk. "You were hungry. Where do you live, sweet girl?" After the cat finished the last drop of milk, Molly laughed when she jumped up and started purring loudly, nestling herself comfortably in Molly's lap. Molly stroked the cat's back and kissed the top of her head. "You're so cute and friendly, I wish I knew where you lived."

There was a knock at the door and Hailey entered the office. "Did she drink the milk?" Hailey grinned when she saw the cat sound asleep on Molly's lap. "Oh my goodness, look at her? She sure has taken a liking to you."

"I know, right? Yes, she was super hungry and licked the bowl clean." Molly looked up at Hailey. "What am I supposed to do with her?"

"Are you thinking about keeping her?"

"As much as I would love to, I'm sure she has a home close by, but we'll worry about that when I close shop and have to put her outside. I hope she knows her way home."

"I'm sure she'll be okay. Like you said, she probably lives nearby."

"I hope so. Well, as comfortable as she is in my lap, I have work to do and I can't leave her here alone," Molly said, gently picking her up. "Come on girl, you can come outside with me and hang out with me while I work if you'd like."

The surprise visit from the cat couldn't have come at a better time, whisking Molly away from her haunting thoughts of Caroline and relieving some of her stress. To her surprise the cat stuck around, staying close to Molly, and laying in the sun beneath the front window. She was soon sound asleep.

"I'm not sure what I should do with her?" Molly said as she stood in front of the store with Albert and Hailey and admired their work, satisfied with the results. Molly took a step back; "I love how the fairy lights around the frame of the window illuminate the book covers perched on the shelves and the small table," Molly said, ignoring any answers to her first question with regard to the cat.

"Me too," Hailey agreed. "And the vintage typewriter on the small table really sets the vibe with the lamp behind it."

"That was your idea, Albert," Molly said, glancing over at him. "Thanks for that."

Albert smiled, feeling proud. "You're welcome."

Molly rubbed her hands together, feeling the chill of the evening. "Okay, back to the cat; I don't know what to do about her. She's still here and I need to close up shop. I feel awful leaving her here, it's getting really cold."

"I'm sure she'll go home once we leave," Hailey replied. "I'm going to head home now myself. I'll see you in the morning."

"Yeah, I guess you're right. I'm just a softie when it comes to animals. I'll see you tomorrow, and Monday, which is only three days away, we're opening the store, so I want to get quite a bit done tomorrow, so expect a busy day," Molly told her.

"I'll come with extra ammo," Hailey replied, laughing as she walked towards her car parked on the street.

After Albert and Hailey left, Molly grabbed her things from the office, turned off the lights, leaving only the fairy lights on in the front window, pulled the front door shut and locked it. She looked to her left and saw that the cat was sound asleep beneath the illuminated window. She knelt down to pet her. "Hey sweetheart, you need to go home, it's getting cold. I hate to leave you here, but I have to go home, too." The cat looked up at her and purred, making it harder for Molly to leave. "Please go home, sweetie. You can't stay here," she said, giving the cat one last pet before she stood. Refusing to turn around and look at the cat fearing it may encourage her to follow, Molly began her walk home, hoping the cat would do the same. When she reached the crosswalk at Main Street, Molly sneaked a peek over her shoulder and was relieved to see the cat hadn't followed. "Thank god," Molly said, quickening her pace, anxious to get home and out of the cold.

CHAPTER 41

When Molly returned home, she found Stacey working at her desk and Henry sound asleep on the couch, snoring loudly.

"You're still working? It's after dark," Molly said, throwing her jacket on the couch and startling Henry who let out a subtle growl before going back to sleep. "Sorry, Henry," Molly whispered.

Stacey looked out the window. "Is it really? I had no idea; I must have lost track of time." She spun around in her desk chair and faced Molly. "I've been *so* busy, and I can tell you that without a doubt I'll have no problem paying my share of the rent next month," she said, wearing a triumphant grin.

"Really? That's great! And you've only been in business a couple of days."

Stacey clapped her hands, "I know, I'm so excited! I got three more clients today. I met two of them in town, and one came by a few hours ago. I should have started this business much sooner and not waited to finish school." She emitted another satisfying grin. "In fact, I'll be finishing up my classes next week."

"Wow, look at you go! Sounds like the word is getting out."

"Yes, it is," Stacey said excitedly. "Apparently Riverbanks doesn't have a certified web designer or developer. There are a few locals that know quite a bit and help out the small businesses, but they don't have the knowledge I have." She leaned back in her chair and grinned again. "It looks like we came to this town at the right time."

"It seems that way. You may have to rent an office in town at this rate."

"Or get my own place."

Her comment startled Molly; she relied on Stacey's share of the rent right now. "So soon? We've only been here a few weeks."

"I know, but the way things are going, I shouldn't have a problem affording my own place. That was the plan, right? We weren't planning on being roomies forever, were we?"

Molly slowly eased herself down onto the couch next to Henry, careful not to wake him again. She was stunned by her statement. Everything was moving so fast for Stacey; a new business that was gaining traction quickly, her client Craig a potential new boyfriend, and finishing school. "No, but why rush things? This place is working out great for us."

"It is, but you have to admit we *are* pretty cramped. And look at my desk area," she said, pointing out the files strewn everywhere, even on the bistro table in the kitchen. "It doesn't look very professional when I have clients come by."

Molly nodded reluctantly and knew she was right. "Yeah, I get it, but why the rush? Next week might be slow."

"Don't worry, I'm not moving out tomorrow or next week, I'm just saying if business keeps going like it is I should be able to move out soon." She slapped the side of her thigh. "Anyway, enough about me, how was your day?"

Molly leaned back on the couch and closed her eyes. "Oh, don't ask."

"Oh dear, that doesn't sound good," Stacey said, leaving her desk and taking a seat in the armchair across from Molly. "What happened?"

Molly opened her eyes and sat up. "Caroline came by."

Stacey gasped. "What? Did you know she was coming?"

Molly shook her head. "No, she just showed up. I wasn't prepared at all, and she totally caught me off guard."

"What did she say?"

"Oh Stacey, it was awful. She'd been crying, and I took her into the office and made her a cup of tea, then she just started pouring her heart out to me. How am I ever going to tell her? I just can't."

Molly was shocked when Stacey's mood suddenly changed. She rolled her eyes and gripped the arms of the chair, curling her fingers. Her jaw tightened and her lips narrowed as she spoke. "You can't go on like this, Molly. You *have* to tell her; you keep saying that you're waiting for the right moment."

"Well, I am."

Stacey raised her voice. "But there may never *be* a right time, you've said so yourself. You always have some sort of excuse. Just tell her for heaven's sake and get it over with. At least you'll know where you stand, because going on like this is ridiculous, and it's driving me nuts."

Molly matched her tone. "Driving *you* nuts? How the hell do you think *I* feel? I'm living it, you're just along for the ride."

"And let me tell you, it ain't no friggin' joy ride, Molly, you have to end this so you can get on with your life, it's really messing with your head. And, in all honesty, you're becoming a pain in the butt to live with. This is all I hear about every day since we got here. Just friggin' tell her!"

Molly crossed her legs, folded her arms and gave Stacey a hard stare. "Why are you being such a bitch all of a sudden? You knew what you were getting into when you came here. I told you how I would be doing this. I don't want to rush into anything; I need to make sure she likes me and that she knows what a great job I'm doing with the store which hopefully will make it more difficult for her *not* to like me."

Stacey matched her stare and also crossed her arms. "If she's pouring her heart out to you, I think she not only likes you but also trusts you. And as far as the store goes, Caroline has told you that you've gone beyond her expectations and anything she's ever imagined, so don't give me this crap about her maybe not liking you or the store not being ready. You're using any excuse you can think of not to tell her." Stacey's jaw tightened and her eyes narrowed as she continued staring at Molly. "And, you want to know something? If you don't tell her soon, I will!"

Molly's eyes grew wide. "You wouldn't dare!" she hissed.

"Don't dare me Molly, I haven't lost a dare yet."

Molly stood up from the couch, her fists clenched as she paced the room. "This is *my* business, not yours, and you have no friggin' right to tell Caroline *anything*. Just stay out of it, okay?" she hollered, staring hard at Stacey who didn't flinch an inch.

"It *is* my business when I have to live with you. You've been planning this shit for over three friggin' years, and now that you have the chance to finish it, you're backing out."

"I am *not* backing out!" Molly yelled, still pacing the room. "It's hard, okay, especially with her losing her husband and everything she's told me. Put yourself in my shoes."

Stacey didn't back down but instead raised her voice. "I *have* put myself in your damn shoes, many times. The only difference is I'd have told her by now."

Molly turned around and stopped pacing, placing her hands on her hips. "I knew it was a mistake bringing you here. We haven't made it two weeks and we're already fighting. Now, I want you to stay out of my fucking business, do you hear me? And if you want to move out, fine! Go ahead." Molly grabbed her purse and laptop and marched across the room. "I'm going to bed," she yelled, slamming her bedroom door shut.

Alone in the solitude of her room, Molly refrained from turning on the lights, threw her things on the edge of the bed and laid down, curling her body into a fetal position and allowing the tears to fall. "Fuck you, Stacey," she hissed between sobs.

A few minutes later she heard a knock at her door and yelled, "go away!"

She heard Stacey on the other side of the door. "Oh, come on, Molly. I'm sorry, okay? Can I come in?"

"No! Just leave me alone."

Stacey ignored her request and opened the door; she saw that it was dark and turned on the lights. "Come on, let's not let this get between us," she said, as she stood next to the bed looking down at Molly who was sobbing.

"I said, go away," Molly hissed between clenched teeth, covering her face with her hands.

"I'm not leaving until we're okay." She sat on the edge of the bed and rubbed Molly's shoulder. "Come on, I said I was sorry, okay? I won't bring it up again. Especially if it causes us to fight like this. You're right, it's none of my business."

Molly wiped her eyes and turned her head to look at Stacey. "I'm sorry too, but you're right, I *do* need to tell her."

Stacey was shocked by her admittance. "Really? So you agree with me?" Stacey paused. "Not to push you, but do you have any idea when?"

"I haven't thought that far ahead, I'm more upset over us fighting right now."

Stacey rubbed her shoulder again. "Me, too. Poor Henry ran into the kitchen and is hiding under the bistro table. I think our shouting scared him."

"Poor guy." Molly looked at Stacey and gave her a weak smile. "I'm sorry, and I really didn't mean it when I said 'go ahead and move out.'"

"I know, because you'd miss me too much," Stacey said with a cheeky grin. "So, back to my question - any idea when you plan on telling Caroline?"

"She's coming in Monday afternoon to see how the soft opening is coming along. Construction will still be happening and she's okay with that; I can't keep the store closed until everything is done, we need to bring money in."

"Okay then, that gives you three days to prepare yourself," Stacy told her before standing. "I'm going to let you get some sleep, and I need to get back to work. I have some deadlines to meet." Before leaving the room and turning off the light, she turned and looked at Molly lying in bed. "You're doing the right thing, so don't back out, okay?"

Molly didn't respond, but instead closed her eyes. "Goodnight, I'll see you in the morning."

CHAPTER 42

Molly awoke early, anxious to start her day at the bookstore, and tiptoed around the apartment so as not to wake Stacey who was sleeping on the couch with Henry lying at her feet. Coffee in hand, she was out the door by 7:00 to start her brisk morning walk to work, something she looked forward to every day. By the time she arrived at the store, she felt rejuvenated and energized, had a clear mind, and was ready to start her day.

The weather was still somewhat mild, a bit on the chilly side, but she'd yet to experience brutal winters or walking in freezing temperatures and snow. Her attitude may not be so pleasant when winter arrives, Molly chuckled to herself as she approached the bookstore. She was surprised by what she saw then.

"Oh, my goodness! Have you been here all night?" she said, kneeling next to the Calico cat sleeping on the cold pavement beneath the window. Her fur was cold, so she stroked her back and kept rubbing her, moving her hand down the entire length of her body to the tip of her tail in order to warm her up. Instantly the cat purred and then rolled onto her back, inviting Molly to rub her belly. Molly smiled and obliged. "I've missed you, too. Why don't you come inside where it's warm, and I'll give you some milk. I may have to go to the store and buy some cat food if you stick around much longer."

When Molly stood up to unlock the door, the cat stayed close by, rubbing her body up against her shin, waiting patiently for the door to open. When it did, she pranced inside the store, like she owned the place, purring loudly and leading Molly to the office, already familiar with the surroundings and feeling right at home.

"Wait for me," Molly laughed, quickening her pace to keep up with the cat. "You certainly know where I keep the milk, don't you?" Molly said, unlocking the door to the office.

After pouring a dish of milk, Molly sat in one of the office chairs watching the cat lap it up, and had a one-sided conversation with herself. "I need to find out where you live. I'm sure your owner is missing you, but if I put an ad in the paper, it won't get published until next week, and you can't sleep outside until then." Molly continued to watch the cat, who was obviously hungry by the way she cleaned up her dish in no time. "I'll run to the store when they're open and get you some real food, okay sweetie? Albert and Hailey should be here by then and they can watch the store."

Molly leaned back in her chair when her phone pinged letting her know she had a message. She pulled out her phone from her jacket pocket and saw it was a Facebook message from a local author in the group asking if she'd stock her books in the store. Suddenly, Molly had an idea. "I know!" she said excitedly, looking at the cat, "I can post your picture in the group, surely *someone* will recognize you!"

Molly wasted no time; within 30 minutes her post went live on Facebook. She pet the cat as she curled up on her lap and went to sleep. "Now all we do is wait," she said, petting her head and stroking her ears.

Within minutes her phone pinged again with another message. Molly leaned back in her chair and read it.

Hi, I saw your post about the cat. I'm pretty sure it's my neighbor's, but my neighbor died last week and lived alone. The cat ran out of the house when the ambulance was there and hasn't been back since.

"Aww, how sad," Molly whispered before texting her back.

That's so sad. So the cat doesn't have a home? Does she have a name? And how can I be sure it's your neighbor's cat?

Molly received another text immediately.

Check her tail; it's slightly bent at the end, about an inch down, from when a dog grabbed her. It never healed properly. She's about three years old, and the owner always called her Kitty. I'm not sure if she had another name. She needs a home, and it would be great if you could keep her. I have two jealous dogs, so I can't take her.

Molly looked over at the cat, now stretched out and snoozing on the carpet. She patted her lap and instantly the cat jumped up and began purring. "Hey girl, let me take a look at your tail." Finding no resistance from the cat, Molly inspected her tail closely. "Well, I'll be, it *is* bent at the end. You must be her." Molly smiled and kissed the top of her head. "Hey, do you want to live here? You can be our mascot and watch the store after closing. You'd be the most popular kitty in town," Molly laughed. "People would come by the store just to see you." Molly pet her on the head. "You need a name, though." Molly picked up her phone and texted the woman back.

Yes, it's her. I checked her tail, and it's bent. I'm going to keep her. She will live at the bookstore, and you can come by anytime to visit her. I'll have to think of a name for her, though. Kitty doesn't work for me, LOL.

While waiting for a reply, Molly picked up the cat and held her in her arms, welcoming the soothing feel and sounds of her pleasant purring. "You make me happy too, sweet girl," Molly whispered, kissing her nose. "I'm glad you found me. I needed a pick-me-up after last night." She looked at the cat's face and smiled. "Welcome to your new home."

The woman who went by the name *Sassy2348* texted Molly back a bunch of smiley emojis and said she'd come by the store soon. A few minutes later there was a knock at the door and Hailey entered, noticing the cat straight away sitting in Molly's lap.

"Oh, she's back."

"Not back, she slept outside all night beneath the window, poor baby. She never left." She looked at Hailey and smiled again. "And, we're going to keep her!"

"We are? And she'll live here at the bookstore?" Hailey asked, beaming.

Molly nodded. "Yep." She proceeded to tell her the cat's history. "So, the poor girl has no home, and she's obviously chosen this place to be her new residence, so I've decided she can live here and be the store's mascot. I just need to come up with a name for her."

"That's so cool, I'll try and think of a name, too," Hailey said, petting the top of the cat's head. "She's so cute, and I can see she's grown quite fond of you."

Molly laughed. "The feeling is mutual." She tickled the cat's belly. "Now, because of this little girl, my plans have changed, I'm going to step out and buy some supplies for her. Before I do that I'll need to walk home and grab my car, so I'll leave her in the office with the door closed. When Albert gets here, I want both of you to unpack the boxes from the local merchants and display their products on the shelves and tables next to the counter. I shouldn't be gone too long."

"Sounds good," Hailey said. "See you soon."

MOLLY RETURNED to the store an hour later with a car full of cat supplies. "How can one cat need so much stuff?" she chuckled to herself, putting her car in park in front of the bookstore. She'd never shopped for a cat before and knew she'd gone overboard with all the tempting choices in the cat aisle, but she couldn't resist. Once outside of her car, she opened the back door and giggled. "My goodness, I'm going to need some help carrying this stuff in," she laughed, staring at the back seat packed full of cat supplies which included three litter boxes, four beds, lots of toys, cat litter, dry and wet food, bowls, and cat treats.

Hailey saw her pull up from inside the store and came out to help her.

"Can you give me a hand?" Molly called out, her arms full of cat goodies.

"Sure," she said, and then laughed when she looked inside the car. "Wow! Will you be my mom?" she said, reaching for two of the beds. "Why did you get so many beds?"

"For different areas of the store, of course. One for the front window, one for my office, one for the kid's area, and one near the counter. She's going to be out here in the store a lot, and she needs plenty of options on where to rest. I want people to get to know her."

Hailey laughed again. "She's going to be one spoiled kitty."

"Did you come up with any names yet?" Molly asked, walking into the store with her arms full.

"No, how about you?"

"Nope, I never realized that naming a cat would be so challenging."

"It'll come to us," Hailey said, following Molly into the store.

"Well, we only have two days to come up with a name. I'd like her to have one for the soft opening Monday." Her words triggered another thought; in two days she'd tell Caroline the real reason why she came to Riverbanks, and wondered how it would change her world, fearing the worst.

CHAPTER 43

When it was time to lock up and go home, Molly felt comfortable leaving the cat in the office. She'd settled in well, testing every bed Molly had placed around the store, always choosing the one closest to wherever Molly was at the time. Pleased to see money wasn't wasted buying an abundance of toys for her, Molly enjoyed watching Kitty spend part of her day entertaining herself by chasing and batting toys around the store. "Welcome home, Kitty," Molly said, petting her as she stretched out in the cozy red bed in the office. "I'll see you in the morning, okay?"

It was almost 8:00 in the evening when Molly closed shop. She was looking forward to spending a quiet evening with Stacey, hoping to make up for the horrible evening they'd had the night before. Carrying her purse and laptop and bracing the chilly evening temperatures, she began her walk home, but abruptly stopped a few minutes later. "Shit, my car's here," she said, shaking her head, forgetting she had gotten it earlier to pick up cat supplies. Amused by her forgetfulness, she laughed, turned around and walked back to her car.

When she arrived home, she was surprised to find that Stacey wasn't home. "Hey buddy," she said to Henry, who was lying on the couch. "Where's your mama?" Molly checked for any messages on her phone and found none. "Huh, maybe she's with a client?" she said aloud, setting her things down and walking to the kitchen.

After fixing a frozen pizza for dinner, Molly grabbed a beer from the fridge and joined Henry on the couch. She decided to spend her time researching cat names online. "Why is this so hard, Henry?" she said, patting his head. "How did Stacey come up with *your* name? I'll have to ask her."

After spending the next 20 minutes looking up names, Molly was distracted by female laughter in the courtyard that grew louder as it approached her door.

"Come on in," Molly heard Stacey say between giggles. "You gotta meet Molly."

"Okay," an unfamiliar female voice replied.

A few seconds later the front door opened, and Stacey walked in with their neighbor Audrey, both engaged in uncontrollable laughter. "Hey Molly, you remember our neighbor Audrey, don't you?"

Molly smiled, setting her laptop on the coffee table. "I do," she smirked. "Have you two been drinking?"

"What makes you say that?" said Stacey, her words slurred. "We went out for pizza, and did you know that if you buy a large pizza, you get a free pitcher of beer? And the second pitcher is half off!" She turned to Audrey and laughed. "How can anyone pass up such a deal?"

"Right?" Audrey agreed, giggling.

"Why didn't you text me?" Molly said, "I would have joined you; it sounds like you had fun."

Stacey stumbled over to the couch, somehow avoiding Henry in her path, who ran to greet her, and let her body drop onto the seat next to Molly. "I thought about it, but I didn't want to bother you at work; besides, you've been telling me how you want everything to be perfect for the soft opening. I couldn't pull you away from *that*."

Audrey followed Stacey and slumped into the chair across from them. "It was a spur of the moment thing anyway. We bumped into each other in the courtyard, and I asked Stacey if she'd like to go for pizza with me," she giggled, closing her eyes. "I can't remember the last time I got this drunk."

Stacey laughed. "And the rest is history." She leaned into Molly. "Did I tell you that the place was packed?"

Molly leaned back to avoid her beer breath. "Do you think free beer had anything to do with it?"

"Probably," Stacey chuckled, then noticed the laptop on the coffee table. "Are you still working?"

"No, I'm researching cat names."

Stacey knit her brow, "you're researching *what*?"

"Cat names. The store has acquired a cat and she'll be living in the store."

"How cool! How did you get a cat?" Stacey asked, straining to keep her eyes open.

"She just showed up the other day, and after posting about it on Facebook so we could locate her owner, a woman contacted me and said the owner had died."

"Oh no, how sad," Audrey said, slurring her words.

"That *is* sad, but it means you get to keep her, right?" Stacey asked.

"Yes, that's right, but I need to come up with a name for her. The owner just called her Kitty, and I want to do better than that. I want her name to have meaning."

"Well, Kitty means she's a cat," Stacey laughed.

"How did you come up with Henry? It suits him to a tee," Molly asked.

"You don't wanna know," Stacey said, shaking her head. "It's pretty sad."

"Yes, I do want to know," Molly insisted.

"An obituary."

Molly's jaw dropped. "You're kidding me, right?"

Stacey sniggered, "no, I'm not. I'd only had Henry for a few hours and was trying to think of a name for him and he was sitting in my lap when I was reading the local paper, and for whatever reason, I read the obituaries, and the name 'Henry' just jumped out at me and that was that, I named him Henry."

"Wow! So, Henry is named after a dead guy," Molly chuckled.

"Sssh, don't tell him," Stacey giggled, holding her fingers up to her lips.

Molly leaned back. "I can't very well name the cat after a dead person," she laughed.

"I've always liked the name Roxie," Audrey said. "We had a cat named Roxie once and, like you, my mom put a lot of thought into it. She'd researched every name."

Molly was intrigued. "So, what does Roxie mean?"

"I remember my mom telling me that it's associated with new beginnings and a fresh start; that's why she chose it."

Molly leaned forward and beamed. "Oh my god, that's perfect! This is a new beginning and a fresh start for her; I'm going to name her Roxie! Thank you!"

Still in a drunk state, Audrey nodded. "You're welcome, I always loved that name." She patted the arms of the chair where she sat. "I think I better be getting home, the room is spinning, and I hope mine won't be."

Molly laughed again, wondering if she'd ever looked so foolish when she was drunk. "Okay, I'll walk you home," she said, concerned she may go to the wrong apartment, or worse, fall.

Audrey stood up, her body swaying. "You don't have to," she said, then quickly fell back into the chair and laughed. "Okay, maybe you should."

"I'll be back in a minute," Molly said, leading Audrey to the door.

Stacey nodded, her eyes closed. "Take your time, I'm not going anywhere."

When Molly returned, she expected Stacey to be passed out on the couch, but to her surprise she had turned on the TV and was scrolling through the channels. "I'm surprised you're still awake," Molly said, closing the front door behind her.

"I'm fine, just got a buzz going on. Did Audrey make it home okay? She had way more to drink than me, I think she drank a damn pitcher by herself."

"Yeah, she's good, but I'm sure she'll be paying for it in the morning."

"She's really nice, she kinda reminds me of my mom, except I never went drinking with my mom," Stacey laughed. "She told me how lonely she's been since her husband died. How sad is that? That poor woman."

"Does she have any kids?"

Stacey shook her head, "Nope." Her eyes suddenly lit up. "Hey, we should invite her to go out with us tomorrow night."

"Yes, I agree, that's a good idea. I have to work tomorrow; do you want to ask her?"

"Sure, I'll invite her over for coffee in the morning, too." She shook her head, changing the subject. "I can't believe you got a cat. I want to meet Roxie."

"You'll meet her the next time you come in to work on the website; when will that be, anyway?"

"I thought I'd wait until after the soft opening, so is Tuesday, okay?"

"No, what you meant to say is, you're waiting until I've told Caroline and hoping the storm will have passed," Molly said, correcting her.

Stacey didn't reply.

CHAPTER 44

After working all day without any breaks Saturday, and with Albert and Hailey's help Molly looked at the large new clock hanging prominently in the store, surprised to see it was already 4:00. "Well, that's it, I've done all I can for the soft opening," she said, looking at Roxie purring in her new blue bed on the large counter. She reached over and stroked her. "You've settled in really well, girl, and I think you already know your new name." Molly looked around the store - what a transformation she'd made. All of the bookshelves were in place, stocked with a variety of genres including best sellers and new releases, which the store had never had. Comfortable chairs and couches were placed around the store. The Children's corner was bright, colorful and friendly. The front windows showcased bestselling authors, and the left window featured local authors and artists. The new counter not only displayed collectables and antique books, but nearby tables and shelves were reserved for local merchant's products and author's books. The beverage and pastry counter would be completed in the morning, giving Molly enough time to stock it.

She turned to Hailey who'd just joined her. "So, what do you think?"

"I think it looks amazing. You've really outdone yourself. I could never imagine this place looking quite like this, and the town is super excited about it, too," she smiled. "We've never had a real bookstore."

"Thanks, but I couldn't have done it without you and Albert. You guys have been a tremendous help. I hope Caroline likes it."

"How could she not? Look at this place."

"Thanks, I needed to hear that. Well, you and Albert will be happy to know that we're done for the day because Stacey and I are going out tonight, so I'm closing up shop early."

"Well, it's about time you went out on the town. Where are you going?"

"Jake's Steakhouse has a live band, so we'd thought we'd go and check it out."

"Oh, great, I'm going there too, with my boyfriend. We'll probably see you there."

"Fantastic, the more the merrier. Can you find Albert and tell him that we're done for the day? I need to lock up."

"Yeah, he was moving boxes around in the storeroom last time I saw him."

DRESSED IN BLUE JEANS, brown cowboy boots and checkered shirts, Molly and Stacey arrived at the restaurant with their neighbor Audrey, surprised to see the place already in full swing with the local all-male band, *Soaring Eagles*, playing upbeat country music. Everyone seemed to know the lyrics and sang along.

"This place is massive!" Molly hollered over the loud music. "It doesn't seem that big from the outside."

"I was thinking the same thing," Stacey shouted. "They have a dance floor and a bar in the back. I see a couple of empty tables across from the band, do you want to grab one?"

Molly nodded. "Yes, I think those are the last two."

The band continued to play as they made their way to the table, stopping to watch the line dancers on the dance floor, dancing perfectly in-sync.

"I would so suck at that," Molly hollered, laughing. "How do they all keep in time with each other?"

"It's not as hard as it looks," Audrey said. "My husband and I came here all the time. It's a lot of fun; you just copy the people next to you. No one ever laughs at you if you miss a beat, you just try to keep up and have fun with it."

"We should give it a try!" Stacey squealed, taking a seat at the table.

"Give me a few beers and then ask me," Molly shouted, followed by a loud laugh. "I won't have a care in the world by then!"

"Deal!" Stacey screamed. "You're not leaving this place until you've done a line dance." She turned to Audrey sitting next to her and nudged her arm. "Now, Audrey, she's a pro, she'll show us how it's done."

"I sure can," Audrey said proudly. "It's been a few years, but it's like riding a bicycle - you never forget."

Stacey looked across the table at Molly. "You should wear makeup more often; you look really pretty."

Molly laughed. "Are you looking for a date?"

"No! I just don't see you wearing makeup often enough, and you always look good when you do. It makes your eyes stand out," Stacey grinned. "I taught you well."

"Thanks, and yes you did."

When the band finished their song, they announced they were taking a ten-minute break. Molly was relieved she could talk now without having to shout. After ordering their food, Audrey took a sip of her beer and smiled at Molly and Stacey. "I want to thank you ladies for inviting me tonight, it feels good to get out, and, might I add, that'd be two nights in a row."

"You're welcome," Stacey told her. "You're a hoot to hang out with."

Molly looked at Audrey and smiled. "Sorry I missed last night's outing, but hey, I'm making up for it tonight."

"I don't have many friends, even though I've lived here over 20 years. My husband George and I used to keep to ourselves mostly. He was a freelance writer and worked from home. Now that he's gone, I don't know what to do with myself, so being here with the two of you is really special, thank you!"

"I'm sorry, it's probably still really difficult, and quite a transition after spending so many years together. Do you have any hobbies?" Molly asked.

"I like to read, knit and crochet, but after I've made a blanket, I don't have anyone to give it to." she chuckled. "I have ten blankets and no idea what to do with them."

Molly matched her chuckle. "I'm sorry, I didn't mean to laugh, but I have an idea; we could sell your blankets in the bookstore!" She grinned, "who doesn't love a cozy knit blanket draped over their knees while reading a book?"

Audrey's eyes turned into saucers. "Really? That would be awesome! You mean you could display them in the store, and someone might actually buy one?"

"Yes, that's how it usually works," Molly chuckled. "I have another idea too, but it's okay if you say no."

"Well, I'm dying to know what it is!" Audrey said, anxious to hear Molly's proposal.

"How would you like to read to the kiddies once a week in the store? I know you've never had any kids; I don't know, is it because you don't feel comfortable around children? If that's the case, it's not a problem."

"I don't dislike children, I love them, but sadly I could never have any of my own. I suffered five miscarriages, and George and I couldn't go through with losing another baby, so we stopped trying. We accepted the fact that it just wasn't meant to be."

"Oh no, I'm so sorry," Stacey and Molly said in unison.

"So, what do you think about reading to them? You have such a calming voice when you speak, and, not to offend you, but you give off that loving motherly vibe," Molly chuckled.

"Well, I'm probably old enough to be your mother, but all jokes aside, I think it's a wonderful idea, and I look forward to it! I need something to inspire me, and get me out of the house."

"Really!" Molly squealed. "I think you'd be brilliant at it, and the kids will love you."

"Thank you so much for asking me, it's just what I need, and I think it'll be fun, too."

Molly turned to Stacey. "I have a proposition for you, too, if you're interested?"

Stacey set down her beer glass. "You do? What's that?"

"What do you think about bringing Henry into the store once a week and hanging out with the kids? They could even read to him! I think the kids would love it, and it'd be kind of cute. And, I bet Henry would get a kick out of it, too!"

"Oh my god, what a brilliant idea! I think Henry would *love* it - I *know* he'd love the attention," Stacey laughed. "I'm sure he gets bored hanging around our place all day." Stacey had a thought and paused. "Wait, what about Roxie? Do you think they'd get along? You know Henry used to love chasing the cats in Texas; remember, you got hit by a truck when he raced across the road after one."

Molly leaned back in her seat. "Oh, I didn't really think about that. Well, I could keep Roxie in the office when Henry's around. That wouldn't be a problem, and over time we could slowly introduce them to one another so they could get acclimated."

"That should work," Stacey agreed.

"Great! We'll figure out a day and time that works for both of you," Molly said, glancing over at Audrey.

"Anytime works for me," Audrey said. "It's not like I have a full schedule."

Stacey suddenly sat up straight, straining her neck to look across the room, "Shit! He's here."

Molly followed Stacey's eyes. "Who?"

"Craig; he's over there with two other guys," she said pointing their way.

Molly glanced over and remained quiet as she saw three pretty girls join them, each one kissing a guy on the lips.

"Fuck!" Stacey hissed. "He has a girlfriend - just my luck."

"I'm sorry," Molly said. "I know you liked him."

"Why the hell does it say he's single on Facebook? Does his girl-friend even know that he portrays himself as single?"

Molly tried to refrain from laughing, but failed. "Not everyone puts their entire life on Facebook. Maybe they just started dating and he hasn't had a chance to change it."

Stacey leaned back, folded her arms and frowned. "Well, he needs to update his status so women like me don't get their hopes up."

"Maybe you jumped the gun a bit. I know you're itching to date, but I'm sure it'll all happen soon enough."

"I'm itching to get laid," Stacey corrected her. "Do you know how long it's been? I've never gone without sex this long - it should be a crime," she laughed.

"Okay, enough talk about your sex life," Molly announced. "We're here to have fun, eat some great food, and drink lots of beer."

Audrey raised her glass, "sounds like a good plan to me. Cheers, ladies."

After eating their meals and drinking two more rounds of beer, Molly and Stacey had enough liquid courage inside of them to give the line dancing a go.

"Okay Audrey, show us how this line dancing is done," Stacey said as she stood up, her words a bit slurred.

Molly took a large swig of beer before she got up. "I'm ready, let's do this!"

"Okay then, follow me and just do exactly what I do. Don't worry if you mess up, I'm sure you'll catch on pretty quick," Audrey told them.

Molly and Stacey followed Audrey onto the dance floor where 20 people stood in line, waiting for the band to start playing.

"Are we ready?" the lead singer shouted to the crowd.

"Yes!" the crowd roared back, raising their hands, with some raising their hats.

As soon as the music started, the crowd immediately cheered and began moving in sync to a line dance, leaving Molly and Stacey behind.

"How the hell do they do this?" Molly laughed, trying hard to keep up with the steps Audrey was doing next to her, the blonde guy wearing a beige cowboy hat on her other side. She was able to keep up with a few of the steps, then quickly broke out in a belly laugh when she messed up. Molly looked over at Stacey, impressed to see she was keeping up. "Wow, Stacey, you're a natural!"

"I don't know what I'm doing," Stacey laughed.

Molly looked down at the guy's feet dancing next to her and started copying his moves. She smiled when she found herself keeping up and was surprised when he cupped his arm around her waist and smiled at her.

"There you go, you're getting it."

Not missing a beat, Molly gazed into his eyes and smiled. "Thanks!"

The guy winked, still holding onto Molly's waist. "One, two, three, and kick," he said, guiding Molly through the steps.

Molly followed his instructions and realized after three routine steps they simply repeated themselves. "I think I'm getting the hang of this."

The guy squeezed her waist. "You're doing great. My name is Gus, by the way."

Molly felt her cheeks turn pink. "Hi Gus, I'm Molly."

"Nice to meet you, Molly," he said, smiling and taking her hand to spin her around.

"Oh wow! You're good at this. Where did you learn to line dance so well?" Molly asked, feeling proud of her dance moves.

Gus wrapped his arm around Molly's waist again. "Just like you - I got on the dance floor not knowing a thing and just followed everyone else."

Molly continued to follow Gus's lead, enjoying the feel of his strong hand holding her waist. She couldn't remember the last time she felt the touch of a man. She breathed in the musky scent of his cologne each time he leaned in closer to talk to her. He was taller than her by a good four inches, slender, wearing blue jeans, a black shirt, a beige cowboy hat, and black cowboy boots. His hair was a dusty blonde, wavy, falling just above his shoulders. He had a sharp, prominent jawline and was clean shaven. Molly couldn't help but notice his dreamy, light blue eyes.

"I've never seen you here before," Gus said, leaning in again, giving Molly another whiff of his cologne.

"My girlfriend and I just moved here a few weeks ago from Texas. I'm fixing up the bookstore in town."

"No shit! I saw your post on Facebook, and I've driven by the store - it looks great! I love the new paint job outside and the new sign."

"Thanks, it'd be great if you could come and see the inside. It's been a lot of work, but we're ready for the soft opening Monday. You should come by then." Molly suddenly feared she was being too forward by inviting him to the store. When the music stopped, she wasn't sure of what to do.

Gus released his arm from her waist. "I think I'll do that, I saw the ad in the paper about it."

Standing in the middle of the dance floor, Molly folded her arms, unsure of what do with her hands. She glanced around, noticing that a few people had left, including Stacey and Audrey.

"We're heading back to the table," Stacey told her as she walked by.

Molly nodded, "I'll be right there."

The band began playing again, and the crowd cheered. Gus smiled at Molly. "Do you want to stay for another dance? The more you do it the better you'll get."

Molly nodded and smiled. "Sure."

Molly followed his lead, smiling to herself when she felt the touch of his hand around her waist again. She laughed, tossing back her head when he spun her around not once, but three times, and when the music stopped, he pulled her in and whispered in her ear, "you did great. I told you that you were a natural."

Molly patted his chest, surprised by how firm it felt beneath her hand. "Thanks, would you like to meet my friends?"

"Sure, lead the way, pretty lady," Gus said as he took her hand.

When they reached the table, Stacey gave Molly a smirk. "You looked good out there, girl, I was watching you." She glanced over at Gus. "Who's your teacher?"

Still holding Gus's hand, Molly smiled. "This is Gus, and he made it look so easy."

"Nah, Molly just follows really well," Gus said, holding out his hand to Stacey. "Nice to meet you, and you are?"

"I'm Stacey, Molly's roommate," she said, shaking his hand. "And this is our neighbor and new friend, Audrey."

Gus took Audrey's hand. "Nice to meet you too, Audrey." He looked over at Molly. "Would you ladies like another beer? I'm buying."

"Sure, that would be great, thanks," Molly said, smiling.

"Now, I'm not intruding on a girl's night out, am I?"

Molly laughed. "No, not at all. There's plenty of room for you here."

"Great! I'll be back with a pitcher of beer."

Before sitting down, Molly watched Gus walk away and liked what she saw. His jeans fit him well, enhancing his perfect behind and toned calves. She moistened her lips with her tongue, taking a seat at the table. "Damn, he's fine," she said, wearing a devious smile.

"Where the hell did he come from?" Stacey said, letting go a high-pitched laugh. "He's friggin' hot!"

"He was dancing next to me, helping me keep up with the steps, and he's not *hot*, he's friggin' gorgeous!" Molly squealed.

"Well, it looks like he's really into you. I saw how he grabbed your waist and held your hand on the way over here. And let's not forget the way he looks at you," Stacey laughed, kicking her legs under the table. "Damn it Molly, I'm so jealous."

"You think he likes me?" Molly said nervously.

"Heck yeah he likes you, are you *blind*? He ain't hidin' nothin' baby," Stacey hollered above the music.

"What do I do?" Molly said, her voice tense, clasping her hands together to calm her nerves. "It's been so long since I dated or even been around a guy I liked. I'm like a fish out of water, and I have no idea what to do."

Audrey spoke next. "Just go with your feelings. Don't fight it and don't question it." She gave Molly a reassuring grin. "Just have some fun if that's what you're looking for."

"I don't know what I'm looking for. I'm not ready for this, and what about the bookstore?"

Stacey creased her brow. "The bookstore? What has that got to do with meeting some guy? You can have both, you know."

"But I'm so focused on the store right now, when will I have time to date?"

Stacey cracked a loud laugh. "Molly, this isn't a damn marriage. There you go again, overthinking stuff. Just have some fun, like Audrey said."

Molly quickly silenced her, waving her hand in the air. "Quiet, he's coming."

"Am I interrupting something?" Gus said, smiling as he set down the pitcher of beer.

Molly slid over on the bench to make room for him and shook her head. "No, not all, have a seat," she said, patting the space next to her.

"Don't mind if I do." After taking a seat, he picked up the pitcher. "Let me do the honors, ladies," he said, picking up a glass and filling it with beer. After all four glasses were filled, he leaned back and stretched his arm out on the back of the booth behind Molly.

Stacey noticed his subtle move and smirked at Molly from across the table. "So, Gus, what do you do for a living?"

"Ahh, it's interrogation time," he joked, causing Molly and the others to laugh. "I'm in logging and run a sawmill. It's been a family business for three generations, and I took over the reins five years ago when I turned 30, shortly after pop passed away."

"Oh, I'm so sorry," Molly said. "Is your mom still alive?"

"Yeah, she is, but she left us when I was ten. She met some city guy and moved to Chicago with him, leaving me and my two sisters behind with our dad."

"Wow! That sucks," Stacey said, shocked by what she heard. "Are you still in contact with her?"

"Stacey!" Molly hissed. "It's none of our business."

Gus patted Molly's knee, taking her by surprise. "It's cool, I've seen her maybe three times since she left. She apologized, said that country life wasn't for her, and that we could come visit her in Chicago whenever we pleased." He chuckled, "I told her city life wasn't for me and that I'd pass." He shrugged his shoulders. "It is what it is. I guess her priorities ain't like mine, so I just let her live her life the way she wants to, and I live mine."

"That's pretty noble of you," Molly said.

Gus shrugged his shoulders again. "I can't tell anyone how to live or what they should do with their lives, I just worry about my own life and doing what makes me happy."

For the next hour Molly listened to Gus talk about himself and was touched when he gave them a candid smile and said, "I have nothing to hide ladies, ask away." She listened when he talked about how proud he was to be an uncle to his older sister's two young sons, Edwin and Lucas, both now in middle school, and sees them every chance he gets. He was unashamed to show his feelings about how hard it was when his sister Ashley moved to Billings because of her husband's job, but he makes the drive at least once a month to spend time with them and their sons. "Hey, at least my little sister Jessie ain't goin' nowhere, her husband works at the mill, and they plan on starting a family soon."

"What about you?" Stacey asked. "Do you want a family someday?"

"Of course I do," Gus replied. "But I gotta meet the right woman first. Just ain't happened yet."

Stacey kicked Molly under the table, causing her to flinch.

"You okay?" Gus asked, turning to Molly.

"Yeah, there was a bug on my leg," she said, giving Stacey a piercing stare.

Gus took a final swig of his beer. "Well, ladies, I've interrupted your night enough, and I appreciate you letting me crash your party, but this guy has to be up at the crack of dawn, even on a Sunday." He turned, looked at Molly and smiled. "It sure was a pleasure meeting you, Molly, and if you don't mind, I'd like to come to the bookstore Monday."

Molly blushed. "It was a pleasure meeting you too, Gus, and yes, I'd love to have you come by. I'll be there all day, so stop by anytime."

He leaned in and gave her a light kiss on the cheek, "I'll certainly do that, now y'all enjoy the rest of your night."

After he left Molly leaned back and closed her eyes. "Did all of that just happen or was I dreaming?"

Stacey grinned. "Oh, it happened, sweetie, and man, does he have the hots for you."

Molly sat up and rubbed her forehead. "Isn't he the sweetest guy?" She shook her head in disbelief. "Is he for real? My god, I could listen to him talk all night," she said and looked over at Stacey. "What the hell am I doing?"

Stacey reached over and grabbed her hand. "Don't you *dare* fight it. He seems like a really nice guy, just go with it."

Molly shook her head, flustered by her emotions, unsure how she should react. "You're right, I'm just going to relax, not overthink it, and see where it goes." She shook her head again and raked her fingers through her hair. "I need another beer."

CHAPTER 45

For the first time since she'd arrived in Riverbanks, Molly fell asleep without Caroline invading her thoughts. For the past two nights she'd smiled, hugging her pillow and thinking of Gus, a man that had dropped into her life unexpectedly out of nowhere and now consumed her thoughts morning till night since the day they first met. She couldn't remember the last time she had been drawn to a man and had forgotten all about the butterflies in one's stomach, the racing of the heart, and the constant distraction from everyday life. She loved everything about him, from his charm, his morals and his old-fashioned family values, not to mention his good looks. He had every quality she was looking for in a man. Molly didn't want to admit it, but he had literally swept her off her feet, something she'd only read about in a good romance novel, and here she was, experiencing it in real life. She refused to question why he had showed up in her life and what she had done to deserve it, instead deciding to take Stacey's advice, roll with it, and see where it went.

Molly spent the day alone Sunday in the bookstore with Roxie, who stayed close by her side as she stocked the beverage and pastry bar after the contractors had finished their work. In the afternoon she received a text from Lucy letting her know that she and Caroline would be at the store by 10:00 in the morning. Molly instantly thought of the promise she'd made to herself and Stacey; to tell Caroline the real reason why she came to Riverbanks. She surprised herself by remaining calm, unlike in the past when she'd feared Caroline's reaction after she found out the truth. All she had to do was switch her thoughts to Gus, and her life was suddenly great with him in it.

"ARE YOU READY?" Stacey asked from the couch where she laid with Henry stretched across her stomach. "You're still going to tell her, right? You said you would on Monday, and that's today."

Molly skipped across the room from the kitchen, ready to face the day and whatever it may bring. No matter what happened between her and Caroline, she knew it would be a good day because she'd be seeing Gus. He had said he'd come to the opening. "Yes, I'm going to tell her today," Molly replied, unable to shake off her beaming smile.

Stacey sat up and pet Henry. "You know, I love seeing you so happy and positive. What happened to the old Molly that worried about anything and everything?" she giggled.

"She didn't have Gus in her life."

"You're really smitten by him, aren't you? I've never seen you like this, and I can't even imagine how you'll be after you get laid. How long has it been?" Stacey asked, grinning.

Molly's jaw dropped. "Stacey! Hush."

Stacey laughed again, tossing her head back into the pillow. "Come on, you know it's the truth. You're always so uptight; you need to get laid, woman."

"Well, when I do, you'll be the first to know."

Stacey cracked a louder laugh. "Ha! You won't have to tell me, I'll know straight away. Our eyes are the windows to our souls, and trust me, yours will be shining after you've had some action, I guarantee it."

Molly grabbed her laptop and cell phone. "Okay, enough about my nonexistent sex life, I gotta go, wish me luck."

"Good luck!"

Molly paused after opening the door and looked across the room at Stacey. "Hey, are you coming to the store today for the opening?"

"Nah, I have some deadlines to meet for some clients, and honestly? I thought I'd stay away and give you some space so you can tell Caroline in your own time with no pressure from me."

"I understand and I appreciate that," Molly replied with a smile. "I've decided I'm going to tell her later in the day, I don't want to ruin the opening for her."

"I think that's a good idea, and, if you can, text me after you've told her."

"I will. Hopefully she won't immediately fire me and kick my ass to the curb," Molly stated before leaving, closing the door behind her.

Like every morning when she arrived at the store, Molly's first call of duty was to check on Roxie who slept in the office and always greeted her with a loud purr and a gentle rub of her body against Molly's legs. "Hey sweet girl, good job on watching the store last night. Are you hungry?"

After feeding Roxie, Molly opened the door to the office and let her roam the store freely while she posted the soft opening on Facebook. Between the ad in the local paper and the numerous posts on Facebook, Molly hoped for a good turnout.

Albert and Hailey arrived five minutes apart a little after 9:00 and helped with the last-minute details before opening the doors. "Okay guys, we are officially open for business," Molly said, turning the Open sign around and switching the fairy lights on in the front windows.

"Yay! I'm so excited," Hailey said, clapping her hands before heading over to the beverage and pastry bar where Molly had assigned her for the day; she had Albert mingling with the customers and helping them find things.

Within five minutes of the store opening, six people had entered the store, all of which Molly greeted with a friendly handshake and a smile before introducing herself. Two had children and she immediately led them over to the Children's section where Audrey had offered to help in the store today and was ready to greet them and show them around.

After making a couple of sales within 30 minutes, Molly glanced at the clock on the wall and saw that it was almost 10:00. She took a deep breath knowing Caroline would be arriving soon. She also wondered when Gus would show up. The loud ring of the bell on the front door grabbed Molly's attention; she turned and saw Caroline, holding her daughter's hand, and Lucy enter the store.

Molly was pleased to see at least 15 potential customers roaming around the store. A few sat in the comfortable chairs and couches enjoying pastries and beverages, while others scanned the many books on the shelves. Others were with their kids in the Children's section playing games and reading with their parents.

"Wow! This looks amazing," Caroline said excitedly, walking through the store towards Molly who stood at the counter. "Am I in the right bookstore?" she joked. "You've outdone yourself Molly, this is incredible."

"Thank you, I'm so happy you like it. We have much more planned, especially in the spring and summer; we'll have tables outside and maybe some live music. I have lots of authors booked to do signings, and I'm also in the process of booking a famous author for the Grand Opening in December."

"Really? Who is it?" Caroline asked, her eyes wide. "We've never done an author signing."

"I don't want to say yet," Molly said nervously. "It's not confirmed, and I don't want to jinx it. I'm waiting to hear from her agent."

"I understand," Caroline said. "I can't wait to hear who it is."

"You'll be the first to know, I promise; after all, you *are* the owner," Molly laughed. "I just don't want you to get your hopes up until it's confirmed," she said, before hooking her arm in Caroline's. "Come with me and let me show you around." She looked down at Caroline's daughter. "Maybe Emma would like to check out the Children's section and listen to Audrey read a story?"

"Yes please!" Emma squealed, jumping in the air.

Laughing at Emma's enthusiasm, Molly, Caroline and Lucy escorted Emma to the Children's section, staying with her for a short while to make sure she was comfortable before leaving her with Audrey so that Molly could show Caroline and Lucy around the store.

For the next hour Molly gave them the grand tour, showing them all the new features of the store, as well as introducing Caroline as the owner to the many customers that came in. They were spending money here, buying not only books, but beverages, snacks and merchandise from local artists and crafters. A few recognized Caroline and thought that she handled herself well as she told them the sad news about her husband.

"I've never seen so many people in this store all at once," Caroline said after speaking to another customer.

"And this is just the *soft* opening," Molly reminded her, feeling proud of herself. "I expect at least half the town to be here for the Grand Opening."

"You know, after what I've seen today, I wouldn't be surprised. Thank you so much for everything you've done," Caroline said, her eyes misty.

Molly nodded without replying, distracted by the back of a dusty blonde-haired man leaning on the counter of the beverage bar wearing faded jeans and a suede jacket. But it was the cowboy boots she recognized. They were, without a doubt, Gus's boots. She smiled at Caroline, her heart racing. "Will you excuse me for just a moment?"

Not waiting for an answer, Molly quickly left Caroline and made her way over to the bar, walking behind it so she could see the face of the man that caught her attention. When he looked her way and smiled, Molly's heart melted, and everything in the world was suddenly good.

CHAPTER 46

Molly grinned as she made her way over to Gus. She stood in front of him and smiled. "Hey, why didn't you tell me you were here?" she asked, drying her sweaty hands on her pants before placing them on the counter.

Gus smiled again and took her hand, surprising Molly. "I've been here for about ten minutes, and you were so busy talking to the blonde lady that I didn't want to interrupt you." He squeezed her hand and glanced around the store. "You have quite a turnout - you should be proud of yourself."

"I am, and the blonde is my boss, Caroline, I was showing her around." She gave his hand a gentle squeeze. "Thank you for coming, I wasn't sure if you would."

"I told you I'd be here, and I always do what I say. You'll find that out really quick if you keep hanging around with me," he chuckled and then paused. "I've missed you; it's been a long two days."

Molly quickly lost herself in his gaze. "I've missed you, too. You've been quite the distraction," she laughed.

"Is that a good thing or a bad thing?"

Molly tossed her head back and laughed louder. "Oh, it's a good thing. It's a nice change to have other things to think about besides this store."

"Well, the feeling is mutual, I've done nothing but think about you since I left you at the restaurant, and let me tell you, that wasn't an easy thing to do. My biggest fear was that another guy would come along and sweep you off your feet and I'd be nothing but a distant memory."

Molly felt her cheeks blush, no one had ever talked to her with such sweet words before. "You have nothing to worry about, the only guy that swept me off my feet was you."

Gus patted his heart. "Thank god, you've done quite the number on me, but hey, I don't want to keep you from your job. Do you want to meet up later for a drink?"

"Sure, that'd be great. I'll be ready for a drink after today." She glanced at the clock on the wall. "I get off around 8:00 if that's not too late?"

"That's fine, where do you want to meet?"

Molly hesitated. "Would you mind picking me up? I usually walk to and from work and we can decide then."

"That works, I'll be here at 8:00," Gus said with a bright smile. "I'm going to look around the store and then I'll see you tonight," he said, squeezing her hand again.

Molly watched as Gus walked away, noticing the chemistry between them was more intense than Saturday night. Standing behind the counter gazing into his dreamy eyes, she had a strong urge to reach over, grab the fleece collar of his suede jacket and forcefully pull him towards her, then kiss him passionately on the lips. It took all of her self-control not to act on her desires.

She smiled to herself when she saw him stop at the Fishing and Hunting section, pull a book from the shelf and begin browsing. "Not only is he a charmer, but it seems he's also an outdoorsman, too," she whispered to herself. Then added, "he's a real man; does it get any better?!"

After helping Hailey at the beverage counter for a bit and in between managing the checkout counter where many sales were taking place, Molly checked the time and saw it was almost 2:00. She'd been so busy she hadn't talked to Caroline in a few hours and wondered when she'd be leaving. She'd seen her mingle with shoppers, as well as spend time in the Children's section with Emma and Audrey. Lucy had left an hour ago, telling them she had to 'get back to her real job,' as Lucy put it, followed by a laugh.

Molly's nerves intensified, knowing what had been haunting her for years would soon become a reality; she just wished she knew the outcome *now*. Expecting Caroline to announce she'd be leaving soon, it was crunch time for Molly. The time had come to tell her. Whatever happened after Molly would need to accept it.

Molly sat behind the counter after helping a customer, contemplating how to tell Caroline, when she spotted her walking towards her, holding Emma's hand. "Did she read my mind?" Molly whispered aloud, then glanced at her daughter. "How am I supposed to tell her with Emma present?"

Caroline put her free hand down on the counter, giving Molly a big smile. "This has been an amazing day, but I think we need to get going." She looked down at her daughter. "Emma is getting cranky, she's ready for a nap."

"She's been such a good girl" Molly noted. "I really need to talk to you before you leave though," Molly pleaded. "We have bean bags in the Children's section, and Audrey can read to her until she falls asleep," Molly suggested.

Caroline looked down at her daughter. "What do you think, sweetie? Do you want to take a nap in one of the big bean bags while Mommy talks to Molly?"

Emma looked up at her mom and smiled. "Yes, that would be fun!"

Caroline turned and looked at Molly. "Let me take her over there, I'll be right back."

"Okay, and I'll have Albert watch the counter because I'd like to talk to you in the office."

Caroline creased her brow. "Is everything okay?"

Molly glanced away for a second. "I hope so."

Caroline released a nervous laugh. "Now you have *me* worried."

Molly ignored her comment. "Let me go find Albert and ask him to cover for me, then I'll meet you in the office."

Caroline nodded. "Okay, I'll be there as soon as Emma is settled."

As soon as Caroline left, Molly reached for her cell in her back pocket and called Albert, asking him to come to the front counter. To Molly's relief, he showed up within a few minutes.

"Thank you, I shouldn't be too long. Call me if you need me."

"Will do, take your time," Albert replied, walking behind the counter.

Without stopping to talk to anyone, Molly made a beeline for the office and quickly closed the door behind her, embracing the silence. Her nerves were peaked, her heart was racing, and no matter how much she rubbed her palms on her pants, the sweat would not dissipate. Afraid her knees would give way, Molly walked over to her desk chair and quickly sat down, leaned her head back and closed her eyes, gripping the arms of the chair. "Maybe I don't have to tell her," Molly whispered under her breath, but then quickly shook her head, "No! I'm not backing out now. I've been waiting for this moment for years. It's now or never," she said, raising her voice in defiance.

Molly wasn't sure how long she'd been sitting there trying to calm her nerves, but nothing seemed to be working. Her heart was still racing, and her palms were sticky. She had practiced her speech over and over in her head, as well as out loud, of what she wanted to say to Caroline, but now she couldn't even put two sentences together. "Fuck!" she yelled in a panic, knowing Caroline would join her any minute. Then, there it was, a knock at the door.

Puzzled that Caroline would knock, Molly quickly sat up. "Come in."

Hailey stuck her head around the door and smiled. "Hey Molly, do you have the keys to the storage? I'm out of coffee cups."

Relieved it wasn't Caroline, Molly smiled and handed her the keys. "I'll get them back from you when I come back out."

"Okay," Hailey said with a smile before closing the door.

A few minutes later the door opened again, and Caroline entered the room. Still gripping the arms of the chair, Molly sat up straight and gave Caroline a nervous smile. "Thank you for meeting with me, please have a seat," Molly said, and decided to get straight to the point while she had the nerve. "How did Emma like the bean bag?"

"She loves it! What a great idea for the children. Was that your idea?"

"Yes, it was. Emma is a sweet little girl; you must be so proud."

Caroline shared a smile that only moms owned. "I am. She's my world now that her father's gone."

Molly took a deep breath. "Is she your only child?"

"Yes, she is."

"You've never had any other children?"

"No, I haven't. What is this about, Molly? Why are you so interested in my daughter?"

Molly's heart was shattered, it was NOT the answer she wanted to hear. Tears pooled in her eyes; her voice quivered as she spoke. "Why are you lying to me?"

Caroline creased her brow. "Excuse me? How dare you accuse me of lying! I have one daughter, and her name is Emma."

"You've never had a child with someone else?"

Caroline uncrossed her legs and then crossed them again. "THAT is none of your business. Is this why you wanted to talk to me? To find out how many children I have?"

"So you HAVE had a child with someone else; you didn't say no?"

"The answer is NO, okay?" Caroline snapped.

Molly remained still in her chair and kept her voice calm; the only thing she couldn't control were the tears falling down her cheeks. "Why are you lying to me?" she demanded again.

"I'm not lying to you; Emma is my only daughter."

Molly narrowed her eyes and gave Caroline a piercing stare through her tears. "That's not true, because I'm also your daughter."

CHAPTER 47

Molly remained frozen in her chair, intensely waiting for Caroline's reaction. After all these years, all the tears shed and the endless anxiety, the moment had finally arrived; she had just confronted her mother. Numb from the flood of emotion overwhelmed her, and a massive feeling of relief came over her from saying the words that'd been bottled up inside of her for so long, "*I am your daughter.*"

Caroline remained silent, avoiding her piercing stare.

Molly's chest heaved from anxiety, her heart beating like a drum. "Well, do you have anything to say? Did you hear me?" She raised her voice a few notches. "I'm your daughter, Caroline!"

Caroline finally met her stare and spat out her words. "You're a liar! Your parents died in a house fire. What kind of game are you playing? Is this some kind of sick joke?"

"They were my adopted parents. My mother told me about you on my sixteenth birthday, and when they died, I decided to look for you."

Caroline stood up and began pacing the room, her nostrils flared as she spoke. "Your mother, or should I say adopted mother, was wrong. I'm *not* your mother. How dare you come here with such nonsense! I just lost my husband and now you're trying to disrupt my world even more; what kind of evil person are you?" She continued to march around the room, stomping her feet in rage. "Is it money you want? Is that why you're here?" She released a callous laugh. "Ha! As you very well know, I'm struggling to raise my daughter, so it looks like you've wasted your time and targeted the wrong woman."

"I don't want your money!" Molly snapped. "I just want you to acknowledge me as your daughter; is that too much to ask?"

Caroline returned to her seat, leaned back and gave Molly a hard stare. "So, the real reason you're here isn't because of the bookstore, but because you think you're my daughter. You lied to me."

"I didn't lie to you; I just waited to tell you. Admittedly, I wasn't expecting to love my job as much as I do. It took me by surprise, but I really love working here, and you can't deny that I've done a pretty damn good job of turning the bookstore around."

"Why didn't you tell me your intentions before coming here to Riverbanks?" Caroline hissed. "I had a right to know."

"Would you have hired me if I did? Of course you wouldn't, let's be real. I wanted to get to know you, to prove to you that I'm a good person and a hard worker." Molly shifted her gaze to the floor. "The bottom line is, I wanted you to be proud of me before revealing to you who I was."

"But I'm not who you think I am," Caroline insisted.

Molly shook her head in disgust; she wasn't expecting Caroline to be in denial. This had never crossed her mind. "Why are you refusing to accept that your past has caught up with you? It's obvious you've never spoken of me to anyone." Anger consumed all the other mixed emotions Molly had been dealing with. "You owe me, god damn it!" Molly shouted. "Because of your selfish reasons, you denied me the life I was supposed to have, which was with you. We could have had a real loving mother/daughter relationship." Tears poured from Molly's eyes. "Why won't you admit that I'm your daughter? Do you hate me that much?" Molly cried.

"Right now, I don't like you much, if you're looking for me to be honest. How *dare* you come into my life with this absurd story of yours and accuse me of being an uncaring person *and* your mother? I can tell you for a fact that I'm *not* your mother."

"And how's that?"

Caroline took a deep breath and spoke in a calmer voice. "If you're my daughter, then I'd like to know where your twin sister is. Yes, I was pregnant before Emma, but I had twins, Molly. I had twin girls, and they were adopted together. So where is she? Where's your twin sister?"

Molly gasped and fell back into her seat. "What? You had twins? You mean to tell me I have a twin sister?"

Caroline rolled her eyes, "What I'm telling you is that whatever research you've done has led you to the wrong person. I'm not your mother, and I'm sorry you wasted your time."

Molly wiped away her tears and closed her eyes. "This doesn't make any sense; everything I've uncovered in my research leads to you. I've not left a stone unturned."

"Well, you missed something, because you never found out that I had twins. I didn't just have one daughter, I had two."

"But my adopted mother told me I was an only child."

"Then that should tell you that if you *are* an only child, then I'm not your mother. I'm sorry to disappoint you."

"Do you know who adopted the twins?"

"No, I have no idea. I was young, and my parents were told they wouldn't be separated but would be adopted together."

Molly shook her head again, refusing to believe what she was hearing. As she stood there raking her fingers through her hair, she said, "something's not adding up."

"Molly - you need to let it go and accept the facts. Now, I'd appreciate it if you would never bring this subject up ever again, and PLEASE, keep my personal life to yourself. I only told you about the twins to prove to you that I'm not your mother. I was young, and I've not spoken of that time in my life to anyone else and I'd like to keep it that way."

"You mean I still have a job?"

"Yes; as long as you don't mention this conversation to anyone, I'll allow you to keep working for me. You've proved yourself in that department. You've done an outstanding job with the bookstore, and I don't believe I could find anyone better."

"Thank you, I thought you might hate me for this."

"I'm a little disturbed by the way you approached me with every-thing else that's going on in my life, but I'm an understanding person, and I realize after your years of research you want answers, and of course closure, but sadly I cannot give that to you."

Molly still wasn't convinced but kept her thoughts to herself. She needed this job, so she refrained from arguing anymore and cordially agreed. "Thank you, I appreciate that. I promise I won't bring the subject up again."

"Thank you, now I'm going to pretend this conversation never happened and I suggest you do the same." She stood and rubbed her hands together. "I must get Emma now, it's time I took her home. I appreciate everything you've done, and as long as your work continues to excel you have a job here."

"Okay. When will you be in the store again?"

"Now that the store is open, I'd like to be here more often and get to know the clientele, mingle with them, and, of course, help you as well. I'll come in Wednesday when Emma's in preschool."

Molly managed to bring up a weak smile. "Okay, sounds good. I'll see you then." She paused. "Can I ask you one thing?"

Caroline rolled her eyes, anxious to leave after the disturbing conversation they had just had. "What is it?"

"Do you ever think of them?"

Caroline furrowed her brow and curled her lip. "Who?"

"The twins, of course. Don't you ever wonder where they are, what they look like? Maybe they have children and you're a grand-mother and don't even know it."

Caroline raised her hand. "Stop! That's enough. I've told you too much already, and I will *not* discuss this subject with you any further. Now I must go!" she snapped, marching out of the office.

After Caroline had left, Molly remained seated, wondering about the outcome of the research she had put in over the years. She was still convinced Caroline was her mother, but now she was shocked by the news she had a twin sister. Did her adoptive mother even know, she wondered? "I'm going to get to the bottom of this and prove her wrong. Somewhere out there is my twin sister, and I'm going to find her," Molly said aloud, leaving her seat and returning to the store.

CHAPTER 48

Shocked by everything that had unfolded in the last 20 minutes, Molly had a hard time concentrating when she returned to the store, forcing a smile every time someone approached her. She wanted nothing more than to go through her records and pages of research. As it played over and over in her mind like a broken record, she kept asking herself: *'What did I miss?'* After she'd had it out with Caroline, she felt nothing but utter disappointment which cut through her like a knife. Molly hoped there would've been rejoicing from both sides, tears of joy, a wonderful reunion where they'd catch up on years missed together. But her heart was torn instead, confusion clouded her mind; she had no idea who she was at this point. She craved a sense of belonging and thought Caroline might be the answer. Molly still believed she was, but now she needed more proof. "How much more time do I have to spend researching?" Molly hissed under her breath as she poured herself a cup of coffee.

"What did you say?" Hailey asked from the other side of the counter.

Molly quickly shook her head, not realizing she'd spoken out loud. "Nothing, just thinking to myself."

"Okay then. Are you good?"

"Yeah, I'm fine, just a bit tired. Why don't you go ahead and take a break, I'll watch the counter." She scanned the store, looking around for the cat. "Where's Roxie?"

"In the Children's section. She's been there all afternoon with the kids, and they love her," she told Molly before walking away.

After Hailey left, Molly picked up her phone sitting next to the cash register, thinking she should text Stacey, then quickly decided against it. There was too much to go into right now, and she decided it would be best to talk to her in person. "God, this is too much for one person to deal with. Why is nothing ever easy in my life?" she snapped, taking a sip of her coffee.

Molly pushed through the rest of the day, finding it a challenge to stay focused and engage with the customers, but she miraculously managed to pull it off. Five minutes before closing she managed to give Gus a genuine smile when she spotted him coming into the store. Embracing the warmth that traveled through her body as she stared at him walking towards her instantly calmed her nerves and the anxiety from today's events. "Why does he make me feel so good?" she mumbled as she walked over to meet him, her smile growing by the second.

Dressed in the same jeans, boots and suede overcoat plus the cowboy hat, Gus matched her smile and embraced her. "Hey, I'm not too early, am I?"

"No, not all. The last customer just left. I've already closed out the register, I just need to put Roxie in the office and lock up," Molly told him, gazing into his eyes.

A few minutes later they were sitting in Gus's black Ford truck parked in front of the store.

"So, how did the day go?" Gus asked, firing up the motor.

"Don't ask."

Gus turned and looked at her. "Hey, are you okay? I thought today was a huge success; you had quite the crowd of people in the store when I was there."

"Oh, the store did great, it's the other stuff that ruined my day."

Gus reached over and rested his arm behind her on the seat. "Do you want to talk about it?"

"Not really, I may scare you off," she said, looking over at him and giving him a weak smile. "Hey, would you mind if we went somewhere quiet? I'm not in the mood to be around a bunch of drunk people."

"First off, you'll never manage to scare me away, let me just make that clear, okay?"

Molly smiled again, he knew exactly what to say to make her feel better. "Okay," she said softly.

"We could grab a couple of hot chocolates and take a walk through the park. Is that quiet enough for you?" Gus asked with a caring smile. "It might be chilly, but I have another coat behind the seat if you need one."

"That sounds perfect. I've not yet seen the park."

"Great, the park it is. We have about an hour of daylight left," Gus said, pulling away from the curb. After grabbing two cups of hot chocolate from the nearest diner, they arrived at the park five minutes later.

"I love living in a small town, everything's close by," Molly said, stepping out of the truck.

"Yep, it does have its advantages. You can pretty much walk to anywhere in town."

"I know. It's great for my roommate Stacey, she doesn't have a car right now, and she's not having any difficulty getting around."

"Can't she use your car if you walk to work?" Gus asked.

"It's a rental through my car insurance; she's not on the policy. My car got stolen in Denver on our way here." Molly stopped at the large wooden arbor entrance to the park and looked up at the tall evergreens scattered thoughout the park. "Wow! This is really pretty, and so peaceful," she said, walking under the arbor. She stood inside the park and admired the tranquility before her. Green grass, shrubs amongst the trees, and plenty of wooden benches made it an inviting place to sit and visit, and unwind from one's day.

Gus spoke in a serious tone. "I'm so sorry to hear about your car. Any chance you'll get it back?"

Molly shook her head. "I doubt it. I should be getting a replacement check soon. They told me it takes about 30 days and it's going on three weeks." Molly laughed when a flock of ducks walked in front of her path about 20 feet away. "Oh my goodness, they're so *cute*. Is there a pond here?"

Gus handed her his spare coat he remembered to grab before locking up the truck. "Put this on before you get cold, and yes, there's a pond here."

"Thanks, you were right, it's cold," she said, letting Gus help her with the coat. "Where's the pond?" she asked eagerly, looking around.

Gus took her hand and smiled. "It's just over that knoll," he told her, pointing straight ahead. He squeezed her hand. "Come on, I'll show you."

Molly's heart fluttered from the protective grip he had on her hand and allowed him to lead the way. She scanned the park as they walked down the trail and over the knoll, enjoying the sound of the children playing tag in the distance and dogs barking playfully. "This is a beautiful park, Texas never had anything like this. It's so cold though, I'm surprised kids are out here playing."

"They're used to it. They grow a tough skin growing up in this climate. Naturally it's much busier in the summer months, but it's one of my favorite places to relax and read a good book when it's not so cold."

Molly smiled. "You like to read? Me too. I hope to write a book someday."

"I do. It's my escape from the mill, where I can be by myself, relax, and escape the burdens of work," he chuckled. "You're seriously thinking about writing a book? That would be incredible. What will it be about?"

"My life, once I've sorted it out," Molly giggled nervously.

They stood at the top of the knoll overlooking the pond, their hands still entwined. Molly took in the view and was surprised to see more ducks taking a last swim before they looked for shelter for the night. "Wow! This is awesome. Do people fish in this pond?"

"When it's stocked with trout they do, and they stock it three times a year. Nothing like a fresh trout dinner," Gus said with a big grin, letting go of her hand and wrapping his arm around her shoulders. "Are you warm enough?"

Molly leaned in, enjoying his embrace. "I am, thanks."

"So, what did you mean when you said 'after you've sorted your life out?' Is everything okay?"

Molly rested her head on his chest. "It's fairly complicated and messy right now."

Gus squeezed her shoulder. "Is there anything I can help you with? If you need someone to talk to, I'm here; I hope you know that."

Molly lifted her head and lost herself in his eyes. "I've just met you, Gus, I don't want to burden you with my problems."

"I don't call it a burden, I'm here as a friend, offering my help."

"Thank you."

"I don't want to pry, but you've only been in town a few weeks and you've done an amazing job with the bookstore. And Caroline seems like she's a great boss. If I didn't know any better, it would seem as though things are going good for you right now, and you've settled in quite well."

Molly let out a heavy sigh, returning her head to his chest. "Yes, it's been a great start. This is a great town, and the people are so nice and helpful, but I'm afraid I may have just ruined everything, including the best job I've ever had, along with my friendship with Caroline."

"Can I ask why?"

"Like I said, it's complicated. I accused Caroline of something today that she took offense to, and until I get to the bottom of it, I really don't want to talk about it." She rested her hand on his chest and raised her head. "Please don't hold it against me for not telling you. I just can't right now until I get some answers."

"No, of course not. I'd never do that, but like I said, I'm here if you want to talk."

Molly smiled. "I'm so glad I met you. Whenever I'm around you everything seems so much better. You're such a soothing person, and no matter how crazy my life seems at times, when I'm with you a sense of calm takes over."

Gus lowered his head and leaned in, cupping her chin in his hand and kissing her softly on the lips. "I'm glad I met you too, you're so beautiful."

Molly blushed from his words, savoring the gentle kiss that left her lips tingling. She couldn't remember the last time she'd been kissed. "Your lips are so warm. How is that when it's so cold out?" she chuckled.

Gus laughed, pulling her in closer. "You must bring out the warmth in me."

Molly lost all track of time as she devoured his embrace, looking out at the pond watching the sun begin to set and the reflection of the moon glistening on the surface of the water. "This is amazing; if it wasn't so cold, I'd stay here all night."

"Are you cold? Do you want me to take you home?" Gus asked.

"If you don't mind, yes, I think I should be getting back. Stacey's probably wondering where I am. I didn't text or call her." Molly paused then pulled away from Gus and held his hand as she spoke. "Gus, I really like you and I want to keep seeing you, but I'd like to take it slow. I want to be honest with you so that you have the option to walk away. I haven't dated in three years because I've devoted all of my time to something which is very important to me. I'm still dealing with it, and it continues to take up quite a bit of my time. And honestly, I can't be distracted until I get closure. I know I'm not making a lot of sense right now, but when I'm ready I will tell you everything. I know this is a lot to ask, but please be patient with me and let me do what I need to do."

Gus squeezed her hand. "I have no intentions of walking away - even though it's only been a few days, I'm emotionally invested in you already. I can't expect you to drop everything for me, we've just met. I appreciate your honesty, it tells me you have a lot of class." He pulled her in and held her tight. "Molly, I'm not going anywhere, and the offer will always stand; if you need help with *anything* or just someone to talk to, I'm here."

Molly smiled and kissed his neck. "I've never met anyone like you; are you for real?" she chuckled. "Most guys would take it personally and storm off, but not you."

"My parents always told me all good things are worth waiting for. Well, I have no problem waiting for you." He kissed her on the lips and smiled. "Come on, let's get you home before you freeze to death."

CHAPTER 49

W hen Gus pulled up in front of Molly's house, Molly pulled her phone out of her purse to check her messages, thinking it was strange she hadn't received any in the past few hours. When she looked at the screen, she saw she'd missed four texts from Stacey.

"Oh shoot!"

"What's the matter?" Gus asked, rubbing her shoulder.

"I had my phone on mute when I was talking to Caroline in the office, and I forgot to unmute it when she left; Stacey texted me four times. She's probably wondering where the hell I am."

"Well, in a few minutes she'll know you're fine. Just tell her I kidnapped you for a while," he joked.

Molly patted his knee. "Thank you for tonight, it was a nice way to end the evening, and I *do* enjoy being with you, even though I said I wanted to take it slow. Once I have things sorted, I'm all yours."

A huge grin burst out on Gus's face. "I'll be anxiously waiting. Can I call you in a few days? Or is that too soon?"

Molly loved how polite and thoughtful of her feelings he was. "I'd like that. Yes, please call me."

"Maybe we'll go to the park again?" Gus suggested, running his fingers through her long hair.

Molly leaned in and ran her fingers gently across his mouth. "You have the softest lips."

"All the better to kiss you with," Gus smirked. "Here, I'll show you."

Before Molly could reply, his warm lips were upon hers, embracing her mouth as he cupped her face with his hands, caressing the soft skin of her cheeks. She instantly melted from his touch, wrapping her arms around his neck. Molly closed her eyes - nothing in the world mattered right now except for the sensual kiss she was experiencing with the new man in her life. It was slow and magical, and it took her breath away. She'd never been kissed like this before and had no desire for it to end. Her chest heaved when he gripped her hair tightly and kissed her harder, pushing her back against the seat. She savored his taste on her lips, exploring his mouth with her tongue. Suddenly he pulled back, gasping for air and breathing heavily.

"My god Molly, I have to control myself. I'm not usually this forward when I first meet a woman." He laughed and gave her a loving smile. "I think you've put a spell on me. I'm going to let you go, no matter how hard it is, before you get the wrong idea about me." He held her hand and smiled. "I really like you and I don't want to lose your respect. You asked me to take it slow, and well," he chuckled, "seems I'm not off to a good start."

Molly giggled and wiped her lips. "It's okay, I still respect you, and I think you've put a spell on me, too. I don't normally kiss a guy like that after just a few days of knowing him." She patted his knee. "Call me, okay?" she said, leaning in and giving him a kiss on the cheek.

"Oh, you can count on that. I'll be counting the hours. Have a good night."

Molly waved from the curb as he drove off, then sombered her mood to face Stacey who she'd promised to text after talking with Caroline. She was expecting Stacey to be in a foul mood for not keeping her promise and took a deep breath before opening the front door.

When she entered her home she found Stacey at her desk, her back towards her. Henry instantly got up from his spot at Stacey's feet and came over to greet her, stopping to sniff her shins. "Do you smell Roxie?" Molly said, petting the top of Henry's head.

Stacey spun around in her desk chair to face her. "Where the hell have you been? I've texted you four times," she hollered. "I was worried sick about you."

"I'm sorry, I just saw your texts. I had my phone on silent when I talked to Caroline and forgot to unmute it. Then Gus picked me up, and well, I never got around to checking my messages."

Stacey shook her head, her brow creased. "Wait! You were with Gus? The guy from the other night?"

Molly nodded and smiled. "Yes, he came into the store today and then took me to the park before dropping me off here."

Stacey leaned back in her chair and folded her arms. "Wow! How romantic. So, you like him, eh?"

Molly sat on the couch and rested her arm on the back of the cushion, facing Stacey. "Like him, he's friggin' amazing! What I *really* like about him is that he's always considerate of my feelings, and such a gentleman. I've never met anyone like him."

Stacey leaned forward and grinned. "So? Did you kiss him?"

Molly laughed. "Yes, we kissed, and it was incredible."

"Oh my god! You have a boyfriend! So does that mean next time you see him you're gonna sleep with him?"

Molly grabbed a magazine from the coffee table and smacked her in the face with it. "Stacey! That's none of your business, and if you must know, we've decided to take it slow."

"Why?"

"It was my idea, and Gus is fine with it. I have all this shit going on with Caroline; I can't devote all my time to a relationship. Gus says he understood, which I admire him for, and I love that he's not trying to rush me into anything."

"Sounds like you have a real gentleman there." Stacey quickly changed the subject. "So, tell me how it went with Caroline, did you tell her?"

"Yes, I told her, and now it's even more of a mess than I ever imagined."

Stacey quickly stood and joined Molly on the couch. "Oh no, what happened? Come on, tell me."

Molly's smile disappeared. "You're not going to believe this, but after I told Caroline, she insisted that I wasn't her daughter. We argued back and forth until she finally admitted that I couldn't be her daughter because," Molly paused and grabbed Stacey's arm, "get this, she had twin girls! Something's not adding up Stacey; I'm telling you, she's, my mother. I need to look through my documents and see what I'm missing."

Stacey patted her knee and took a deep breath. "You don't have to look at anything, I know she's your mother."

"How can you be so sure?"

Stacey took another deep breath. "Because, Molly, I'm your twin sister."

CHAPTER 50

Molly quickly stood, shaking her head vigorously in disbelief, her eyes wide, stunned by Stacey's words. "What the hell are you talking about?" Molly hissed. "Are you crazy? We don't even look alike."

Stacey remained unfazed by Molly's outburst and remained calm. "No, I'm not joking, Molly, we're fraternal twins and Caroline is our mother."

Molly shut her eyes tightly, her jaw tightening when she spoke, confused by what Stacey was telling her. Still standing in the middle of the room, she raked her hands through her hair when she spoke. "But how can we be twins, Stacey, we don't even have the same birthday? I don't know what kind of game you're playing, but it's not funny."

"It's not a game, and what I'm telling you is the truth. We do have the same birthday; I just didn't want you to find out right away that I'm your sister, so I gave you a different date. Why do you think I didn't want to be on the lease of this place? I'd would've had to give you my real birthday, and you've always known it to be April 10th. Then you would have asked why I lied about my birthday." Stacey tugged at her hair. "It's why I dyed my hair blonde. It's a distraction from my facial features that look like yours - my eyes, my nose and my awful thin lips. Yours are the same."

Molly quickly disagreed. "No, they're *not.*" Then she spat out her next words. "So, you lied to me, and all those times we celebrated your birthday it wasn't even your friggin' birthday." Molly shook her head again. "What kind of sick person are you?"

Stacey stood and approached Molly, reaching for her arm.

"Get the hell away from me!" Molly screamed, pulling away. "I can't believe you lied to me, why? You've seen all the work I've put in looking for Caroline; if you're my sister like you say you are, then you knew I was looking for *your* mother, too! What the fuck, Stacey! So, you just let *me* do all the work?"

Stacey smirked. "I did exactly what you did to Caroline."

"What are you talking about?"

"Think about it. Did you tell Caroline right away that you were her daughter? No, of course you didn't, and why is that, Molly? It's because you wanted to get to know her, is what you told me. You also said you wanted her to like you and be proud of you after you turned the bookstore around. In other words, you wanted to prove yourself to her by seeking her approval." Stacey folded her arms. "Well, I didn't tell you for the exact same reasons. I wanted to get to know you, hopefully bond with you, and I wanted you to like me. I, too, was seeking your approval."

"But I've known you for three years, I've only known Caroline for a few weeks. Why wait so long to tell me? I don't understand, and I'm sorry, but I don't believe you."

"You told me that you were certain Caroline was your mother, but you still had some doubts. I knew that the only way Caroline could defend herself and deny she was your mother was to confess she had twins. If she told you that, then I knew she was our mother, and that didn't happen until today."

Confused, Molly shook her head. She felt like someone had punched her in the gut. She returned to the couch feeling nauseous. "But Caroline told me the twins were adopted together; we weren't, so that tells me we're not sisters."

Stacey remained standing, her arms still folded. "Wrong. My mother first told me I was adopted when I was five. When I was ten and a little older, we had another talk, and it was then she told me I had a twin sister. I asked her why she wasn't with us. She told me that your adopted mom, Fiona adopted us together a week after we were born, but after having us for a month, Fiona realized she'd made a mistake and couldn't handle raising two girls but wanted to keep one. I guess I was the one she sent back, then my adopted mom adopted me."

"Why didn't my mother tell me any of this? And how does someone pick which child to keep? That's just horrible. I could never do such a thing."

With their moods a little calmer, Stacey took a seat next to Molly on the couch. "My guess is that she was ashamed of giving me up, I know I would be. So, I think she led you to believe that you were an only child to protect herself."

Molly's nerves were frayed as she played nervously with her fingers. "She didn't even tell me I was adopted until I was 16."

"She probably didn't know how; in fact, I'm surprised she even told you, what with the secret she was hiding. She probably thought you'd never look for your real mother."

"I didn't have any plans to until after the fire and I was left with no family." Molly changed the subject. "Is it true you were raised in Florida?" Molly asked.

Stacey nodded. "Yep, that part is true. When I found out I had a twin, after I finished school, I did a bunch of research just like you did, which led me to Texas. The fire and the loss of your parents confirmed my belief that you were my sister. The story was in the paper with your adoptive parent's names, and it confirmed everything I knew."

"So, you were stalking me?"

"Just like you were doing with Caroline. I admit, I did follow you at times. I needed to find out where you went to live after the fire, and it was pure luck when I followed you to the apartment building where we met. On a whim one day I drove to the house where you were staying with Ted and Doris and saw you getting in your car, so I followed you and waited in the parking lot of the apartment building until you came out. When you did, you had a big smile, and you were reading some documents. I knew it was the lease and that you'd rented an apartment there. So, after you left, I went and talked to the manager; he told me he'd just rented an apartment and only had one left. I knew he was talking about you. I told him I would take it and asked when I could move in. I laughed to myself when he told me exactly what I needed to know. Get this, he said, *'well I told the new tenant I just rented to that it wouldn't be ready until after the weekend and she could move in on Monday, so I'll tell you the same, you can move in on Monday.'* I took the apartment and figured you'd arrive early Monday morning to move in, so I got there at 7:00. You finally showed up at 10:00 and it was the perfect scenario to meet."

"Back then you didn't know I was looking for Caroline, did you?"

"No, I didn't, and maybe I was wrong not to tell you who I was when you told me about your search for her, but I wasn't sure if she was our mother back then. I was still trying to build up your trust in me, and it seemed there was never a right time to tell you."

Molly's eyes got big as she glared at Stacey. "Wait a minute! I was supposed to come to Riverbanks alone, and then you talked me into taking you with me. You were so distraught after Doug broke up with you and I felt so sorry for you that I couldn't leave you behind. Was that all an act? Did he really break up with you?"

Stacey raised her hands in admittance. "Okay so, yes, that was a lie. He didn't break up with me, I broke up with him, but in my defense, I needed to find a way for you to invite me to go with you. And what better way than getting dumped by a guy? Better yet, one that cheated on me?"

Molly couldn't believe what she was hearing. "Stacey! That was a horrible thing to do. How could you? I hated Doug for what he supposedly did to you, but it turns out you slandered his name for your own gain. That poor guy."

"He had no idea what I told you and only you. It was a clean break. There were no nasty words exchanged between us; in fact, he was surprisingly okay with it. Maybe our relationship had already run its course, and I hadn't even realized it, so what I did was a good thing actually if you look at it that way. I saved him from breaking up with me."

Molly rolled her eyes. "Slandering someone's name is never a good thing, Stacey." Molly paused, and for the first time since hearing the shocking news, she managed a faint smile, rested her hands in her lap, and stared at Stacey. "So, you really are my sister?"

Stacey grinned. "Yes, I am."

Molly couldn't take her eyes off Stacey; she had a sister. And the more closely she looked at Stacey's facial features, she realized Stacey was right, they had the same eyes, they were even the same color. They both had the same high bridge on their nose, and yes, they definitely had the same thin lips. "I'm in shock, I don't know what to say," Molly said with a big smile. "I have a sister," she whispered, tears pooling in her eyes. "So, what do we do now?"

Stacey held out her arms and grinned. "How about a hug, Sis?"

Molly burst out laughing, she couldn't believe she had a sister. Then, just as quickly, a sadness crept in. She leaned in and embraced Stacey, sobbing heavily. "Oh Stacey, we've missed out on so much. We were both denied the lives we were supposed to have. We should have grown up together with our real mother, Caroline. Why did she have to separate us? We should have been a family."

"You said she'd told you that she was really young when she had us, right?"

"Yes, she did, and it's strange, but I've never found out anything about our father. Wouldn't it be amazing if we found him too?"

Stacey chuckled, pulling away from Molly's embrace. "Let's cross one bridge at a time. The first one is to tell Caroline. Do you want to call her now?"

"Oh god no. This is not something you tell someone over the phone, and besides, I need all of this to sink in before we confront her."

"So, when?"

Molly thought for a moment. "She's coming into the store Wednesday. I want us both to be there and tell her together."

"Sounds good to me, Sis," Stacey laughed. "I like calling you Sis." She stood up. "Why don't I grab us a couple of beers from the fridge, we need to celebrate."

"Sounds good Sis, I want to talk to you all night and compare our childhoods, find out what we've missed."

CHAPTER 51

The next morning Molly struggled to pull herself out of bed as she had just gone to sleep a few hours earlier at 3:00 am. She and Stacey had their first and probably not their last sister-to-sister talk, drinking a few beers together. When the beer ran out, they'd switched to wine. Her head was feeling the consequences not only from her consumption of alcohol but also the lack of sleep, but the suffering was well worth it.

She had learned so much about Stacey - her childhood and their similarities, some of which surprised her. Stacey grew up in Orlando, Florida, and spent all her life there until she moved to Texas to find Molly. Her father died of a stroke a year before she left and her mother who is still alive, lives alone in the same house where Stacey grew up. She was an only child and was thankful her mother told her at an early age that she was adopted. Because of her honesty she has and continues to have a good relationship with her mother, calling her weekly and reminding Molly that she'd visited her a few times since moving to Texas. When Stacey decided to look for Molly, her mom gave Stacey her blessing and said she would help her any way she could.

Molly discovered that they both hated heights, something Molly had shared with Stacey, but Stacey had never shared with Molly. They were shocked to learn they both didn't like apples or grapefruits. What shocked them the most was discovering they could both touch their nose with their tongue. How the conversation and discovery came about Molly couldn't remember, she was pretty drunk by then, but clearly remembers the high-pitched laughs when they both accomplished the strange task.

Reminiscing the night before while wrapping herself in her bathrobe, Molly remembered sharing with Stacey the disappointment she felt regarding her adopted mother Fiona who hadn't been truthful with her, not only waiting until she turned 16 to tell her she was adopted, but also never telling her she had a twin sister. She wondered what else Fiona hadn't told her. Molly felt Stacey had a much healthier and more honest relationship with her parents. What excited Molly the most was next year; they'd be celebrating their birthdays together for the first time. *'We have to have a huge party to make up for all the ones we've missed,'* Molly had insisted to which Stacey quickly agreed.

After adjusting her eyes to the morning sun beaming though the bedroom window, Molly left her room and headed to the kitchen to make a much-needed cup of coffee. She found Stacey sleeping on the couch with Henry in his usual spot at her feet. Being careful not to wake her, Molly tiptoed to the kitchen, but as soon as the coffee machine began making its gurgling sounds and the aroma of coffee filled the air, Stacey stirred and rubbed her eyes.

"Shoot, I'm sorry. I was trying not to wake you," Molly said, adding sugar and milk to her coffee cup.

"It's fine, I have an appointment at 9:00, and it'll take me that long to make myself look decent," Stacey chuckled.

"Do you want some coffee?" Molly asked.

"Yes please, just give me the pot," Stacey joked. She sat up which caused Henry to jump off the couch and immediately run to the front door.

"I'll let him out," Molly said. "Then I have to get dressed and get out of here," she added, grabbing Henry's leash.

WHEN MOLLY ARRIVED at the bookstore, she was pleased to have 15 minutes to spare before opening the store. She immediately went into the office to check her emails, having neglected them yesterday after her emotional conversation with Caroline, meeting up with Gus, then chatting with her newfound sister until early in the morning.

The first email she opened was from her insurance company telling her that they'd be closing her case and issuing her a check for the loss of her car within seven days. "Sweet, time to go car shopping," Molly said, clapping her hands. She continued to scroll through her emails, bypassing all the junk and spam, then gasped when she saw one from *Emerald Literary Agency.*

Molly paused before opening it, hoping it would be good news. She needed something to butter up Caroline with before she and Stacey confronted her. After reading the email a few times, Molly squealed and danced in her chair, waking Roxie who was lying in her bed, out of a deep sleep. "Yes!" She couldn't believe what she was reading; the Literary Agency had confirmed that the newly famed author Patti Levenick from Alaska had agreed to do a book signing at the *Read More Books* bookstore's Grand Opening while on her two-month *Detour Book Tour.* Molly had inquired about the unusual name for the tour, and the agency had told her that since she'd left her prestigious life in New York City and moved to the small town of Hope in Alaska, Mrs. Levenick had grown fond of small, forgotten American towns and wanted to make a detour through some of them while doing signings in the big cities, so the agency was booking bookstores in small towns across the country close to cities where Patti Levenik is signing and *The Read More Books* bookstore location was perfect for Mrs. Levenick as she would be doing a signing in nearby Billings, Montana.

"This is unbelievable!" Molly screamed, staring at the screen. When she'd reached out to the agency a few weeks ago asking if Mrs. Levenick would be available to do a book signing, she thought her chances were slim. Patti Levenick was the hottest author in the book world right now. She was on a massive tour promoting her debut novel *I'm Home*, and rumors of a movie deal were spreading across the country (which the agency wouldn't confirm at this point). Molly had read her book and watched how the author instantly rose to fame, telling her story of how she'd led a rich and prestigious life in New York City with her two daughters, Savannah and Jewel, and was one of the best and highest paid lawyers on the East Coast, only to give it all up and move to Hope, a desolate town in Alaska, with her ex-husband, Bryce.

Molly leaned back in her seat, making room for Roxie in her lap and smiled. "This is amazing; the famous Patti Levenick is coming to our little bookstore in Riverbanks. I can't wait to tell Caroline," she grinned. "How can she be upset with me after booking this?"

When Albert and Hailey arrived shortly before 9:00, Molly decided not to tell them about the exciting news, fearing it may spread across town before she'd had a chance to tell Caroline. She'd learned quickly that living in a small town, news spreads fast, whether or not it's true. The only person she planned on telling was Stacey when she returned home, who had expressed the same anxiety as Molly when it came time to telling Caroline they were her daughters. She needed something to ease Stacey's nerves, and booking the most famous author in America was perfect. She knew Stacey could keep a secret, heck, she'd kept one since they'd met three years ago. Now it was just a matter of getting through the day with no hurdles and hopefully lots of book sales.

CHAPTER 52

Since learning Stacey was her sister, Molly immediately noticed the difference in their relationship. Even though they'd missed out on so much as sister and believed they were denied the lives they were meant to have because of Caroline's decisions, the bond between them had strengthened instantly. She came to the realization that Stacey was no longer just a friend who could walk out of her life anytime, but a sister who would now be a part of her life forever. It was a massive transition that affected her emotionally, bringing her to tears. No longer was she alone in the world, she had Stacey, and hoped Caroline would welcome them into her world as their mother.

Molly couldn't wait to tell Stacey about Patti Levenick. As soon as she arrived home after a successful and busy day at the bookstore, she insisted Stacey tell no one at this point. Stacey had agreed by crossing her heart.

"Oh my god, you're kidding me! How the hell did you manage that? I see her everywhere online promoting her huge book tour, and she's also on all the talk shows."

"I know, I can't believe it, and I can't wait to tell Caroline. Nothing should piss her off after this."

"You've got that right," Stacey agreed. "Good plan, Sis. I'm feeling much better about telling her our news."

Molly smiled when Stacey called her Sis. She'd never get tired of hearing those sweet words.

During the excitement, Molly stopped and sniffed the air. "Hey, what smells so good?"

Stacey grinned and got up from the couch. "To celebrate our newfound sisterhood, I've made us dinner." Still smiling, she skipped to the kitchen. "We're having roast beef with all the fixings'" she said, opening the oven door. "It'll be done in about 20 minutes." She turned and looked at Molly sitting in the armchair. "Want to help me set the table? Henry will have a special plate too."

"Sure," Molly replied leaving her seat. "We can discuss how we're going to tell Caroline over dinner."

After serving up the delicious meal and pouring two glasses of red wine, Molly and Stacey spent the next few hours trying to figure out the best way to tell Caroline they were her daughters. The conversation led to sharing more childhood stories.

"I wonder where we'd be today if Caroline had kept us and we grew up together?" Molly said, taking a sip of her third glass of wine. "Caroline has lived here most of her life, which means we'd probably have grown up here too," she added.

"Sounds weird to think we could have been natural country folk," Stacey said, reaching down to pet Henry sitting at her feet. "But then I wouldn't have this little guy."

"Our careers would have been different, too. I wouldn't have gone into advertising and trade shows, there's none here, and I'm sure you wouldn't have gone to college to study web design. I wonder what we'd be doing if we'd grown up here, away from the big city life and everything we've ever known?"

"I'd probably be working as a waitress somewhere, and you'd probably be working in Caroline's bookstore just like you are now. She's had it for a while."

"I'm not so sure. If she'd stayed with our father, she wouldn't have had the bookstore." Molly paused and gave Stacey a hard stare. "Do you think she'll tell us about our father? We know nothing about him." Her eyes got big. "I've just had a shocking thought."

"What's that?"

Molly leaned forward, holding the rim of her wine glass. "What if he still lives here? We may have walked past him and not even known it."

"Oh, wow! I never thought of that. What if Caroline never told him about us and he has no idea he's a father?" Stacey questioned.

"Tomorrow will be a big day, and I'm going to insist Caroline tell us about our father. After all these years I think we have a right to know." Molly glanced at her phone to check the time. "It's almost midnight. We've been talking for hours, and I think we should call it a night. We need plenty of sleep so we're well rested and prepared for whatever tomorrow may bring."

"You're right, Sis," Stacey agreed, finishing her glass of wine.

CHAPTER 53

With winter just around the corner, the mornings were turning much cooler. The next morning Molly decided to drive her car to work and take Stacey with her rather than brave the chilling temperatures.

"I have plenty of work I can do on the website until you decide a good time to talk with Caroline," Stacey told Molly as they got out of the car in front of the bookstore.

"She won't be here until after she's taken Emma to pre-school which will be about 10:00. How are you feeling about all of this? Are you nervous?"

Stacey stood behind Molly, waiting for her to unlock the door and shook her head. "Surprisingly, no, I'm not. I thought I would be, but I think it's because we're doing this together." She gave Molly a caring smile. "We're in this together, Sis."

Molly looked over her shoulder, matching her smile. "I feel the same way. Two days ago, I was facing all of this alone, but now with everything that's happened the stress level has diminished down to practically nothing. What's even more surprising is that I'm okay with whatever Caroline wants to do, whether it be accepting us as her daughters and being a part of her world or, sadly, she may want nothing to do with us. For years I've been saying that if I was rejected it would destroy me, but now that's not the case because I'll always have you as my sister and knowing that has given me strength."

"I agree with you one hundred percent; she can't take *that* away from us."

Stacey followed Molly to the office where she met Roxie for the first time. "Oh, my goodness, she's *gorgeous*," Stacey said, picking her up from the desk where she lay. "And it looks like she's made herself right at home here."

"Yep, she has a brand-new bed over there," Molly said, pointing. "But my desk seems to be her sweet spot. When I'm working that's where she always lays. It's a battle between petting her and getting my work done."

"And she just wanders around the store all day?" Stacey asked.

"Yes, she loves being among the customers, they give her all kinds of attention. We've also put a kitty door in the office so she can come and go, that way she can use her litter box whenever she needs to."

"I'm so glad you found each other. She's a beautiful cat, and so friendly. I hope Henry likes it here as much as she does when I bring him in to meet the kids."

"I'm sure he'll be fine," Molly told her. "We could start next week if you'd like to see how he does. I'll make a post on Facebook introducing Henry to the community after you let me know which day works for you," she said, taking Roxie from her arms. "Okay, I'm going to let you get to work; I have a few emails to answer before opening the store."

Being her usual punctual self, Caroline arrived at precisely 10:00 as Molly was ringing up a customer's purchase. Molly looked her way and smiled. "I'll be right with you."

Caroline raised her hand, pleased to see the store had so many customers, some browsing books, others lounging on couches, some enjoying a beverage, chatting with friends, or reading as soft music played in the background. "No rush, take your time," she told Molly, who now had three people in line at the checkout.

After a few minutes Molly called Albert over to relieve her from the counter and left to join Caroline. "Sorry to keep you waiting."

Caroline smiled, glancing around the store. "No problem - I'm impressed with the number of customers we have in the store this early."

"We have a steady clientele all day from the moment I open the doors. We're doing quite well I have to say."

Caroline glanced around the store again. "I can see that, well done."

"I have some other exciting news that I'm itching to tell you," Molly said with a huge smile. "Would you like some coffee?"

"Yes, that'd be great. So, what's the big news?"

"Let me grab us some coffee first, and I'll meet you over at that couch," Molly told her, pointing.

A few minutes later Molly joined Caroline at the couch where she was talking to a customer and smiled when the customer praised her on the new store.

"You must thank this young lady, Molly; all the credit goes to her."

"It's incredible, and just what this town needs. I'm Shawn by the way, nice to meet you," he said, extending his hand.

Molly shook his hand. "It's nice to meet you, too. Let me know if I can help you with anything," she told him before he walked away.

After placing the coffee cups on the table, Molly took a seat next to Caroline, thankful she was in a good mood and not showing any displeasure towards her after their fiery conversation the other day.

"So, what's the good news?" Caroline asked, smiling.

"Do you remember when I told you I was waiting to hear from an author's agent about booking them for a signing and didn't want to say any more until I'd heard from them?"

"Yes, I do, and?"

"They emailed me and confirmed the booking!" Molly squealed.

"Patti Levenick is going to be doing a book signing here at the store's Grand Opening."

Caroline gasped. "What? Oh, my goodness, you're kidding! How did you ever manage to book a big author like Patti Levenick to come to our little store in the middle of nowhere?"

Molly explained the *Detour Book Tour* to Caroline and how the *Read More Books* bookstore was in the perfect location for a detour from her signing gig in Billings.

"Wow, this is such amazing news," Caroline said, leaning back into the couch. "No other news today can top that," Caroline laughed.

After Caroline's last statement Molly dove right in, seizing the opportunity to grab the bull by the horns and get it done. "Well, I also have some other news to tell you, but it's a private matter which I'd like to discuss in the office."

Caroline's smile quickly disappeared. "You're not quitting on me, are you?" she said hesitantly.

Molly stood without replying, thinking to herself, '*That's for you to decide, Caroline, after Stacey and I tell you the news.*'

Carrying her coffee, Caroline followed Molly to the front counter. Molly told Albert she'd be in the office for a while and to call her if he needed anything.

"Oh, hi Stacey, I didn't know you'd be here today," Caroline said, closing the office door behind her. "How's the website coming along?"

Stacey looked up from the computer. "Hi Caroline, it's going great. I'm just working on some last-minute updates."

Caroline turned and looked at Molly who'd walked over to Stacey's desk and stood behind her looking over her shoulder.

"You said this was a private matter, Molly, but Stacey's here. Would you like to talk later?" Caroline asked.

Molly looked up and gave Caroline a smug smile. "No, it also involves Stacey."

Caroline creased her brow. "It does, how?"

"You might want to take a seat, Caroline," Molly told her, resting her hand on Stacey's shoulder.

"Okay," Caroline said, asking no questions and placing her hands in her lap.

Molly gave Caroline a piercing stare, keeping her hand on Stacey's shoulder. "You are my mother, Caroline."

Caroline immediately rolled her eyes, "Oh no, not this again. This is why you brought me in here?" she said, raising her voice in disgust.

Stacey interrupted her. "You're *my* mother, too."

Silenced by Stacey's words, Caroline's face quickly lost all color. "What?"

"You heard her correctly," Molly said, not taking her eyes off Caroline. "You're also Stacey's mother. We're sisters, and not just *sisters*, but fraternal twins." Molly continued to stare at her. "We're your daughters, Caroline."

"I don't understand, you told me last week you were an only child. Is this another sick game of yours?" she said, raising her voice.

"I only found out two days ago that Stacey's my sister, and no, this is not a game, Caroline. Believe it when we tell you that you're our mother."

"But if what you're telling me is true, how did you get separated? I thought you were adopted together," Caroline asked, tears pooling in her eyes, not believing what she was hearing.

Molly and Stacey walked over to Caroline and sat in the two empty chairs next to her. For the next half an hour they shared their stories with Caroline, proving they were her daughters.

When they were finished, Caroline sobbed and reached out for their hands. "I'm so sorry, I never wanted to give you up, I was forced to."

Molly was the first to take Caroline's hand, relieved she hadn't pushed them away. She held her hand tightly as tears streamed down her face. Stacey, also crying, leaned forward and took Caroline's other hand.

"Why were you forced to give us up?" Molly asked.

Caroline took a deep breath and wiped away her tears. "I was only 15, almost 16 at that time, but still a young and stupid teenager who rebelled against her parents. They were embarrassed to have an out-of-control pregnant teenager for a daughter and made the decision to have you both adopted. They were told you'd be adopted together, and after the decision was made, we moved from Billings to this small town where no one knew us. They kept me in hiding until you were born and began their new lives here after you'd both been taken away to be adopted, never mentioning my pregnancy to anyone." She began to sob again, her tears increasing, her sniffles louder. "No one took my feelings into consideration or even asked me if I wanted you both to be adopted. You were my babies - I never wanted to give you up. For years after, I was a mess, going back to my old ways like I was still living in Billings consuming copious amounts of alcohol, and my parents never talked about you two again once you were gone. Any mention of you both was forbidden - I was supposed to act like it never happened."

"I'm so sorry," Molly said, squeezing her hand. "What about our father? Where's he?"

Caroline let out a sarcastic laugh through her tears, surprising both Molly and Stacey. "I'm not sure, because if we're being brutally honest here, I have no idea who your father is..."

"What?" Stacey said, confused.

Caroline broke free from their hands and stood up quickly, holding her hand up to her brow in shame. "It could have been one of four guys which was another reason why my parents left Billings so quickly. My father's exact words were, *"We're ashamed to have a tramp for a daughter."* Caroline rubbed her forehead harder. "He's right, I *was* a tramp back then. My parents paid no attention to me; I was a lonely child seeking attention and comfort through alcohol and men that used me for sex. They made me feel good and knew all the right things to say. I'm not proud of what I did, but I was young and stupid, and I'm sorry, but your father could be any one of those men."

"Wow! You don't seem like you would have been that kind of girl," Molly said, shocked by Caroline's words, and disappointed knowing she'd never get to know who her father was.

"After you were taken away from me and I found myself going back to my careless ways, I told myself I could never go through that again and lose another child, or possibly even two, so when I turned 18 I knew the only way I could get away from my parents, whom I have never forgiven by the way, was to join the military and rehabili- tate myself. When I returned to civilian life four years later to start a new life, the only place I knew was this town. My parents had already moved to Wyoming, so I decided to stay here, and it's worked out fairly well, especially after meeting Pete and having Emma."

"Do you ever talk to your parents?' Molly asked.

Caroline shook her head. "No, I have no idea if they're dead or alive, and honestly, I don't even want to know. They're in the past, and I've never wanted to go back there."

Molly approached Caroline, her eyes still misty. "Are *we* a part of your past that you don't want to go back to?"

Caroline looked at Molly and held out her arms, sobbing heavily. "You're a part of my past that I wished *never* left me. I have thought about the two of you so many times - wondering where you were, what you looked like, and if you'd ever forgive me if by some miracle we'd ever meet."

Molly met her embrace and cried when she felt the arms of her birth mother wrap around her and hold her tight. "A miracle did happen, we're here and we do forgive you. I understand now that everything that happened was *not* your fault."

Stacey joined them in the middle of the room, tears rolling down her cheeks. She embraced her mother and sister. "I'm so sorry for everything you went through, I never want to lose you again."

Caroline held her daughters tight. "I'm sorry too, thank you for finding me. I've been too afraid to look for you because I feared that you'd probably hate me, and I wouldn't be able to handle that, it would have destroyed me."

"I had the same fears too," Molly said, still holding Stacey and Caroline tight. "But I kept wondering how my life would have turned out if *you* had raised me. I wanted to know what kind of life I was denied, and I now know that *you* didn't deny me that life, your parents did."

Caroline nodded and then pulled back. "You also have a half-sister, Emma, and I know over time she'll grow to adore you both. This is just what she needs after losing her father. You are going to be wonderful big sisters to her. Thank you for never giving up on your search for me; I promise I won't let you down again, this is just the beginning for us," she said, embracing them again and allowing her tears of joy to fall.

CHAPTER 54

In the midst of their emotional reunion Molly's phone rang. Reluctant to answer it, Molly pulled away from her mother's arms and seeing that it was Hailey, she quickly picked up. "Okay, I'll be right out," she said before hanging up. "That was Hailey, the store is getting busy and she needs my help."

"Well, let me help you," Caroline said brightly. "That's why I'm here," she added, giving her daughters a loving smile. "After all, this store will be yours one day; I plan on keeping it in the family."

Molly wiped her tears, her smile big and bright. "That's what we are, we're family. I thought I'd lost everything after my adoptive parents died. I thought I'd be alone for the rest of my life, but now I have my real mom *and* two sisters I never knew existed. I can't wait to see what the future has in store for us."

"We have to make up for lost time and cherish every moment," Stacey added.

"And we will," Molly said, looking at Stacey. "I'd love nothing more than to spend the day with you, but I'm needed in the store," she said, stroking Roxie. "Are you ready, Caroline?" she asked, returning Roxie to her bed.

Caroline smiled. "Yes, sweet daughter of mine, show me the way."

Molly turned and looked at Stacey who'd returned to her desk. "I'll see you at home tonight."

"No!" Caroline chirped loudly. "I'd like to invite you both over for dinner tonight to meet Emma. Please say yes, I haven't had any company since Pete died, and it would be our first family dinner."

Molly glanced at Stacey who quickly gave her an approving nod. "We'd love to, and we'll bring the wine. Text me your address and we'll leave from here after we close up."

"You'll have to come by our place and pick me up," Stacey told her. "I'm leaving in a couple of hours."

"I can do that," Molly replied, opening the office door and leaving with Caroline.

MOLLY SPENT the next few hours showing Caroline everything she needed to know about the store and introduced her to some of the customers. Since beginning her quest to find her real mother, this is just how she'd hoped it would be. Her search couldn't have ended any more perfectly; in fact, it was better than she'd ever hoped for - she had a twin sister she never knew existed and a half-sister, Emma.

All afternoon Molly floated around the store, grinning like a Cheshire Cat and bonding with Caroline, sharing their life experiences as they worked together. She felt she could talk to her about anything; there was an immediate connection when the truth was revealed, and one they both promised would never be broken again. Molly thought the day couldn't get any better but was soon proven wrong when she spotted Gus entering the store.

"Caroline, will you excuse me for a moment?" Molly said, placing some books in the Romance section where they were stocking the shelves.

Without waiting for a reply, Molly rushed to meet Gus, her heart racing, her cheeks flushed. When she approached him, he smiled and opened his arms to embrace her before giving her a warm kiss on the lips.

"Gus, what are you doing here? I thought you were going to text me later today."

"I know, but I just wanted to see you. I've missed you." He paused and smiled. "Maybe we can get together tonight? I'd like to take you out for dinner."

"Oh dear, I can't, sorry. Stacey and I are going to Caroline's for dinner."

Gus's smile quickly disappeared. "No problem, maybe some other time."

Guilt swept through Molly; she hated to hurt his feelings. Then she had an idea. She smiled and took his hand. "Come with me," she said, dragging him through the store to where Caroline was stocking shelves.

"Hey, Molly," Caroline said, and then glanced over at Gus. "Who's this?"

Molly hesitated, unsure of how to introduce Gus. "This is Gus, my boyfriend," she said, looking over at Gus who instantly smiled at her words, giving his approval of the title she'd given him. "I wanted to ask if I could bring him to dinner this evening?"

"That would be wonderful! The more the merrier," Caroline said excitedly, putting the books she was holding down on the shelves.

"Oh no, thank you, but I don't want to intrude," Gus protested.

Molly squeezed his hand. "It's okay, I want you to come. It's a celebration and I want you to be there, I have so much to tell you."

"Now you have me intrigued," he chuckled. "I'd love to come."

"Good, because I won't take no for an answer," Molly joked. "I'm picking Stacey up after work - meet me here at 6:00 and we can all ride together. I can take you back to your truck after dinner."

"Sounds good, I'll see you then." He turned to Caroline. "Thank you, it was a pleasure to meet you."

Molly leaned in and hooked arms with Gus. "Come on, I'll walk you out. If you stay any longer, I won't get any work done."

"She's right about that," Caroline laughed. "I'll see you tonight, Gus, it was nice meeting you."

Once outside Gus took Molly in his arms and kissed her softly on the lips. "So, it's official, I'm your boyfriend? I thought you wanted to take it slow, what happened?"

"So much has happened; it's why I want you to be at the dinner tonight, and yes, if you're okay with it, I'd like to call you, my boyfriend."

Gus kissed her again. "Yes, you can, but on one condition."

A look of worry swept over Molly's face. "What's that?"

"That I get to call you my girlfriend."

Molly gave him a big smile. "Deal."

CHAPTER 55

Molly honked her horn for the second time outside her house. "Come on Stacey, we're gonna be late," she hissed from the driver's seat.

Gus laughed from the back seat. "Did you text her to let her know you were on your way?"

"I did, several times, but she never texted back."

After a few minutes of waiting, Molly's patience was diminishing rapidly. The front door finally opened, and Stacey stepped out dressed casually in jeans, a red sweater, a beige wool jacket, and brown cowboy boots. Molly rolled down the passenger side window and hollered, "come on Stacey, we're already late."

"Coming!" she said, opening the car door. "Sorry, I had to feed Henry." She turned and smiled at Gus. "Hey Gus, good to see you again."

"You too, Stacey. I hope you don't mind me tagging along, Molly insisted."

"Not at all, Molly already filled me in."

They arrived at Caroline's house within ten minutes. After stepping out of the car, Molly stood and admired the quaint, one-story family home made of brick with red trim around the windows. A wooden children's swing set sat on the front lawn, and rose bushes, now trimmed and dormant, were planted beneath the two front windows. Molly looked to the left where a driveway led up to a two-car garage and a small shed. "It looks like she has quite a bit of land in the back," Molly said, opening the black metal gate to the front yard.

Caroline opened the front door before they got a chance to knock. She smiled, holding Emma in her arms. "Hello, and welcome. Please excuse the mess, I'm still having a hard time going through Pete's things."

Molly entered first and was surprised by how large the inside of the house was. It seemed much smaller from the outside. She loved the open floor plan with the large kitchen bar and wooden barstools overlooking the family room that had two yellow walls, a great contrast against the white walls. "This is beautiful, and so big and bright!" Molly beamed, scanning the large living area.

Caroline closed the door after everyone was inside and led them to the kitchen. "Thank you, we remodeled it just before Pete got sick. It was our last major expense before the medical bills kicked in. We had plans to do the two bathrooms next, but life threw us a massive curveball. I'm not sure when I'll ever be able to afford to have them done." After setting Emma down, Caroline pulled out a bar stool. "Please have a seat, I'll get you something to drink."

Stacey held up two bottles of white wine. "We brought wine."

"Great! I'll get some glasses," Caroline said, opening one of the kitchen cabinets. "We have about 20 minutes before we eat."

"It smells so good," Molly said, taking a deep breath. "What are you making?"

"We're having homemade pizza that Emma helped make," Caroline told them, smiling down at her daughter standing close by her side. "It's Emma's favorite; she loves choosing the toppings, and tonight she's decided on pineapple, ham and sausage."

"Sounds delicious," Molly said, smiling at Emma.

Gus took a seat at the bar next to Molly and rested his hand on her thigh. "I'm so sorry for the loss of your husband, Caroline. If you ever need anything fixed, I'm happy to help."

Molly gazed at Gus with loving eyes. "That's awfully nice of you."

"Thank you, Gus, that's very kind," Caroline said from the other side of the kitchen counter. "It's been an extremely trying time; you don't realize how much you depend on someone until they're gone." She took a deep breath. "We had so many plans for this place, and now I'm not sure if they'll ever get done. We have ten acres - Pete wanted to build a huge barn and get Emma a pony."

"I'd like to help in any way I can," Gus replied with a friendly smile.

"And we'd like to offer our help too," Stacey pitched in, looking at Molly. "Right, Sis? After all, we're family and that's what family does."

Molly set down her glass after taking a sip. "Absolutely! Just say the word and we'll be here."

Gus shook his head, his brow furrowed. "Wait, am I missing something here? Stacey just called Molly 'Sis' and said you guys were family."

Molly tossed back her head and laughed. "Yes, you've missed quite a bit. This is why I wanted you here tonight, I wanted you to be a part of our first family dinner."

Gus creased his brow again. "I'm so confused; what's going on?"

Molly spoke up, a big smile on her face. "Today was an amazing day! Stacey and I are Caroline's daughters, and little Emma here is our half-sister. It's been an incredible journey to find our real mom, but after all the years of worrying and being terrified of Caroline's reaction, I can honestly say I've never been happier. Not only did I find my mom, but also a sister I never knew I had."

Gus's jaw dropped. "Oh my god? That's amazing! I'm so happy for all of you. What an incredible story. You'll have to give me all the details later about how you found each other." He paused and circled his hand in front of him. "Wait, is that what you meant when you said you needed to get your life sorted?"

Molly grinned and nodded. "Yes, it is. I told you that before telling Caroline, fearing her reaction. I plan on writing a book about it someday now that I know my story has a happy ending." Molly gazed into Gus's eyes. "Not only did I find my family, I also found what may be true love."

Gus leaned in and kissed her gently on the lips. "You just may have." He paused and smiled again. "So does this mean we don't have to take it slow in our relationship now?"

Molly kissed him back and looked into his eyes. "No more taking it slow."

"Okay, get a room guys!" Stacey hollered jokingly. "I'm happy for the two of you. Now I want to know when *I'm* going to find my true love?"

"When you're not looking for it," Molly said, smiling at Gus.

Molly suddenly realized something and pulled away from Gus. She sat up straight and looked at Caroline. "Do you have a picture of Pete?"

"Yes, I do, over here," Caroline said, walking to a bookshelf in the family room and grabbing a framed picture off the top shelf, returning to Molly's side. "This is one of Emma and him," she said, handing her the picture.

Molly took the picture and looked at in silence. Pete was holding Emma in his lap on a swing she recognized from the park. Emma was around two years old. "It just dawned on me that Pete is our stepdad," she said, not taking her eyes off the picture.

Caroline's smile was weak when she spoke. "My goodness, you're correct. That never crossed my mind, but yes, even though he's no longer with us, he is your stepdad, and I know you both would have loved him." Tears pooled in her eyes. "He was such a wonderful father to Emma, I just know he would have welcomed you into our family with open arms."

Stacey quickly got up from her seat and marched over to Molly's side. "Oh my god, I never thought of that either! Let me see the picture," she asked, holding out her hand.

Molly handed her the picture. "He was so handsome. I'm so sorry we never got to meet him," Molly said softly.

Stacey stared at the picture. "Me too."

Trying to avoid bursting into tears, Caroline quickly changed the subject. "Okay, I'm getting all misty-eyed, are we ready to eat? I know Emma is."

~

FOR MOLLY DINNER couldn't have been more perfect, and from the joy, laughter and tears that were shared, Molly knew everyone felt the same way. They were all family, including Gus, her new love. For the first time in her life her heart felt full, ready to burst at the seams.

Caroline shared wedding photos, pictures of Emma since birth, and older photos of her in the service. Emma showed Molly and Stacey her bright pink and white room that had more stuffed animals than a toy store, and a large dollhouse against the wall across from her bed. Before leaving the room to return to the others, they sat on the edge of the bed so Emma could show them her favorite toys.

Holding a plush dolphin, Emma swung her legs in front of her and casually remarked, "Mommy said you're my sisters."

Shocked by her words, Molly and Stacey shared a look. "That's right, we're your big sisters, do you like that idea?" Molly asked gently.

Emma nodded and smiled. "I've never had a big sister before, and now I have two."

Stacey tickled her side, and Emma let out a high-pitched giggle. "How lucky you are! I have two sisters also, you and Molly."

"And so do I," Molly said, giving Emma a big smile. "You and Stacey."

Emma raised her hands. "We each have two sisters. We're all lucky."

"Yes, we are," Molly said, giving Emma a gentle hug before joining Caroline and Gus in the kitchen, where they were found peering under the sink.

"What are you doing?" Molly asked, taking a seat at the counter.

Caroline stood up and took Emma in her arms. "I have a leak, and

Gus offered to come by and fix it this week." She smiled at Molly. "You've got a great guy here."

Molly smiled at Gus. "I'm beginning to see that."

After Gus finished checking under the sink and announcing that it would be an easy fix, Caroline led everyone into the family room and took a seat on the white couch, making room for Emma on her lap. The others took seats on the couch and adjoining chairs. The discussion soon shifted to the unbelievable signing of the famous author, Patti Levenick.

"If this doesn't put us on the map, I don't know what will," Caroline said, raising her glass. "A job well done, Molly."

"I still can't believe it. I have a call scheduled with her agent this week to work out the details." She shook her head in disbelief. "Is this really happening? Someone needs to pinch me."

Gus reached over and pinched her thigh.

"Ouch!" Molly screamed in a high-pitched voice.

"Well, you said 'pinch me,'" he laughed. "It's happening - the number one author in the country is coming to your bookstore."

"And we only have a few weeks until the Grand Opening to make sure her visit is perfect as well as memorable. I want people to be talking about it long after she's left," Molly said enthusiastically.

CHAPTER 56

3 WEEKS LATER

Molly woke up early Saturday morning spooning with Gus in his big, beautiful brass bed, his arms around her waist. Molly lifted one of his hands to her lips, kissed it gently and smiled. This was the third time this week she'd woken up in his bed. Since consummating their relationship just over two weeks ago, they'd become inseparable. Gus had ensured their first time making love was romantic and special. Molly knew two hours into their date on Sunday she'd be sleeping with him by the end of the day. She'd wanted him much sooner, but didn't want to come across as too easy, and hard as it was, she'd put her desire on hold.

He had picked her up early Sunday morning dressed in Levi's, a beige sweater, leather work boots, and the suede coat which was part of his regular attire during the colder months. Molly dressed warm for their date as the temperatures were in the low 20's for most of the day with chances of some snow in the afternoon, but not enough to affect any roads. Gus had booked them a cabin on the outskirts of town for the day, knowing Molly had to work the next day. He also had a logging shipment going out early the next morning, the last one of the season and also needed to return home later in the day, before dark.

It was the first day in over a week they'd been able to spend an entire day together as Molly'd been so busy at the bookstore booking local authors for signings and readings, as well as launching the weekly book club and the writer's workshop. The store had come full circle and was now a prominent gathering place for the community. Parents brought their children to listen to Audrey read once a week, and on Saturdays Stacey enjoyed bringing Henry in to chill with the kids and have them read to him. Surprisingly, he and Roxie got along great from the first day and she would lie next to Henry on the days he visited.

"This is our special day," Gus told her, driving to the cabin. "I have an ice chest full of food and wine, so we don't need to go anywhere. We'll just enjoy each other's company."

For Molly the day was perfect. The two-bedroom log cabin was just 30 minutes away, surrounded by tall pine trees with no neighbors in sight. Gus lit a fire in the fireplace after unpacking their food and served her a glass wine before seasoning the steaks he planned to cook for their late lunch. Molly felt like they'd stepped back in time playing board games, curling up on the sheepskin rug in front of the fire, and reading classic books to each other that they'd found on one of the cabin shelves. Refusing Molly's help, Gus fixed a sensational meal for them, poured two more glasses of wine, and led her back to the sheepskin rug where the magic happened. Molly immediately caved to his gentle touch and soft kisses, allowing him to caress every inch of her body, savoring every moment as he devoured her body and became one with her. Molly had fallen hard for him that day, and Gus let her know that he'd never had such strong feelings for a woman such as he did now.

Since that unforgettable date, Molly's days were consumed with fond thoughts of Gus, missing him when they weren't together, yearning to be in his arms and breathe in his scent. On the evenings she couldn't bear to pull herself away from him, she'd spent the night; sleepovers at his place were becoming more frequent now.

Last night they took a bath by candlelight, and he'd shocked Molly as he held her in his arms, the hot water soothing her body. He said, "why don't you just move in? I have a big farmhouse house with four bedrooms, and it's even bigger after you leave. I miss you when you're not here."

Molly couldn't believe how fast their relationship was moving. She'd only met him three weeks after arriving in Riverbanks, and he'd literally swept her off her feet in that short time. They'd only been officially dating for six weeks, and he wanted her to move in with him. Her heart was screaming 'yes!' But she knew there was no way at this time, not with everything going on at the store. She just knew that she couldn't add moving into the mix. "I can't move in with you, Gus. Patti and her family are arriving in two days for the Grand Opening, and we still have a lot of Christmas decorations to put up before the big event which happens in three days. I want everything to be perfect; this is her last signing before she flies back to Alaska on the 7th for Christmas, then her tour resumes in mid-January in states where the weather is not so severe."

Molly's heart ached when Gus's smile soon disappeared. "I'm sorry baby, I understand, and it's selfish of me to ask. Let's get through the Grand Opening and Christmas, which is only two weeks away."

She rubbed his arm and kissed him on the lips. "It'll be something to look forward to in the new year, and besides, I have to think of Stacey. Her web design business is doing great, but I need to make sure she'll be able to afford our place on her own. I don't want to abandon her or put her in a situation where she's struggling."

Gus leaned in, wrapped his arms around her neck, and kissed her softly. "I know honey, I just hate being away from you."

The morning after, Molly stirred beneath the sheets and smiled, thinking of their passionate lovemaking the night before after their bath. Gus was the gentlest, kindest man she'd ever been with. His touch was always slow and soft, his kisses long and deep. He caressed her with care, never rushing her, winning her heart each time he said her name.

Feeling her body move, Gus opened his eyes and rested his head on Molly's shoulder. "Hey, beautiful. You're awake."

Molly turned her head and squeezed his arm still wrapped

around her waist. She kissed him on the cheek. "I am. We've got a big day ahead, there's so much to do. Stacey is meeting me at the store in an hour to help, and our neighbor Audrey is coming too." She squeezed his arm again. "Also, thank you so much for helping me, you've been a lifesaver. I can't wait to see the tree you're bringing in today," she said, beaming. "It'll be fun decorating it."

Gus gave her a loving smile before he sat up. "My pleasure, I'd do anything for you."

Her big smile was evident when she spoke. "And, we have the kids from school coming in at 1:00 to hang their homemade decorations. That was Audrey's doing; she called the school and suggested the idea, and they loved it. They had grades K through 5 make them."

Gus took her in his arms and kissed her again. "I love how the bookstore is bringing this town together. There're so many reasons to like you, look what you've done."

Molly blushed and freed herself from his embrace, sitting up and reaching for her phone on the end table.

"Who are you calling this early in the morning?"

"No one, I'm checking the weather, I've been checking it every day. I hear rumors of snow and I'm trying to find out how much."

Gus chuckled. "Those apps are never reliable, half the time they're wrong."

"Well, you're no help," Molly laughed, giving him a friendly slap on the arm. "What if we get a big snowstorm and the highway is closed before Patricia arrives? Our event will be ruined, and people may not show up if there's a lot of snow and the roads are closed. That would be awful after all the hard work we've put into this." Molly let out a heavy sigh. "God, I hope that won't be the case."

Gus squeezed her shoulder and kissed it before getting out of bed. "All we can do is hope for the best. So far, we've had a pretty fair winter except for the frigid temperatures, but don't you worry, the folks in this town will show up. Weather has never stopped anyone around here."

Molly smiled. "That's what Caroline said when we were planning the events."

AFTER KISSING Gus numerous times in his driveway, Molly drove to the store in her brand-new, white Subaru which she'd purchased just a few weeks ago. Stacey had joined her to look at new cars, and with her web design business doing so well, was able to purchase one too, and had also decided on a Subaru, choosing a Forest Green color.

When Molly arrived at the store, Hailey was already waiting outside, rubbing her hands together to fight the chilly temperature. After parking she got out quickly and raced over to her. "I'm so sorry, it's freezing out here. Have you been waiting long?"

Hailey shook her head, still rubbing her hands. "No, just a few minutes. I thought I'd get an early start."

Molly hurriedly unlocked the front door. "Come inside, I'll make us some coffee."

Hailey followed her into the store. "Thanks, that sounds great."

From behind the counter of the beverage bar Molly fired up the coffee machine. "Hey, can you let Roxie out of the office? I'll feed her in a bit."

"Sure," Hailey said, removing her hat and scarf as she walked through the store.

By 10:00 the store was bustling with customers. Audrey and Stacey had arrived to assist her, along with her other hired help, Albert. Molly hadn't stopped since she'd arrived. In between helping customers, she and everyone else hustled on decorating the store with festive decorations, hanging Christmas lights in the windows and around the store, and placing small, artificial trees in the front windows. They cleared an area for the large tree Gus would be carrying in and hung garland on the bookshelves and counters as the sounds of holiday music played in the background. Stacey and Audrey decorated Santa's Corner in the Children's section, while Audrey found a perfect bright red armchair at the local thrift store which Gus had brought over in his truck the day before.

Molly continued to check the weather and looked outside frequently as she was working, but so far nature had been on their side. As promised, Gus arrived at noon with a beautiful, eight-foot tree.

"Oh Gus, it's perfect!" Stacey cried. Her staff as well as some of the customers helped her carry it inside.

"I'll grab the lights," Stacey said once the tree was in place.

"I love this time of year, it's so magical," Molly said, swaying in Gus's arms admiring the tree.

"Me too," Gus replied, holding her tight.

Molly looked at the large clock on the wall. "Come on, let's get some lights and decorations on it, the kids will be here in half an hour." She turned and looked at Hailey holding a box of decorations. "Can I put you in charge of making the hot chocolate?"

"Sure, I'll get right on it," Hailey replied.

Stacey returned with the lights and handed them to Gus. "Hey Molly, is Caroline coming in today?" Stacey asked. Even though Caroline was their birth mother, both preferred to call her Caroline, for now anyway.

Molly shook her head. "No, she was here all day yesterday, and I think she wants to spend some time with Emma. She'll be here tomorrow for a few hours," she said, looking out the window. "It's snowing!" she squealed excitedly. "What perfect timing. I just hope it doesn't dump a foot down on us," she laughed.

"And look, there's the school bus pulling up," Stacey said, pointing.

For the next hour the bookstore was in full festive mode, with children hanging their ornaments proudly on the tree as Molly, the staff, and customers admired their work. Roxie mingled with the boys and girls, rolling on her back every chance she could for a belly rub, while Hailey served hot chocolate with a peppermint candy cane to each child before they boarded the bus to return to school.

"Now this is what Christmas is all about, the children," Molly said, flopping her body onto the nearest couch. "I'm exhausted."

Gus joined her on the couch. She immediately curled into his arms, resting her head on his chest. "Is this day over yet?"

Gus chuckled. "A few more hours." He looked out the front window of the store. "Look, it stopped snowing."

Molly raised her head and looked out. "Oh good, we only got a couple of inches, I'll make it home."

"You mean I'm not going to get to see you tonight?"

Molly laughed; she would like nothing more than to spend another sleepless night making love with him. "As much as I want to, I should go home and get a good night's sleep. We only have one more day until the Grand Opening, and Patti arrives tomorrow afternoon. She's going to be calling Caroline here at the store, and Caroline wants me here when she does."

Gus gave her a hard squeeze. "I know, but a guy can try, can't he?" he joked.

"Any other day and I would have said yes with no hesitation, you know that, but this is the culmination of all the hard work I've put in over the last few months, and I want it to be perfect."

"And it will be. The whole town will be here celebrating with you, I guarantee it."

CHAPTER 57

Molly woke up at 6:00 the morning of the Grand Opening, anxious to get to the bookstore. As was the case on the previous two mornings she quickly jumped out of bed and raced over to the window to check for any snowfall. "Phew," she said, relieved to see that only six inches of snow had fallen during the night. She grabbed her phone and checked the Weather app and saw that no more was expected until tomorrow afternoon. "Thank god," Molly said, wrapping herself up in her bathrobe.

When she opened her bedroom door, the aroma of coffee hit her senses. Shocked, Molly walked to the kitchen and found Stacey faced away from her, pouring herself a cup of coffee. "Stacey, you're up already!"

Stacey looked over her shoulder and smiled. "I couldn't sleep - I'm so excited about today and meeting Patti and her family. Especially after reading her book and the fascinating life she's had," she moaned, holding her heart, "and about her and Bryce, oh my god, what a love story."

"It's quite the story, I agree; I hope they make it into a movie,"

Molly said, surprised to see Stacey so perky after they'd both unintentionally stayed up past 1:00, lost in sister talk.

As soon as Molly arrived home after work last night, Stacey wanted to know everything about the phone conversation she and Caroline had with Patti. Molly told her that they'd talked for over an hour and that she sounded really nice. Giggling, Molly confessed to Stacey, "from what I'd read about her in the book, I expected her to be a snob coming from the corporate world, but she was quite the opposite. She was really down-to-earth and super friendly. She thanked Caroline for having her, and that her and her family looked forward to seeing the bookstore. She also said how much Riverbanks reminded her of her true home in Hope, Alaska, where she's been living for the past three years and has never been happier. It's an incredible story," Molly repeated, pouring herself a cup of coffee and joining Stacey at the bistro table. "Where's Henry?" she asked, looking under the table.

"Being a lazy dog sleeping on the couch. I think our chatter last night kept him awake; he's not a happy camper this morning."

"Are you bringing him to the store?"

Stacey shook her head. "No, there's too much going on, and I don't want to spend half the time wondering where he's at."

"Yes, that makes sense." Molly checked her phone. "It's almost 6:30. I want to leave in an hour. Caroline and Emma will be at the store at 9:00, and Patti will be there at 11:00, an hour before her event scheduled at noon. I want to make sure the table we've set up for her with the book display and signs are all in place before she arrives."

"Okay, sounds good. I'm bringing Audrey with me, so we'll be there around 10:00; can you tell Caroline? I was going to call her last night, but we got to talking, and well, we know how that turned out."

AFTER CLEANING the snow off her car Molly was relieved to see the roads had been plowed, making her drive easier as she had very little experience driving in the snow. She'd questioned herself on her ability to drive in this weather and had relied on Gus to pick her up from work a few of those evenings, leaving her car overnight to be picked up when the road conditions had improved.

Molly turned onto the street where the bookstore was and instantly slowed down when she saw at least a dozen news vans and numerous cars parked outside. "What the hell?" she whispered under her breath. "The news people are here! Wow, I was NOT expecting this; I can't believe they're here this early, it's freezing, are they nuts?!"

Seeing the spot where she usually parked taken up by a Billings news station van, Molly kept driving until she saw an open space a few buildings down. Grabbing her purse, she then wrapped her wool scarf a few times around her neck and stepped out of the car. She'd decided to dress casually for the event, assuming everyone else would as well because of the wintery weather. Dressed in blue jeans, a thick, white polar neck sweater, a long, white wool coat and tanned suede and leather boots, she carefully walked on the snowy pathway, stepping in the footprints left by other people.

When she neared the store, she was instantly approached by three reporters who'd quickly jumped out of their vans when they saw her. Molly recognized them from the morning news out of Billings. She smiled even though her nerves were peaked.

"Are you associated with the *Read More Books* Bookstore?" a female reporter bundled in a parka and jeans asked.

Molly looked down at the large microphone the reporter had rudely pushed in her face. "Yes, I am, I work here," Molly replied.

Two other reporters joined them, both middle-aged men. "And what do you do here?" one of the men asked.

"I'm the store manager, and I help Caroline Moor, the owner, with anything she needs."

"Are you excited to have the famous author Patti Levenick visit the store today?" the woman reporter asked.

Molly beamed for the camera to her left; she'd never been on TV before and suddenly felt like a star. "Yes, all of us at the store are extremely happy she's included our store on her book tour. We're honored to have her; she's the talk of the town," Molly laughed into the camera.

The cameraman matched her laugh before turning off the camera.

"Why are you guys here so early? Patti won't be here for a few more hours, and it's freezing outside," Molly asked, her eyes wide.

Three other reporters had joined the circle. One replied, "we're covering for the morning news and would love to see the inside of the bookstore."

"I have quite a bit of work to do before I can let you in, I'm afraid, but you're welcome inside once we're open for business."

Once she was in the store away from the reporters, Molly took a deep breath. 'Wow! I was just on TV,' she chuckled to herself as she group texted Stacey, Gus and Caroline to tell them about the media presence. She headed to the office where she was greeted by Roxie.

Molly picked her up and held her in her arms. "Hey girl, you just might become a famous kitty by the end of the day - the news is here." She pets the top of Roxie's head. "Be sure to put on a show for the cameramen and be the sweetest kitty ever, just like you were when we first met."

After feeding Roxie, Molly spent the next hour on some final touches. After she'd finished everything looked perfect. She glanced at the clock and saw that it was almost 9:00. "Where is everyone?" she asked aloud, walking to the front door. "Albert and Hailey should be here by now." Then she laughed as she looked out the window. She folded her arms and stood watching the buzz from the media. Stacey and Hailey were being interviewed by the female reporter, and further down the street she saw Caroline, holding Emma in her arms, being interviewed by a male reporter. "Oh, my goodness, this is crazy! You'd think we were in Hollywood!" Molly laughed, unlocking the door, only to be approached by two more reporters.

Molly opened the door wide and hollered, "Please come inside out of the cold, hot chocolate for everyone!"

The media gladly accepted her invitation and quickly followed her into the store. She directed them to the areas where they could film without interfering with the event.

"I can't believe the media is here," Caroline and Stacey said, finally managing to break away from the journalist and join Molly in the store.

"Did you invite them?" Caroline asked Molly, taking off her coat and Emma's.

"No, they've been following Patti's tour. We're going to be on the morning news!" Molly squealed, clapping her hands. "I wonder if Gus will see it. He always watches the news when he has his coffee, and he's not going to be here until around 11:00."

"This is insane!" Stacey laughed, looking around the store at the many cameras and microphones. She laughed when she saw Roxie rolling on her back in front of a reporter, noticing that the cameraman was filming her. "Look at that, Roxie is loving the attention. She'll be a star by the end of the day."

"That's what I told her," Molly laughed, looking over at Roxie. "She's certainly working the crowd."

Molly looked at Caroline and took her hand. "Will you be giving a speech today? We'd talked about it a while back, but it was never mentioned again; it's okay if you don't. I wouldn't want to pressure you into anything you don't want to do."

Caroline squeezed her hand. "It's okay, and yes, I'd love to speak. Look at all these wonderful people who came here to support us," she said, looking at the crowd entering the store along with the cameramen. "The least I can do is thank them."

"Oh, I'm so happy to hear that. When do you want to do it?" Molly asked.

"I thought perhaps right before Patti's speech, then I'd introduce her if that works?"

"Caroline, you're the boss, but yes, I think that'd be perfect!"

By 11:00 the store was the busiest it had ever been. Christmas music played in the background, while the customers, many of them with their children, browsed the store, talking to the local merchants showcasing their products, and visiting Santa sitting in his red velvet chair in the Children's section, where every child there received a gift donated by the community. Molly couldn't believe the turnout; Gus was right, the freezing temperatures didn't stop these people, and after mingling with many of them, she was surprised to learn some had driven all the way from Billings and other surrounding communities.

Stealing a moment for herself before Patti arrived, which could be any minute, Molly sat on one of the stools at the food and beverage bar, savoring a much-needed cup of coffee. She scanned the store, beaming, her eyes bright. It was a beautiful sight. Then she spotted her mother Caroline standing in the middle of the store with Emma, laughing with Lucy and Joyce, the real estate agent, who'd helped Molly immensely when she first arrived in Riverbanks. Molly smiled again when Caroline called Stacey over and hugged her before Stacey took Emma to the Children's section. Just a few months ago Caroline had confessed to Molly that she was afraid to return to the community, unsure of how people would react to her with the passing of her husband. It warmed Molly's heart to see Caroline glowing and embracing her new life. She hoped she and Stacey, her newly discovered daughters, had something to do with her new happiness.

A few minutes later Molly saw Caroline look towards the front door then hastily leave her friends. Chatter amongst the crowd increased, many all looking in the same direction over at the door. Molly turned her head and saw someone who needed no introduction - Patti Levenick, dressed in jeans, a black sweater and black suede boots, stood next to an extremely handsome man with blonde, curly hair and a short boxed beard which enhanced his face nicely. Molly didn't remember him having a beard in the book and never pictured him with one, but it suited him well. Standing on either side of them were their two daughters, Jewel and Savannah; both had long black hair identical to their mother's. Standing behind them was an official-looking woman with long, straight red hair who Molly assumed was Patti's assistant.

Molly quickly left her stool, wiped her clammy palms on a

napkin, and walked hastily to the front entrance to stand beside Caroline and greet them.

Caroline spoke first, holding out her hand. "Patti, it's such an honor and pleasure to have you at our store." She turned and looked at Molly. "This is my Store Manager, Molly."

Molly held out her hand and gave Patti her best professional smile. "It's a pleasure to meet you. We have everything ready for you, and, as you can see, there are many people here anxious to meet you."

Patti hooked her arm in her husband's. "This is my husband Bryce, and these are our daughters, Savannah and Jewel." She glanced around the store, taking in all of the festivities. "What a beautiful bookstore you have here, so warm and inviting."

From a distance the cameramen took pictures of Patti, rattling Molly, who'd requested they *not* approach her until after her event.

"Can we go look around, Mom?" Jewel asked, bored with grown-up talk.

Patti squeezed her shoulder. "Sure sweetheart; your dad and I will join you shortly."

Caroline and Molly walked over to the table where they'd set up everything needed for her book signing. "This is where we'll have you sign your books and do your speech. Does everything look okay?" Caroline asked.

"It looks wonderful," Patti said, then whispered, "I prefer these small signings rather than the large ones in the cities. There's more of a connection with the readers, and these little bookstores remind me so much of home. Hope, the town I live in is small like this, and it could use a bookstore. This is absolutely beautiful."

"Thank you," Caroline said, smiling, "but all the credit goes to Molly. I hired her to save this bookstore that I've neglected for years due to my husband's illness. You should have seen it a few months ago. You never would have agreed to come here if you had," she joked.

Molly saw Stacey walk towards them and waved her over. "This is my sister Stacey, she designed the website for the store," she told Patti.

Stacey held out her hand and smiled. "I'm so excited to meet you, I loved your book."

"Thank you, it's been quite the journey." She turned and looked at Bryce, giving him a loving smile. "And I have this man to thank for it."

Bryce laughed. "Nah, I just gave you a little shove to get you going in the right direction."

After talking for a few more minutes, Molly suggested that they get Patti settled at her table and announce to her many guests that she'd be speaking shortly. Caroline agreed and said she'd make the announcement in ten minutes, giving people plenty of time to get situated.

Checking the time, Molly wondered where Gus was. He'd told her he would be at the store at 11:00, and it was now 11:30. She checked her text messages and saw there was one from him early this morning that she'd missed. She laughed when she read it. *'Hey, I just saw you on the news!'*

"That was really cool seeing you on the news," a male voice said behind her.

Molly turned around and smiled when she came face-to-face with Gus. She leaned in and kissed him on the lips. "Hey, I was getting worried about you."

"Sorry I'm late, I had to park almost two blocks away. This place is packed," he said, looking around. "You outdid yourself, babe," he added with pride.

"Thanks." Molly took his hand. "Come on, let's get you something to drink before Caroline's and Patti's speeches - I don't want to miss either one of them."

CHAPTER 58

Molly and Stacey sat with their baby sister Emma between them on the couch, with Gus on Molly's left, his arm around her shoulders, waiting for Caroline to begin her speech. Hailey finished serving the last of the beverages as Albert turned down the music from behind the counter.

The store fell silent; all eyes were focused on Caroline standing before them looking radiant and happy. Patti stood off to the side holding hands with Bryce, waiting to be introduced, while their two daughters sat close by with Patti's assistant. Camera lights from the media in the back were turned on, causing Caroline to quickly blink to adjust to the sudden beams of bright lights before starting her speech.

Caroline glanced around the store at the people gathered and smiled. "Ladies and gentlemen, children, friends and family, thank you all so much for bracing the cold to be here today. I can't tell you how much it means to me. When my husband Pete and I purchased this store many years ago, this is what I dreamed it to be. Not only a bookstore, but a place where the community could gather, share interests, join in many activities and workshops and make new friends. Sadly, when my husband was diagnosed with a terminal illness, all my time was dedicated to taking care of him and our sweet daughter Emma, and my plans for the store seemed a distant memory."

"That soon changed when I knew my husband's life would soon be coming to an end, and I knew I needed to create a future for Emma and I. Medical bills had consumed our savings and the only thing I had was this store, but I needed help; that's when I hired Molly." She looked over and gave Molly a loving smile. "We would not be here today if it wasn't for Molly, she worked tirelessly to turn this store around and be something we could all be proud of. She has put this store and our little town on the map singlehandedly." Caroline grinned. "I mean, look at us, we're on the news!" she said, waving at the cameras. "Hello everyone at home watching us," she giggled.

The crowd roared, looked over their shoulders and waved at the cameras. Many of the children clapped and smiled for them. Caroline paused, took a deep breath, and with tears in her eyes looked at Molly, then Stacey, giving them both a loving smile. "But this store not only brought this amazing community together and provided a future for my daughter and I, but it also reunited me with my twin daughters, Molly and Stacey, who I regrettably gave up for adoption almost 30 years ago; something I was forced to do by my parents and not by choice."

The crowd gasped, eyes were wide, and the chatter of surprise could be heard. Caroline looked at her daughters with tears rolling down her cheeks and waved her hands. "Come on up here."

Molly stood first, tears flooding her eyes. She turned and held out her hand for Stacey, then Emma, and together they walked over to their mother and met her in a lovely embrace. Tears of joy could be heard from the crowd, and one person shouted, "I need a tissue." Bright lights from the camera shone on Caroline and her daughters for all the world to see. Caroline released her hold on her daughters and smiled. "I would like to introduce you to the family I never knew I had. Because of this store we found each other, and it will always be a part of our family. We may have lost the first 30 years together, but we're going to make up for it and have the best years together going forward." Caroline wiped her moist cheeks. "Thank you everyone, we're all family here. Now I'd like to introduce you to our very special guest. It is such an honor to have her here celebrating this special day with us, please welcome Patti Levenick, author of the best-selling book, '*I'm Home*.'

The crowd instantly erupted into cheers, clapping their hands as Patti stood and embraced Caroline, taking the microphone from her before greeting the crowd. Once the crowd settled, Patti smiled. "Thank you everyone. Wow! What an incredible story! How do I top that?"

The crowd laughed.

Patti chuckled. "You know, I had an opening speech prepared, but after listening to Caroline's story, that has now changed. This is what I love about small towns - the closeness of the community, as Caroline said in her speech, you are all family, and she felt comfortable enough to share with you how she recently reunited with her two beautiful daughters, and that it was this bookstore that brought them together." Patti looked over at Caroline. "I had no idea of this until just a few minutes ago. Caroline's story reminded me of my own; I was also denied a relationship with my father because of a family member's actions. That person molded me into something I wasn't for her own personal gratification, and for many years I lived a lie until my amazing husband Bryce," she looked over at him and smiled, "took me back to my roots in Alaska. That's where I found the *real* me, and I've never been happier."

"I look back on my days as an elite corporate snob, and a real bitch I might add, in New York, and I see now how unhappy I was, trying to prove myself to everyone *except* my husband and my daughters. This is one of the reasons why I'm doing the Detour Book Tour. I wanted to connect with small rural towns across America and the communities, just like we're doing tonight. Small towns are the backbone of America, and in my opinion, the hardest working. Country folk speak from the heart and embrace everyone that crosses their path." She paused and smiled at the crowd. "Thank you for embracing me and making me feel welcome. We moved to Hope,

Alaska, three years ago, and a year later I had the urge to write my story. I lost so many years not being true to myself – do *not* let that happen to you. Live your life to the fullest and do it for you, surrounded by the people you love. Do what makes you happy, not what makes others happy." Patti looked over at Caroline surrounded by her daughters. "Your life has just begun with your girls, and I know it will be full of joy, just like mine has been since I moved to Alaska." She looked at Molly and smirked. "And maybe, just maybe I can borrow Molly from you and use her expertise to open an incredible bookstore like this one in my hometown of Hope. But that's another conversation."

Molly laughed, wondering if she was serious. If she was, then it was definitely something she could bring up in the future. Her heart was full listening to Patti's words. Everything she said was true and relatable to her own life. She'd come to Riverbanks in search of her past, to find her birth mother, not knowing if her research might have led her down the wrong path.

Disconnected from the world with no family to lean on, Molly feared leaving Riverbanks lonelier than when she'd arrived. But instead, everything she ever dreamed of came true, and now she not only had a mother, but two sisters to share her life with, something she never expected. After losing the only parents she'd ever known, she had a family again. She looked over at Gus, a man who had walked into her life unexpectedly and stayed. She gave him a warm smile; she was excited about their future. Riverbanks was her home now, she had a future here and couldn't wait to see where it would take her and what memories would be made.

ACKNOWLEDGMENTS

While writing this book, I couldn't decide on a name for the cat. As always, when I need help, I turned to my Facebook group, *Read More Books*, and asked my readers for suggestions.

After many wonderful ideas and a group vote, the name "Roxie" emerged as the favorite — a heartfelt suggestion from Laura Lindemulder.

Roxie was the name of Laura's beloved late fur baby, and it's an honor to use it in this story. As a thank you, Laura will receive a signed copy of the book. I'm so grateful for my amazing readers!

ABOUT THE AUTHOR

Award-winning author Tina Hogan Grant was born in England and moved to the States in 1979. After moving to California, she became a commercial fisherwoman and spent ten years fishing off the southern coast of California with her husband Gordon. After retiring from fishing, they moved to a small mountain community in CA and spent the next ten years building their dream home, doing most of the work themselves.

Grant enjoys writing suspense romances, stories with strong female characters who know what they want and aren't afraid to chase their dreams.

Favorite quote: "There's no such word as can't "

When Grant is not lost in her world of writing she enjoys riding ATVs, hiking and discovering new trails, and going on long road trips.

Grant's book Better Endings won a gold medal award for Best Fiction Adventure 2020

And The Reunions won a gold medal award for Best Fiction Adventure 2021

Grant has had appearances on FOX NEWS Bakersfield, Bakersfield NOW NEWS, HOMETOWN -KVPA Radio Santa Clarita, Voyage LA Magazine, and The Mountain Enterprise Newspaper, and BOLD Magazine.

Keep in the loop with Tina by signing up for her newsletter on her website www.tinahogangrant.com

www.ingramcontent.com/pod-product-compliance
Lightning Source LLC
Chambersburg PA
CBHW050024120726

47903CB00006B/1902